About the Author

Born in County Mayo, Bernadette Quinn has lived in Dublin since student days when she studied pharmaceutical chemistry. She was a founder member of "AIM group for family law reform" and she helped to found a magazine called "Woman Spirit." She was joint author of the book *Can you stay married?* Her novel *Out of that childhood country* was published by the Book Guild Limited. She was one of 10 prize-winners in the short story competition open to Irish women worldwide and published by Arlen House. Other short stories have been published in various journals and magazines as have over 50 of her poems.

Salvage

Bernadette Quinn

Matador
9 Priory Business Park,
Wistow Road, Kibworth Beauchamp,
Leicestershire. LE8 0RX
Tel: 0116 279 2299
Email: books@troubador.co.uk
Web: www.troubador.co.uk/matador
Twitter: @matadorbooks

ISBN 978 1785891 557

British Library Cataloguing in Publication Data.
A catalogue record for this book is available from the British Library.

Printed and bound in the UK by TJ International, Padstow, Cornwall
Typeset in 11pt Minion Pro by Troubador Publishing Ltd, Leicester, UK

Matador is an imprint of Troubador Publishing Ltd

*This book is dedicated to John, my son and
Deirdre my daughter in law.*

Chapter One

Sally Griffin drove slowly along the coast road on her way to Pat and Pam's house. Each corner she rounded showed a separate and different picture. It was a lovely April evening. The hills were aflame with leaping growths of gorse that perfumed the air round the craggy rocks that pushed their grey noses through the riotous growth. She turned round a sharp corner and there perched on its rocky promontory was the Aerie.

She slowed down to look at the house and the gardens. The white two-storey building had the main block flanked by wings, one wing slightly larger than the other – a witness to Pat's natural dislike for too-obvious uniformity in design. *They are right*, she thought, as she gazed at the house which fitted in so harmoniously with the surrounding scenery.

It is beautiful.

It was too soon to call on Pam. She would drive a little further on. She brought the car onto the beach, deserted except for a man and a dog in the distance. She looked back. She could only see some of the roof and one white chimney. She got out of the car. She would have time to walk as far as the beach shelter.

She thought of the party she had given a few nights ago to celebrate her engagement to Morrison. That night she had met Pam for the first time. She had run into Pat on a few occasions in the company of Morrison and liked what she saw. Morrison thought a lot of him. In fact Pat seemed to be popular with everyone. The same couldn't be said of Pam as she soon found out before the two of them arrived, late as usual, as had been the wry comment of her guests.

She had been more than surprised at the vehemence of the remarks made about Pam, blaming her for this delay as well as for all other delays in the past. But her heart had dropped when eventually the two of them did arrive. Pat, handsome, distinguished, low-voiced. Pam, drab, indifferent, taciturn. Pat had apologised for their lateness and hoped they hadn't spoiled the meal that he knew would be one of Sally's specials, but he hadn't given a reason for the late arrival although she had been told by the others he had become quite expert at thinking up excuses.

She had gone out of her way to be friendly to Pam, but it had been hard going. Pam seemed to be a good deal older than the rest of the women in the room, perhaps two or three years older than Pat. Auburn hair clung to an oval face in an untidy mass, but she had wonderful eyes. They were a shade darker than her hair and the lashes were dark and long. She had never seen such eyes before. She had small even white teeth and when she smiled, which was seldom, the smile never reached her eyes. Her face could be a dead thing except when she spoke. And it could have been beautiful. That was the pity of it. She had been fascinated by those eyes. Her own were so insignificant compared to them. If she wore blue her eyes seemed blue, if she wore grey they looked dull and if she wore green they looked a different colour again.

'I'm sorry for staring, but you have the most beautiful eyes.'

'Thank you.' She said off-handedly. Then with an obvious effort: 'You have beautiful eyes too.'

'Did you say beautiful?' And she had gone on to describe their vagaries.

Pam had laughed, her first laugh of the evening, but then stopped abruptly: 'They have the nicest colour of all. The colour of happiness.'

What an odd thing to say, Sally thought, and *why do I feel uncomfortable in her presence?* There's no doubt about it, she is different from the other women in the room. Pam leaned back in her chair, indifferent to her surroundings. Most of the people stood around in groups talking and laughing and the hostess longed to join them, but she felt obliged to sit with her. Pam held a drink in one hand, a cigarette in the other. Her eyes remained downcast. She raised her eyes suddenly just when Sally expected the cigarette ash to drop on her dress, to flick it onto the nearby ashtray. Sally was at a loss for something to say. She couldn't tell Pam she liked her dress because although the silvery material was beautiful it was all wrong for her colouring. It helped to drain her face of every bit of life. It was also the wrong length. Had Pam forgotten it was 1968 and that women were wearing much shorter clothes? It wasn't as if she didn't have good legs, observing the long and shapely limbs crossed casually underneath the tight-fitting skirt.

'Morrison is hoping that Pat will be able to come over to us for a holiday. And you, of course, when we settle down in the States. Have you been to America?'

'Yes, once, when I was sixteen. I stayed one summer in Los Angeles with my aunt and uncle.'

'Did you like it?'

'Yes, but I suppose everything and every place that is strange or foreign is wonderful when you're that age, but I wouldn't care to settle down in America, at least, not in Los Angeles.'

Sally looked at the laughing guests. They seemed to have forgotten Pam and herself.

'Your husband is very popular. With men and women. I think that tells you a lot about a person. Don't you agree?'

'I've never thought about it.' Pam was plainly not interested. 'But I suppose you're right,' she added as an afterthought. It was becoming impossible to carry on a conversation with her. Should she try any longer? Something prompted her to go on. But what had she to say? What could she say that wouldn't be seized upon and given short shrift? And then she said the next thing that came into her head.

'I think you're very lucky.'

'Lucky, did you say?'

The words had roused her. Her head jerked around. Then the spurt of energy flickered and died. She let her head drop back on the cushion.

'I suppose you could say that,' she said, with the driest of smiles.

Silence stretched between them once more. Sally no longer hunted around in her mind for things to say. If Pam were as happy that way, leave her so.

When she had finished her cigarette she called out, 'Who's hungry?'

During coffee the subject of houses arose. Morrison explained how his problem had been solved. His parents had proposed moving out of their house, which was too big for their present needs, and moving into a smaller place about five minutes ride away.

'Have you seen Pat's house yet, Sally?' Barry asked. 'It's one of the finest in County Dublin, if not the finest. And the cute divil picked out one of the best locations for his masterpiece.'

'No, but I hope to see it sometime.' She looked at Pam. Pam smiled but said nothing.

'It's a monument to Pat's genius,' Margo said. 'There are architects and architects but Pat is a sculptor, painter, what-have-you, all rolled into one. It's a real landmark.'

Pam looked up. 'Like all mausoleums,' she said dryly. 'And for additional authenticity it has got its own mummy. Me.'

There was an uneasy titter. Pam ignored it. 'But you're welcome to have a look-around any time, Sally. I'm always at home for inspection tours.'

Sally sensed the hostility but if Pam liked being rude, let her. She was hurting no one but herself.

'Yes, I would like to see it.' She would like to have said: it is impossible to resist such an enthusiastic invitation, but instead she said, 'We'll make a date before you leave.'

She gave a quick glance in Pat's direction but he seemed to be unaware of anything unusual. Perhaps he is used to it. But she noticed the exchange of glances among her guests.

The party was a great success. No one was anxious to leave. Even Pam let herself go eventually and when she laughed her face looked younger, more attractive. Before saying goodbye to Pam and Pat she said: 'What about my inspection tour? Or have you forgotten?'

'No, but I thought you had. What time would suit you?'

'Would Tuesday evening be all right? Half past seven?'

'That will be fine.'

Sally had reached the beach shelter. She would make it back in nice time for her visit. She brought the car to a halt at the corner of the house. She was so absorbed in admiration of the house and gardens and the wonderful view that she jumped in fright when a boy of about nine crawled from the shrubbery, followed almost immediately by an older boy, screaming and waving a very limp lasso. The first boy tore around the house followed by the other. Then silence. Sally had not yet recovered from the sudden interruption when she became aware of the two children appearing slowly around the corner. They moved hesitantly in her direction.

'Sorry,' said the older boy, smiling shyly. 'We'd gone past you before we noticed you.'

'I can believe that,' the visitor said with a grin. 'I'm Sally Griffin. You must be Mrs McElroy's boys. Your mother is expecting me.'

The visitor wasn't prepared for the explosion of laughter which greeted her remarks. It's uncomfortable to be laughed at, she thought, especially by children. She stood there uncertain what to say or do next. At last the older boy recovered sufficiently to address her, 'Oh, I'm so sorry,' the child gasped, 'but you see I'm not … I am … I mean I'm not …'

It looked as if he were about to lose control once more. Sally did some quick thinking. Of course that's it. They're not Pam's children. Probably two little friends, or perhaps outsiders who shouldn't be here in the first place. Then a thought struck her. Would Pam have forgotten the appointment? Would she be at home? There seemed to be nobody around. She looked at the two children. The older boy had now regained his composure, though the twinkling eyes in the otherwise solemn little face didn't seem to guarantee that he would stay that way too long. He cleared his throat.

'What I want to say is, I'm not a boy. I'm Rosemary and this is my brother Robert. Mummy will have a good laugh when I tell her you thought I was a boy. She's always saying that someday somebody will mistake me for a boy because of the way I behave and this haircut.'

She put up a hand to pull at a curl from the auburn close-cropped hair. 'And now it's happened.'

Sally was amused at the slender child standing before her, so self-assured, yet so innocent. She took hold of Robert's hand.

'Do you know you have the makings of an Olympic runner!'

He was a beautiful child with big brown eyes and curly hair a shade lighter than his sister's.

'Did Rosemary catch up on you?'

'No,' Rosemary answered for him. 'I didn't. When I got around the corner there he was standing stock-still. I said, "What's wrong?" And all he could say was, "That lady. Did you see her? There's a lady back there." So we went back to look and there you were.'

She led the two children to the front door. Rosemary rang the bell. The door opened and the children's mother stood there, hands outstretched.

She smiled warmly: 'Welcome, Sally. I see you picked up my two strays on the way.'

This woman was so different from the woman she had met a

few nights ago. It wasn't that she was out to please her visitor, Sally thought, that caused such a change, but rather that this pleasant humour seemed to fit her more naturally.

Pam led the way into one of the rooms off the hall. Rosemary and Robert automatically took possession of an arm of their mother's chair, their long jean-covered limbs reaching the floor. The group made a lovely picture. Sally became aware that she was under scrutiny.

'You're looking lovely,' Pam said. 'How on earth did you manage to keep the men at a distance up to this?'

'It wasn't easy,' Sally laughed and immediately focused her attention on the children. When Robert left the room Pam said, 'Tea or coffee, Sally?'

'Tea will do fine.'

'Rosemary,' Pam said, 'you can make the tea now.'

After she had gone Sally said, 'She's sweet. And so pretty. You must be proud of the two of them.'

'They're good children.' Pam was wistful, reflective.

Rosemary is the image of her mother, Sally thought, startled by the similarity: the oval shaped face, the delicate bone structure, the huge eyes with their unusual colour and their long dark lashes, the heavy well-arched eyebrows and small teeth.

'I know what you're thinking. How like me Rosemary is. It comes as a bit of a shock to people when they first notice this. And when they do, they see me as a grandmotherly edition of Rosemary.'

'That's not true,' the visitor protested. She realised though that people might be guilty of thinking this if they only knew the Pam she saw at the party. But this other Pam was so vivacious, so young-looking. Her auburn hair had been gathered back into a clasp, curls escaping to frame her face. Her eyes had shed their dullness. Why, she's not much older than myself. And I thought she was forty-four or forty-five. 'For one thing, you look years younger than the other night.' She stopped, embarrassed.

Pam laughed. 'I know what you mean and you needn't feel embarrassed. I did look awful and what's more I acted awful. I could see you weren't quite sure what to make of me, but I must say this for you, you didn't try to flatter me. I can't stand people who flatter me because they feel they have to, or gush over me just because I'm the wife of Pat McElroy. 'Oh, I forgot,' her eyes sparkled, 'you did say something about my eyes.' Suddenly, she looked sad. 'If you only knew how refreshing it is to meet somebody different.' Then brightening, 'I liked you immediately though I may not have shown it. Because you were yourself. Honest. Sincere. You had nothing to hide and you didn't pretend. You see, there was hardly a person there the other night, and I know most of them for a long time, who was being his or her real self. And that goes for me too. Pitiful, isn't it.'

Her eyes were pensive, gazing unseeing ahead. After some moments she uncrossed her legs and sat upright.

'Well, that was quite a speech. My apologies for sermonizing.'

Pam intrigued Sally and she felt she was going to like her a lot. Getting to know her might not be all that hard. She watched her while they talked. She saw the lovely smile which transformed her face. Listened to her rapid articulate flow of words. Watched the quick dramatic movements of her hands. She wore beige trousers and an olive green jumper which did more for her slender figure than the frumpish dress. Pam was just suggesting she might like to have a look-around the house when Rosemary came into the room manoeuvring a trolley laden with tea things. Sally noticed the look that passed between mother and daughter and was unaccountably glad.

'Will you join us?' Sally asked. 'There's enough here for an army.'

'No, thank you. Robert and I are having something to eat with Martha.'

When the child had left the room there was silence for a few moments, each woman occupied with her own thoughts.

Then Sally said, 'She's a lovely little girl,' as Pam poured out the tea. 'She's so self-confident and capable.'

'I hope that will never be knocked out of her.' She paused. 'Having Robert and her makes everything else almost bearable.'

She seemed to be unaware that she had let anything slip out as her voice tapered to a whisper.

It was nearly ten o'clock before Pam got up to show her visitor around the house. They had talked a lot. Conversation came easily to them.

Robert was sound asleep when they reached his room. He lay on his back, little arms curved upwards, the sleeves of his pyjamas having slipped in wrinkles to his elbows. His curly head was resting on the palms of his hands. The mother stood by the side of his bed looking down at him, seemingly oblivious of her visitor. Then she bent down and kissed him.

'You can have a better look at this room some other time,' she said when she closed the door.

She opened the door of Rosemary's room quietly. A pair of bright eyes welcomed the disturbance.

'Just as I thought. Now, I suppose you're going to tell me you were only waiting for us to come before settling down.' Oh no, you don't,' as her daughter sat up in bed intending to make the most of the visit. The mother pressed her back gently onto the pillow.

'You should be asleep. Robert is asleep.'

'He would be,' Rosemary grumbled good-naturedly, allowing herself to be tucked in.

'He doesn't know what he's missing.'

'And I suppose you'd like to stay awake all the time in case you'd miss something.' Pam bent down to kiss her.

'I love you, Mummy. You're the best mummy in the world.'

The mother kissed the little face, white with tiredness, once more.

'I should have gone up to her earlier,' she said, as she led the way to the main bedroom. The visitor marvelled at the beauty of the place. She would have thought it almost too perfect but that here and there was evidence that two children lived in the house, who had not the respect the beauty and perfection demanded. Pam must have read her thoughts.

'It's easily known that there are children around,' she said, bending to pick up a tattered book that lay half hidden under a plant trough. 'Not that they do any real damage, but why they can't open a door without leaving their finger marks all over it I'll never know. But I can't be checking them all the time. This is their home, not a show-house.' There was a slight edge to her voice as she finished speaking.

Sally would have liked to linger, examining and admiring, but it was getting late and it seemed that Pam's interest and enthusiasm in her role of guide was waning. What was it she heard an old man in Leenane say when she remarked about the beauty of the scenery?

'When you always live with beauty, you no longer see it.' Pam must feel the same way. She must get bored at times showing other people around her beautiful mausoleum. Wasn't that what she called it? Automatically they turned in the direction of the front door. They had omitted the kitchen and one or two other rooms, the visitor noticed, but thought it better not to say anything about it. From the time her host had closed the door of Rosemary's bedroom the life seemed to have drained from her face. Even her voice had taken on a bleakness she had not noticed before.

'I suppose you're expecting Pat home any minute,' Sally said, as they stood in the doorway.

'I expect him when I see him.'

Sally felt the curt reply was not intentional. Nevertheless, she was puzzled by it. Pam walked with her to the car. For a moment they stood gazing at the view. City lights twinkled in the distance. Out to sea, the lighthouse split the darkness. The Hill of Howth was a charcoal sketch on the sky line. There was a soft soughing among the trees and way below, the sea, spent itself gently against the rocks. The silence was pierced by a night-bird's call.

Sally said, 'It's beautiful.' She looked back at the house set in tranquillity.

'It is', Pam said. Her voice was so low that Sally scarcely caught the words. They shook hands. As Sally drove down the driveway she saw in the rear-view mirror a lonely figure, tiny against the magnificent backdrop. She was beginning to see a little of the truth.

Pat McElroy had seen what he hoped was Sally's car drawing away from the house, its headlights dipping in and out through the tree-lined driveway. He gave a grunt of satisfaction and accelerated slightly. His wife was brushing her teeth as he opened the door of their bedroom.

'Did Sally come?' he called into her as he began to undress.

'Mmm,' she mumbled, her mouth full of froth.

He could hear the nightly ritual of mouth-rinsing and splashing of water. Then there was silence. What was delaying her? Well, he was tired and sleepy. No point in waiting.

Pam pushed the connecting bathroom door further ajar and took one long ironic look at her husband's still figure. She knew he wasn't asleep. If he wasn't interested in talking, neither was she. She sat at her dressing table and switched on the overhead light. Suddenly she got up and switched off the main bedroom light. Then she sat down again and looked at herself critically in the mirror. She took up her hairbrush and slowly and rhythmically brushed her hair until it began to shine. Somehow, the fresh lovely appearance of Sally triggered off the desire to do something about her own neglected appearance. Once upon a time, in the not-too-distant past, though it seemed it was of another age, she used to look as lovely and as lively as Sally.

She paused in her brushing now and again and was aware of the uneven breathing of her husband. *Idiot! He thinks that I think he's asleep.* She removed the grubby-looking dressing gown

11

from her shoulders and padded out to the main bathroom where the soiled- linen basket was tucked away in its ornate alcove. She knew there was a new dressing gown somewhere if she could put her finger on it. After some searching she found the box, the gown still folded in its original tissue paper. She took it from its box and hung it in the airing closet. Then before settling down for the night she checked, as she always did, to see if the children were comfortable. Rosemary had scarcely moved. *Poor baby,* she thought, *she must be panned out.* She looked in at Robert. He had thrust the bedclothes away from him and was lying, one leg straddled over the eiderdown, an arm encircling the pillow. Her heart ached with love for her children as she made these lonely nightly visits. They looked so sweet and vulnerable. As she gazed at each sleeping child, present thoughts jostling with past memories, pressed the tears to her eyes. Tonight the prayer that was always there was forced from her lips. The stillness added to its poignancy. 'I hope life will be kind to you. I know there will be some pain and suffering, but as long as you love and are loved you can overcome anything. I hope you never hurt anyone, especially those you love or who love you.'

When she got into bed her husband was sleeping soundly. She turned on her side and for the first time for a long while she fell asleep immediately.

She awoke next morning feeling surprisingly refreshed and rested. She could hear the sound of her husband's electric razor through the closed door of their bathroom. Sometimes, she slept on into the morning. Sometimes, she got up for the children's sake as they liked to see her sitting at the table with them. This morning she got up out of bed with a bound. The children were already up and seated at the breakfast when she came downstairs. They had finished their cereal and were now tucking into a plate of Martha's homemade bread. How could they eat so heartily at such an unearthly hour of the morning?

It took her all her time to drink a glass of fruit juice and a finger of toast with her coffee.

'Mummy, where did you get that? I never saw that before,' Rosemary exclaimed.

'Oh, I've had this dressing gown for ages. I got it when you were very small.'

She had good reason to remember the Christmas she got it. It was the first of many occasions she was forced to think for Pat for the sake of the children. He had given no indication he was remembering her. His staff, his cleaning woman would be full of praise for Pat's thoughtfulness and generosity if she cared to visit the office at that time of the year. He never forgot anyone, they would say, not even his past employees. Was there ever such a thoughtful man? Was there indeed, she thought. On that occasion, six years ago, she had left it to the last minute, hoping against hope he would remember her. It was the night before Christmas Eve that she reminded him by referring to the surprise present she had bought for him. Looking contrite he admitted he had forgotten to buy her a present as he had been so terribly busy. Would she run out and get something nice for herself? He wasn't much good at that kind of thing anyway. A stubborn streak was urging her not to buy anything. To let him down in front of people who asked. To be able to smile sweetly and say: 'Oh, Pat forgot. He's such a busy man. But I don't blame him and I don't really mind.'

But to let down her children? To see the disappointment in their faces on Christmas morning? What explanation would be sufficient to cover up the forgetfulness of their beloved Daddy? So she went out and bought the dressing gown. It would have been of some comfort had he accompanied her, but he was busy adding his own personal taste in decorations to the hall and the children remained on to help him. It was a lonely outing and her heart wasn't in the buying. She saw the dressing gown in the window and asked to try it on. It was horribly expensive and another time she would have refused to spend so much money on principle, but now she was indifferent. She brought it home. Having shown it to the children on Christmas morning as they sat around the Christmas tree opening their gift parcels – 'Daddy's present to me' – she had returned it to its box and put it away. From that Christmas on, birthday and wedding anniversaries, the procedure was jostle his memory and hooray! Another expensive present to show the children and friends. It was only just one more re-arrangement of the pattern of their lives.

The children were still gazing at her in admiration.

'Well, do you like it?' she asked as she sat at the table with a flourish.

'It's beautiful,' Rosemary said, her eyes round with wonder. Evidently she had forgotten she had seen it before.

'That velvet makes you look like a princess,' Robert said, the big brown eyes widening in delight.

She held out her hand in royal fashion. 'You may kiss my hand, Sir Knight,' she said in languid tones.

'Oh, Mamee!' Robert said, reverting to his baby enunciation. But he immediately bent over and kissed her hand. His father came into the breakfast room just then. He glanced at the three smiling faces.

'What's all that about?' he asked, as he took his place at the table.

'Her Royal Highness, Princess Galetta has announced she will honour us with her presence for an un-un – for an unspec – for an unspecified time.'

Rosemary's victory over the elusive word shone in her face as she looked at her father.

'Princess what?'

'Princess Galetta. Isn't that a pretty name? I've just made it up for Mummy. Doesn't it suit her?'

Pam smiled. She was continually being surprised by the quick inventive minds of her children.

"Did you see Miss Griffin last night, Daddy?' Robert asked as he gulped down a last mouthful of coffee. 'She's beautiful but not as beautiful as Mummy,' he added.

'No, I'm afraid I missed her.'

Rosemary said, 'Don't worry. You'll be seeing lots of her. She's going to come here often. I hope so, anyway, because I like her.'

The room seemed curiously silent when the children left for school. Pat poured himself another cup of coffee.

'So Sally came last night.'

'You asked me that last night and I said yes.'

'So I did. I was so tired I had forgotten.'

Pam gave him a level gaze. He looked down at his coffee.

'Are you seeing her again? It would do you good.'

Don't talk down to me. I'm not one of the children, she wanted to blaze out at him. Instead she said, 'As it happens we haven't made any arrangement for future meetings.'

He glanced up from a letter he was reading. 'Oh, is that so? Perhaps it's just as well. I don't care for her an awful lot. Of course that needn't prejudice you.'

'Why don't you care for her?'

'I think she's not sincere. A too-good-to-be-true kind of person. But then, she has nothing to do with me.'

'As a matter of fact I think she's a very sincere and good person and she seems to like me and that's not usual for people to do nowadays. You've seen to that.'

'Oh, we're back to that again. I ask a simple question and we have a melodrama.'

'You ask a simple question and I get treated like a child: when am I meeting Sally again? It would be good for me. I'll decide whom I'll meet and when, and I'm not going to worry whether it's going to be good or bad for me.'

'You stop acting like a child and you won't be treated like a child.'

'Are you a paediatrician or my daddy?'

'My God! It's impossible to carry on a conversation with you.'

'We never do carry on a conversation or, haven't you noticed? It's either the great silence or a verbal barrage.'

'Don't blame me for either. You showed very clearly the other night at Sally's place that you were expert in both fields. You were an absolute embarrassment. Only for Sally – and I'll say this much for her – who tried to get you out of your sulks, you could have spoiled the evening for everybody.'

'That's flattering. I didn't know that I was that important. That it was possible for little old unpopular me to make a difference to any party. I seem to remember you telling me more than once that I was a nonentity – I think that was the word you used – that it didn't matter whether I came out with you for the evening or not.'

'Go on. Drag up everything. Typical.'

'Not typical. Tactical. When you get dirty I get dirty. And let me remind you that I wasn't being sulky the other night. I was being my usual self. And if silent is being usual you have made me that way. I'm like that with you at home, which is the way you want it, so why should I change for other people? As you can see by this conversation we have a verbal barrage as a change from the silence.'

She lit a cigarette to hide the trembling of her lips. Two emotions were in conflict. To go away somewhere from this scornful man and cry her heart out, or slap that handsome face until he cried with pain.

He took a sip of coffee. 'When I asked you about Sally was that being silent?'

'You were indifferent last night. You hadn't two words to throw to a dog when you came in, but this morning curiosity got the better of you. Wondering why she came here, and was it possible I could have a friend at last.'

He pushed back his chair noisily and got up from the table scooping his correspondence together viciously: 'You're a right bitch.'

He banged the door after him and with an anguished cry she dropped her head into her hands.

Chapter Two

Sally Griffin got out of bed feeling tired and depressed and wondered why she should feel that way. Was it because of meeting Pam last night? Could she possibly have that effect on her? Should she meet her again? Last night she liked her and enjoyed her company. This morning that picture of her standing lonely against the silhouette of that mausoleum, as Pam referred to her house, gave her a pang. But why should she feel sorry for her? Others openly or covertly disliked her. She had got everything any woman could want. A handsome wealthy husband who seemed to give her every attention. And, she was no great match for him. No, she shouldn't say that. That was only what other people thought. She did seem a very nice person. Then she had a dream? home, two lovely children, a car, a devoted housekeeper, a daily help and a reliable gardener. She had just about everything, and if all that couldn't make her happy then she had only herself to blame.

But there she was, Sally Griffin, adding two and two and making what? How could she, just after a few hours' acquaintanceship, come to any conclusion? Surely Pam wasn't one of those disgruntled people who wouldn't be happy no matter what they had. She couldn't be as bad as she was painted, or indeed as she painted herself. Last night she had seen a facet of her character that she must rarely if ever show in public. She saw a vivacious, attractive woman whose lovely eyes sparkled when she laughed. She saw how naturally the role of an affectionate, loving mother fitted her. Then what? There was something wrong somewhere. Pam and Pat together. The picture blurred a little.

Why was it that Pam seemed to have the unhappy knack of alienating all sympathy when she was in Pat's company? She tried to shrug off disturbing thoughts. She would ring Pam sometime. She had made various arrangements with her friends and she had Morrison to think of. She was meeting him this evening. Her eyes brightened at the prospect. She hummed as she took a last look at herself. Tomorrow she would be meeting Vienna Dalton. They had arranged to have a meal before seeing the play: *When Two Worlds Collapse*. She was looking forward to seeing it. She'd seen so much rubbish in the past masquerading as theatre it would be a change to see a play that didn't insult her intelligence. She would enjoy it all the more having Vienna to share the evening's entertainment with. Next to Morrison there was no company she liked better.

To other people it must seem that Vienna never had any trouble of her own, but she knew differently. Vienna took trouble and sorrow in her stride. Only she knew how Vienna had nearly broken down in the past, but never, never was anyone aware of this fact. Pam was the very antithesis of Vienna. Both were tall and slender but there the similarity ended. Pam was only a shadow compared to the bright golden person Vienna was. Pam let the whole world know how she felt. Vienna was herself, facing the world with a frank, good-humoured, sometimes cynical and self-mocking approach. But in something else they had a common bond. It seemed neither cared a damn what the rest of the world thought of them. If only I didn't feel obliged to meet Pam again it would make all the difference, she thought. What was it about her that tugged at her heart?

The evening with Vienna was a disappointment to Sally. Over the meal they got entangled in an argument over Pam. Vienna dismissed her as a careless slut, too absorbed in herself to give a thought to her husband and children.

'That's not fair. She's a – '

'Correction,' Vienna interrupted. 'Pam isn't absorbed in herself.

If she were she would do something about herself, about the way she dresses. Everything about her is all wrong. Not many women are as lucky as her. She has a wonderful husband and it's obvious he's devoted to her, but even in public that bitch can't behave herself. She embarrasses everyone as well as Pat. No wonder he wears that resigned look when she's around. When she's not around he's a different person. I wouldn't blame him if he had an affair, but of course he's the type of man who would always be loyal to his wife. Do you know, he's the most obliging person you could meet. Nothing is too much trouble for him. I'd swear she's jealous of Pat's popularity.' She sniffed derisively. 'But why am I wasting my time talking about her?'

Sally was shaken by the sheer vehemence of her remarks. She knew Vienna could be frank and outspoken, but never to the point where it could be hurtful or downright cruel as she was now. What had got into her?

Vienna's eyes were still fiery when Sally looked up at her. She waited. Vienna was content to let the silence deepen. Sally was the first to speak.

'I never heard you speak like that before about anyone. Anyone would think that Pam was your enemy.'

She looked at Vienna, her eyes misted with pain and doubt. 'I gather Pam is far from popular and it's difficult to come to any conclusion about her just after a couple of meetings, but there's something about her that makes me think she's more wronged than wrong.'

'Oh, come off it, softie.'

'No, I mean that. Anyway, which of us hasn't faults, the only difference between Pam and the rest of us is that we're more clever than she is at hiding them.' She felt silly for feeling so near to tears and took a mouthful of coffee to steady herself. 'And we mustn't forget that there are always two sides to every story. Surely, Pam can't have been like that always. Can you imagine Pat ever marrying a slut as you so elegantly put it! So, what can have happened to bring about the change in her? Surely Pat must be responsible in some way for the way she is now.'

Vienna was smiling once more. 'My dear Watson, I can be of no possible help to you there. All I know is I can't ever remember seeing Pam any different. She's married, I suppose, about thirteen years and I've known her for at least eight of these years. Sorry to disillusion you and all that.'

Sally Griffin had just returned to her office from her morning break some days later when Pam McElroy phoned. 'I had intended to ring you, Pam, but you beat me to it. How are you?'

Pam sounded full of the joys of life. What are they all talking about? This surely is the real Pam, Sally thought, delighted at the lively tone at the other end.

After answering enquiries about Rosemary and Robert, Pam said: 'I phoned specially to thank you for calling out the other night. I enjoyed it very much and I hope you'll call out as often as you can. So do the children. They fell for you in a big way. Now, I was wondering would you be able to meet me in town sometime for a meal and a chat?'

'Yes, I'd love to. What about next Tuesday? Are you free for that evening?' Pam felt like saying that all her evenings were free but stopped herself.

Sally Griffin was at the meeting place on time. As she ran up the steps of the Shelbourne Hotel she wondered if Pam would be there before her. She gave a quick look around. She needn't have rushed so much. There was no sign of her. She sat down and prepared to wait.

'Sorry I'm late.'

She looked up and saw Pam, hot and breathless, coming towards her. Her initial reaction was, how could Pam wear that awful suit for an evening in town, but then she forgot her disappointment as she gave her one of those rare attractive grins.

'But give a dog a bad name and it seems a pity not to live up to it. Or down to it.'

'You're not too late.' Sally glanced at her watch. 'Only about fifteen minutes. Make it ten the next time. Gradually does it or you might do yourself an injury.'

Sally felt she was going to enjoy the evening. Pam was her kind of person. I don't know how people can misjudge her, she thought. She really has a terrific personality and its impact is immediate. Why does she take such pains to hide it or is she quite aware that she does so? No wonder her children are so attractive. It was from Pam that they got this shining personality, not from Pat. Pat was – well, he was nice in a different way. When they had settled down with their drinks Pam said: 'Tell me Sally, what do you think of me? I mean as you see me, warts and all.' She was smiling but her eyes were serious.

'Why do you ask?' She was embarrassed. This wasn't a fair question.

'Why do I ask? Because I know I'll get an honest answer. Please. Tell me.'

Sally hesitated. 'Do you usually go around asking your friends what they think of you?' She kept her voice light. Pam couldn't really be serious.

'No. I must admit this is the first time I've done it. And the reason is, I think you're going to be a different kind of friend.'

Sally was treated to another of those attractive grins.

'All right. If that's what you want, here goes. When I saw you come in I was disappointed to see you wearing that outfit. I thought you could have done better. I mean, that suit looks expensive but it does nothing for you. Besides, it's the wrong thing to wear this time of the year. It reminds me of the sort of thing you'd wear on a cold day if you were taking the dog for a walk.'

'But I do wear it taking the dog for a walk.'

'But you're not taking the dog for a walk now.'

'That's true. But continue.'

If there was any pain in the giving or receiving the criticism it did not show in their laughter.

It was true, Pam thought, she hadn't bothered very much about her appearance for a long time. All that mattered to her nowadays was personal cleanliness and tidiness. Her days had a great sameness about them, though punctuated on occasions by those various social functions which Pat seemed to think were one of the necessities of life. This evening, with Sally, she felt the faint stirring of something she had thought was dead. She actually wanted to shake herself from the apathy which had crept up and engulfed her so insidiously. It was so easy to give in during the latter years. Now she felt this stirring, and faint though it was, it was there and it was insistent. She hugged the thought to herself.

'Doctor Sally, you've a chronic case on your hands, but I think the cure is in my own hands.'

'Then the cure should be quick.'

After a moment's silence Pam said: 'You must be very excited being engaged. I can remember well what it was like. The wonderful certainty of knowing you were loved and loving in return. It's such a beautiful time of one's life.'

'It is, even though I'm a good deal older than you were when you were engaged. I'm thirty-three.'

'You don't look it. I'm thirty-seven and I'm lucky if I look it as most of the time I look like my own mother.'

'Stop knocking yourself. That's another bad habit you must cut out.'

'Sorry! Sorry! Morrison is very nice. I haven't seen that much of him. Few people call to the house now. Pat prefers to entertain out. But what I've seen of him I like. When are you going to the States?'

'In September. We're getting married over there. Morrison's father has a heart condition and wouldn't be able to make the journey. My family will be going over for the wedding.'

Sally noticed, as she talked about her plans, a certain wistfulness in her listener's face. She pulled herself up abruptly.

'But of course you've gone through all this, Pam. Have you any advice for the innocent and unwary?'

'If you were my daughter and asked for advice there is so much I could say and even then, who is qualified to tell whom what. One can only draw from one's own experience, and is advice or knowledge from one's own experience always the best or wisest to give? But I don't think you need worry. I feel you and Morrison will have a very good marriage.'

Sally veered the conversation away from herself in an effort to encourage Pam to talk about Pat and the children. Without quite knowing how she found herself discussing the recent row in the Dáil between the Minister for Health and the opposition spokesperson. As interesting as that was she realised attention had been diverted from home ground so it must be a touchy subject, or why this avoidance of what was so dear to so many women. Most women didn't need any encouragement to enthuse over their children at least. But she mustn't get bogged down in futile conjectures.

When Sally looked at her watch again it was ten minutes past eleven. The evening had flown. Pam was really a very likeable person and good company. They would meet in two weeks' time at the O'Gorman's tenth wedding anniversary party to which they had been invited. Sally told Pam she was taking a long weekend off to visit her favourite aunt. She promised to phone when she returned.

Why is it, Pam thought as she lay in bed, *that when I'm in good form Pat is at his worst? Does it give him some kind of sadistic satisfaction to see me depressed or cross, or aiming cracks at him when we're alone?*

Because then he puts on his most tolerant act, particularly in company, when I feel like throwing something at him. Why can't we carry on a conversation like two normal people without one or other of us going off the deep end?

This evening as they remained seated at the table smoking a cigarette with their coffee she described her previous evening's outing with Sally. The meal had been one of Martha's special efforts, Pat was in cheerful mood and the children were at their most amusing. One time during the dinner she had flung back her head and laughed at something Rosemary had said when Robert startled her by saying: 'Mummy, why don't you laugh more often?'

She looked at the sober little face.

'That's right. Why don't you laugh more often?' Rosemary had echoed.

'Perhaps because I have very little to laugh about.'

The response was involuntary and seeing the two solemn little faces she hastily amended it. 'If you two keep going the way you've been since we sat down your father and I will have to eat alone. Otherwise we'll get indigestion eating and laughing together. You're better than any comedy team I've seen on television.'

She was relieved to see their faces crinkle in pleasure.

Pam's smile still lingered on her face after they had left the room. The children were wonderful. *Do we really deserve them?* But then they must have some idea how much we love them and that counts, for the moment at any rate. And because of the lighter mood she found it easy to tell her husband about the previous night's events. It was only when she had said something that required an answer she realised that his mind had been elsewhere.

'I've been talking to you for the past ten minutes and you haven't made a single remark. I suppose you haven't been listening to a word I've said.'

'I have been listening.'

'Well, why didn't you answer my question just now?'

'I didn't hear it.'

'Why? Are you deaf or something? Tell me one thing I've said.'

'You were talking about Sally.'

'Go on.'

He stubbed his cigarette savagely in the ashtray. 'What is this? An inquisition?'

'Why can't you be honest and say you weren't listening. You must think I'm blind not to see that you're barely able to hide your boredom whenever I talk to you. Even the children are beginning to notice your rudeness to me. Thank heavens Rosemary and Robert see so little of you. Would you behave with your clients the way you behave with me? You certainly wouldn't. The handsome Patrick McElroy is such a gentleman. So charming. I know your litany of public praise off by heart. I have my own private litany and they end with "Oh Lord, deliver me!"'

'There you go again.'

'Again what?' she blazed back at him. 'I was just talking about someone we both know and you foul things up as usual. Why can't we carry on a conversation like two normal people? And the little conversation we do have is about Rosemary and Robert. And even then we can't agree, because as on everything else you're an authority.'

'What the hell are you talking about? Good God, do I never get a moment's peace? If it isn't one thing it's another. I thought your moan was about Sally. That I wasn't listening to what you were saying about her. Who is Sally anyway to get so worked up about?

'I'm not the slightest bit interested in her if you want to know the truth. It seems to me that I've heard nothing but Sally this and Sally that for the past few weeks. I'm getting sick and tired hearing about this paragon of virtue.'

'Is that so? It would be interesting to see how your friend Morrison would react to such remarks about his fiancée. I might tell him, only he'd never believe me. As to your remarks about hearing nothing but talk of Sally you exaggerate as usual.' She forced herself to be calm and reasonable. 'I have seen Sally three times in as many weeks and have spoken of her exactly three times, and the first of these consisted of one word when you asked me had she called. On the second occasion I indulged in a few remarks as I was getting ready to meet her. This could have taken up no more than two minutes. This evening I was unfortunately a little more vocal. Nevertheless, I couldn't have been more than nine or ten minutes, and even then, it seems I took up none of your precious time.'

Her painful honesty and accuracy stung him into retorting: 'She certainly gets you wound up which is no bad thing in a way.' He got up from the table. 'Which reminds me, if she is all that wonderful, according to yourself, how come some of it doesn't rub off on you?'

Her eyes were cold and hard as she returned his stare but her heart was crying inside. She moved restlessly in the bed. She would not go to the O'Gorman's party. In spite of knowing that Sally would be there she felt a terrible indifference for everything outside her home. If Pat could only realise what he was doing to her. It was as if she were being constantly steamrolled over and over. What was he trying to do to her? Her head ached in torment and despair. She wanted to pray but her mind refused to co-operate. 'Oh God, you don't listen.' The cry was wrenched from her.

When Sally phoned on the morning of the O'Gorman's party, Pam's resolve not to go was shaken, but when she replaced the receiver her face set in stubborn determination. She had forced her voice to be enthusiastic talking to Sally: oh yes, she was looking forward to going. She must dig out something to wear. Sally should look out for the unexpected. After all she would only be responding to the hints she got from her not so long ago. So for her sake she intended to be a hit even if what she wore hit the guests between the eyes.

Sally burst out laughing and she found herself laughing too. That was one thing she hadn't lost yet, the ability to make people laugh. A pity she couldn't make it work for herself more often. But how could she laugh when her heart was so heavy? How could she laugh when there was a millstone dragging her down to utter despair day by day and week by week? When she succeeded in easing the load a fraction or tipped it to one side in an effort to regain the simple happiness her soul craved, relief was short-lived. Pat and she had scarcely spoken a word since they had it out with each other the evening she had talked about Sally. She hadn't seen Sally since. He must have liked that. Probably thought: there's another friendship I've nipped in the bud. But did his mind think along those lines, or was it that it had become second nature to him to destroy anything or anyone connected with her?

One by one in insidious moves she had been deprived of her own personal friends. It had taken her a long time to see through Pat and to realise what was happening to her. She was fully aware of it now, but somehow she felt too drained of energy, physical and mental, to prevent it. But she would not give up Sally's friendship. She would fight for this in spite of everything.

Although the minimum of conversation was carried on between Pat and herself in front of the children she put on an act of cheerfulness. This act had become second nature to her. If only she could shed her personal unhappiness and, forgetting about Pat, make the children the centre of her life it would be so much healthier, and better for the children too. How much longer would they be deceived by her? And now, in the last few days because she had been cool and undemonstrative, Pat had swung the opposite way and become pleasant and chatty. She should have become immune to these fluctuations of his moods, even become bored with them, but always they had this terrible power to inflict just as much pain and heartache as before, on occasions even greater. Something or someone would have to change before an explosion occurred.

Nothing or no one could change Pat. She couldn't change him. The truth was she had not tried or even thought of doing so. It was she who had changed. Had done it for Pat's sake, conforming to his every wish, believing it to be the right thing and had done it with love, thinking: this is what marriage is all about. The giving of oneself all the time, not counting the cost because there was no price that could be put on love. She would do anything for love of Pat.

But there were times too when she had been pricked by thoughts that no matter what she put into their marriage it wasn't enough. True. Pat hadn't set out to change her. The disappointed look, the unhappy face after the arguments, the cold silences that followed, silences that extended for longer periods as time went by, did the work for him. To avoid all this she had given in to Pat no matter what the issue involved was. And so there came a day when she woke up to the realisation that she was becoming a stranger to herself, a creature as far removed from the person she had been before her marriage as Pat was from the person she thought she had married. She was not able to change herself anymore for Pat. She had become the someone else he seemingly wanted and that hadn't satisfied him. She didn't know what he wanted.

She must stop thinking of him, feeling for him. She had to get out of this marriage trap, because that was what it was. It was no marriage union. It was dangerous for both of them. For her it could prove fatal. From now on she would travel alone, guiding the children as far as they needed her. When the need of her was ended she would go her own way. A moment of calm had come to her. She faced the truth for the first time in her married life. Her marriage was finished but her life was not. She had something to give of herself, if not to her husband, to her children, to others: the lonely ones, the neglected, the poor, the disabled. She would have more love to give away, more time, more concentration. She was still a young woman with her whole life ahead. And she mustn't forget she was a doctor, even though she had given up thoughts of practising when she got married because that was what Pat had wished. She might never have qualified, never have sacrificed her career, for all the allusion Pat made to it, or indeed his friends. As far as they were concerned she was just one more stay-at-home wife who had it easy and didn't know how to appreciate that fact.

Well, she would do something about her qualification when she had the clarity of mind to deal with it. In the meantime she would live as if she were a single person, planning her daily life the way it suited her. That was where real single bliss could not equal hers. For she had the love of two children whom she loved with all her heart. It mightn't be a bad life. Pat was her social security for the time being and that was all. In a way it would be a relief to cut adrift from him. She felt more free already. From now on she wouldn't feel compelled to go where Pat went, to do what Pat felt was right for her. Her first independent move would be her refusal to go with him to the O'Gorman's party.

She had no particular interest in going. It would be the same old crowd except for two or three new or absent faces. And as for Sally being there, she could see her at any time.

Pat would go without her of course. He had done so before.

She was doing a quick tidying-up of the landing where there were some stray toys and books left lying around when her husband dashed upstairs to change, and seeing her unconcernedly working, still in her trousers and jumper, paused in the act of opening their bedroom door.

'Are you not ready yet?'

'Does it look like it?'

'Come along. We haven't much time.'

She followed him into the bedroom and closed the door. 'I'm not going.'

'Not going? For heaven's sake what's up now?'

'Nothing. Just that I've decided not to go.'

'You've decided not to go! And at this late hour!'

She looked at him coolly. 'Yes. And at this late hour. I've no excuse. I'm not sick. I'm not tired, at least not in the way you think. You go. You make your excuses for me to your friends. You've become quite an expert at that, you know.'

She waited for his reaction. No matter what he said to her from now on or how he acted, she felt she would be able for it, because now she had removed him from his place in her life.

He looked at her with suppressed fury, then strode into the bathroom and banged the door behind him. She sat down at her dressing table and brushed her hair, examining her reflection critically. She could hear the shower going. For one moment she was pierced by a pang of remorse but quickly brushed away the temptation to change her mind.

The next few days were not easy for her. She had started off with determination if not enthusiasm in her new approach to life, in her new way of thinking. With the beginning of each day she consciously blotted out all thoughts of her husband. In some ways it was easier than she anticipated, seeing him as she did every day. Now she was able to look at him with equanimity, speak to him in a friendly manner, thrusting all desire for anything further from her mind. So what if she realised she was hardly a presence in his company. She should be used to that by now, she told herself.

But during those quiet moments when she was alone her mind would boggle at the thought of the endless future. How wrong it all was. How perverse. Pat was not her husband but neither was he her brother, her father, her lover nor her son. Who was he then? And what were they doing together in the one house? If they were working partners there would be no problem. They would separate after the day's work and go their different ways. It was during these dark moments of despair she would be tempted to give up and

31

go down on her knees in an endeavour once more to make her husband see what was happening to their marriage. But then a moment of calmness would let her see how futile and humiliating that course would be. She had done it so often in the past, and if she stood on the top of the highest mountain and voiced her pleading to the four corners of the earth she would have got as little response, except there, she would not be at the receiving end of a barely tolerant look which told her in no uncertain terms, when it was not repeated in cold anger, that her trouble was all in the mind and that she should see a psychiatrist.

When Sally Griffin phoned her in the morning to enquire how she was, she was about to say she was feeling fine when she remembered that her husband would have given an excuse like an illness for not going to the O'Gorman's party. She was right. Pat had said she had been hit by a sudden bug. She hated deceiving Sally but she didn't want her to suspect anything. She had let herself down too often in the past and had injured nobody but herself. From now on she was holding on to her dignity and pride.

Sally gave her the news. 'You would have enjoyed it.' She stopped suddenly. 'But you must have heard all about it from Pat.'

'Men forget all the important bits.'

She felt much better after the phone-call. She would have understood if a girl so in love as Sally was didn't get in touch with her. No one else took the trouble to phone her.

There's always some crisis or other with Pam, Pat thought, as he stood at the window of his study, gazing into the distance. There was no pleasing her. Now, this new mood of hers. What was that all about? Impatiently he dismissed it from his mind. There were other things to think of. A new architectural competition was coming up; it was being held for a new block of civic offices in the city. Already he knew what he was going to do, what that particular area required and could afford in office accommodation, and how essential that the whole scheme remain in character with the ancient buildings surrounding it. It would be a great moment in his career if he won because he would be winning against stiff national and international competition.

As well as that exciting prospect, Barry Davis had given him the job of designing new premises for his motor-works. Because of the size of this site he was off to a good start, with no restrictions in design or plan. So all his own ideas and the ideas he picked up on his trips to the Continent could be incorporated in these new premises. He loved his work and was proud of his success. Then there was the trip to Europe. He enjoyed those business trips but he missed the children. His face softened as he thought of Rosemary and Robert. Robert was such a manly little fellow and so intelligent. Rosemary would be quite a beauty some day. He often thought how like Laura she was, his little sister who died when she was only twelve. Laura had been a bright and pretty little girl. He had missed her terribly for a long time. The two people whom he had loved so much, his father and Laura, had left him.

He would have liked two or three more children. If they were like Rosemary and Robert they would be no hardship to any parent. But there was no use thinking like that now.

He had two children and he was satisfied.

Chapter Three

The evenings were getting longer and Rosemary and Robert were enthusiastic when their mother suggested outings after dinner. The mother enjoyed them as much as the children. At first they explored all the walks in the neighbourhood, then they went further afield. Rosemary and Robert wanted their father to join them on the outings but he explained that he was often very tired and sometimes he had work to do in the evenings. They accepted his excuses. After much coaxing Martha was roped in to share their outings. She walked and climbed but eventually gave in. She said she wasn't built for such exertions. Rosemary told her if she lost weight she would be able, and she couldn't lose weight if she didn't take enough exercise. It wasn't all she ate that put on her weight, if she ate only what Martha ate she would die of hunger.

'Well, you could be right, about the exercise I mean, but that's not exercise. That's penance. I'll try and think of easier ways of losing weight.'

'Do that,' Rosemary said, putting her arms around the well-upholstered figure. 'Do it as quick as you can. It's such fun having you with us.'

Martha looked with love at the three happy faces. She loved them so much and could not imagine life without them. Reared in an orphanage where, she would always declare, she got her share of care and affection, she realised early in life that the world outside the orphanage would vary little for her, but this did not distress her. She loved housework and had a natural talent for homemaking. The knowledge and experience she had acquired in the orphanage was used in several households, but it was her last employers she had to thank for sending her to the McElroys. They were going abroad, and anxious that she find suitable employment before they left, suggested she might like to take up work with their friends. They had told her she couldn't have nicer people to work for. With the McElroys she was one of the family. She had love and friendship as well as privacy and comfort. She couldn't have been happier. She noticed that Mr McElroy was quiet but she was fond of him and he treated her kindly. She idolized Mrs McElroy and found it hard not to spoil the children. In other houses she had been left in the background and not having any standards to go by, found nothing strange in this. It was only when she was some months in the McElroy family that she realised all that had been lacking in her life. She had celebrated her thirty-ninth birthday two days after her arrival, a birthday that came and went as so many others had gone, marked neither by card nor greeting. But that was the last lone birthday. Remembering those birthdays with the McElroys her eyes misted with happiness.

Five days had gone since Pat McElroy had left for Europe. He would be taking in three countries – France, Germany and Italy. Pam felt no envy or desire for all this travelling. She was standing at her bedroom window gazing at the garden which was in its early summer beauty. Everything was so fresh and alive it gave her a feeling of sadness. The terraced lawns sloped to a natural dell where there was a tiny lake overhung by trees and shrubs. The view of the Sugar Loaf Mountain was unimpeded, aloof and palely blue against the deeper blue of the sky. Two frilly clouds flirted overhead. The sun was warm and polished the evergreens to a new lustre. She heard the children's laughter in the distance. They had holidays a little earlier than usual and she was glad as it was such beautiful weather. Martha called out to Bill, the gardener. She could hear her say something about flowers. Martha wasn't slow to help out Bill with his work but she confined her willingness to the flower section, as she was quick to remind him whenever he teased her about the hard work that was required in the vegetable garden, and how he could do with some help there. Pam saw Bill emerge slowly from the shrubbery with no hint of impatience in answer to Martha's call. Martha joined him at the fountain. They made an incongruous picture standing there in the sunlit garden, Bill in his mud-stained overalls, scraggily thin and under-sized, using a tool to point out something to Martha who towered over him, spotlessly neat.

I should be happy, Pam thought wistfully. Faces from the past came unbidden to her mind. Some were dead like her mother. She remembered school friends and the friends she had gathered in the pre-marriage years. *Where are they now? Why do I sometimes feel as if I am alone in the world except for the children? Even they at times seem to be lost in a world of their own. And my time with them is so short. Too soon they will leave to start a life for themselves. Does Martha ever feel as alone and lonely as I feel?* Tears ran heedlessly down her face.

Oh God, I'm so lonely I feel I could die. Why is it I seem to have everything and yet nothing? Am I a selfish person? Am I cruel, mean? Even as she raised these doubts she knew in her heart and soul she wasn't. She smiled bleakly. *I know I can be lazy, careless in my appearance, indifferent to people's opinion of me. Being indifferent isn't such a terrible fault, though it could be a form of pride, but I'm full of love and want to pour out that love. The one person that matters most to me, and he does matter in spite of what I tell myself otherwise, abuses my love, treats me as if I were something to be endured in his life. There are times I hate him for what he is doing to me, to us. Why can't I let go and live my own life? Why? Is he that important? He is only one person. Nothing very special about him except that he has the power to paralyse me in so many ways. I know there is much good I can do in the world but when I try*

*he does something to me, what it is I'm not even sure I know. All
I know is, I started out with so much enthusiasm that is not there
anymore. Perhaps I'm weak. Perhaps, I'm a coward. Perhaps, I'm a
born failure. I don't know. He is just one man and I am one woman.
Why can't I fight him? Why can't I overcome him? I should be able
to. Do I try hard enough? But this one man is my husband, not my
enemy, and I was meant to love him as he was meant to love me. I
am resigned most of the time to Pat's treatment of me but is there
anything positive or constructive about that? What is constructive
about being resigned to a husband who has forgotten what it is to
act like one? What is constructive about being resigned to a sickness
or disease if you know there might be treatment for it and a cure,
and you fail to look for either? Because there must be a cure. I'm
not going to remain resigned to Pat's treatment of me. Deep down
inside me I don't believe for one moment I'm ever resigned to it. I
only put up with it for the sake of the children and for appearance's
sake and even then, a vindictive kind of streak in me urges me to let
him down in public. I know I'm letting myself down too. It's a pyrrhic
victory for me but it yields a momentary satisfaction just to see his
embarrassment. Besides, it doesn't seem I have anything to lose now.
But all this negativity has got to stop. I want the man I married in my
life once more, not this stranger.*

She slumped on the fitted window-seat that her husband had
put there specially so as to enjoy the view in comfort. But now
her eyes were blind to the beauty that stretched out before her.
Her mind was active, feverishly seeking an answer to some of the
problems that dogged her married life. She tussled with a new
thought. Do men really want love, the kind of love that women
want? Do they want to love or are they capable of giving it? To
think that men were babies once who responded to love as all
babies do. They smiled and cried for the same reasons as little girls.
As toddlers there wasn't any difference between the sexes where
emotions were concerned. Little boys gathered bunches of wild

flowers with the same enthusiasm as little girls to be given to their mothers with the same love, and got the same hugs and kisses in return. Where does the rot set in that eventually causes such a change in the attitude of the sexes? How and when do boys change so drastically in their emotional lives? *At what age will my little son change from the affectionate, thoughtful boy he is to the thoughtless, insensitive male I see in so many walks of life?*

Now she thought she had the answer to how and where boys change. Boys, though influenced by the gentler qualities of the mother in the early years, their father's influence and example whether it was good or bad or simply indifferent, seemed to exert a greater power over them. A mother can work herself to the bone, advising, encouraging, loving. But unless all that is backed by the boy's father, unless they work in harmony, loving their son, loving each other, much of what she does seems futile or impermanent. What can a woman tell her son if the opposite of what she says is practised before his eyes every day until he leaves home? Unless a boy is extra sensitive and extra perceptive to a disruptive home atmosphere, knowing things are not as they should be, what he sees could be perpetuated in his future home.

She shook her head despairingly. It was useless. She wandered aimlessly into the dressing room. She had promised to bring the children for a drive to the Vartry water works. But she felt suddenly deflated. With her husband not at home to notice how well she was managing, the edge was gone from her enthusiasm. She looked at her reflection in the mirror. It wasn't worthwhile changing. She brushed her hair. The children came running upstairs and bounced through the bedroom door.

'Are you ready, Mummy? It's a lovely day. Martha has a huge picnic hamper for us. She said she got up at the crack of dawn to get it ready.'

The mother came out of the dressing room. Their faces fell.

'Oh, you aren't ready yet,' Rosemary said, looking her up and down. 'Do hurry, Mum, it's such a lovely day and we want to get out fast'.

The mother smiled at their eager faces. 'I'm ready. Come along.'

Rosemary stepped back from her in dismay. 'But Mum, you're not going out in that!' She pointed to the tatty trousers, the well-worn jumper. Something in the child's manner irritated the mother.

'I am. And that, as you call what I'm wearing, is good enough for where we're going.' Her voice, which had sharpened at the unconscious rebuke, softened. 'Anyway, who'll see us? Very few people are there at this hour of the day.'

'But I see you,' the child burst out in anguish. 'And Robert sees you'.

Her lovely mother who dressed so well lately and of whom she had been so proud had gone back to the old ways. If there had been no change the child might have gone on unheeding. But she had seen how her mother could look and some of her good example had rubbed off on her. She had also seen there were other choices a girl could wear besides school uniform and stained jeans and jumpers.

'Oh Mummy, please change. You've a lovely pair of trousers somewhere. I think I know where they are. And jumpers too.'

She rushed into the dressing room and slid over a door, pulling frantically at the racks of clothes. The mother's temper snapped.

'Leave my things alone and come out of there,' she ordered. She was not going to be pushed around by her own child. She was sick of being pushed around by people. This was the last straw.

Rosemary came slowly into the bedroom, all joy and enthusiasm drained from her face.

Her mother bent forward accusingly, her face cold with fury.

'Since when did I start taking instructions from you on what and what not to wear?' Her face reached out to the now frightened child. 'If you don't like what I wear that's just too bad.'

The mother found she could barely control herself. All the suppressed resentment, hurt and anger that had been locked inside her found a strange outlet and was suddenly unleashed on an innocent victim. A warning voice told her to stop before she went too far but she ignored it and suddenly she lost control.

'If you don't want to come with us you may stay at home,' she shouted. She saw the fear in the child's face giving way to stubbornness.

'Then I shall stay at home,' she said loftily.

She took Robert's hand to take him from the room. 'Robert and I aren't going anywhere with you.'

The mother held a restraining hand on her son. 'Oh no, you don't. Robert is coming with me.'

The boy started to cry. Rosemary threw a protective arm around him, drawing him away from her mother. The mother gave a push and the child staggered back, eyes blazing.

'Daddy was right. You are a slut!' she cried furiously.

Pam heard the sound of the stinging slap on the child's face. She wasn't conscious of the act until she saw the red smear on the smooth cheek. The girl looked at her mother for an instant, then tore from the room crying hysterically, followed by Robert roaring at the top of his voice.

The mother did not move. She did not know how long she stood there numb with shock. A knock on the door and a worried Martha, on the pretext of something to do with the picnic, called into her. She muttered some reply. She heard her retreating footsteps. And then the whole terrible scene hit home and kneeling on the floor she pressed her face on the bed. Her baby. Her sweet gentle little girl to call her that. Never, never would she have believed that this could happen. And to think that Pat was low enough, cruel enough to say that horrible word to their daughter about her mother. No matter what kind of a mother she was, and she believed she wasn't a bad mother, she didn't deserve that. She had accused Pat of a lot of things in the past, but nothing could go lower than this. The comfort of tears eluded her.

There was a knock on the door. 'May we come in, Mummy, please? I'm sorry, terribly sorry for everything.'

But her child's plea for forgiveness left her curiously unmoved. 'Leave me alone,' she answered tonelessly.

The children moved away silently. She was beyond caring now, even for the children. If this was the result of years of love and devotion, why bother further. She entertained threatening and treacherous thoughts but all the time whether she wanted it or not the thought of her two children kept bobbing up and down through the waves of despair that threatened to engulf her. If she didn't have children … But she did have them and she couldn't remove them from her conscience. She couldn't shift her responsibility of loving them and caring for them to someone else. She wasn't made that way. She might be everything that Pat accused her of being, and sometimes when she was too weary and bewildered to fight the accusations spoken or implied, she found herself believing that there could be truth in them, but no one could ever accuse her of being anything less than a loving, responsible mother.

But children were the innocent victims of an adult world. She was to blame for causing that horrible fracas. Her two little ones mustn't be allowed to suffer like that. She must go to them. But first she would change.

She was brushing her shoulders free of fallen hair when she heard the clatter of tea cups outside the door. There was a timid knock and at her request to come in, the door opened tentatively and Robert's curly head appeared. He stepped inside, opening the door further ajar for Rosemary who moved slowly in carrying a tray laden with tea things.

She smiled at her mother uncertainly. Pam's heart turned

over in painful and suffocating love at the sight of the forgiving little things.

'Just what I needed.'

Her voice was scarcely a whisper. She mustn't let them see how close to tears she was. With an effort she smiled.

'Don't tell me you carried that heavy weight upstairs.'

'Yes, I did. Martha wanted to carry it but I said I could manage.' The mother kissed the top of her head. 'And so you did.'

'She spilled milk on the tray-cloth,' Robert pointed out.

'And you let one of the cakes fall on the stairs. That one there. I've been keeping my eyes on it because you're going to eat it and no one else.'

'I don't want to eat anyone else,' Robert said laughing. 'I'm not a cannibal.'

He pulled the dressing stool into position and Rosemary gingerly laid the tray on it. She looked half-vexed at the widening dampness made by the spilled milk.

'I'm sorry about that, Mummy. It kind of spoils the whole thing.'

'Not at all, darling. Wouldn't it be worse if you spilled the pot of tea over yourself?'

'I suppose so.'

'It's no use crying over spilt milk,' Robert said in a tone that suggested it was his own original thought.

'You're very smart this morning,' Rosemary said.

'I'm always smart except usually I don't have time to notice myself.'

'It's just as well,' Rosemary said. She turned to look at her mother wonderingly. 'Are you going out? You've changed your clothes.'

'We're all going out.'

'That's great,' the two children said.

When they got out of the car they looked over the railings on the scene below. Robert said, 'I don't think I could ever get tired coming here. Isn't it lovely, Mummy?'

'It's beautiful.'

In spite of the artificial divisions of water the setting had a fairy-like quality with the diminutive figures of white-shirted workers going about their business. The boy left mother and daughter and went at breakneck speed down the steep flight of steps, counting loudly as he descended.

Rosemary said: 'He gets a different result every time. I think he believes the men either add a step or two or take them away just to annoy him.'

It was the first time she had spoken more than the word or two in the car. Robert was now well ahead, skimming the edges of the oblong patches of water, darting around the circular wall that enclosed the fountain, standing motionless at points where the spray came heaviest.

Pam's heart twisted once more in an agony of love for her children. How could she possibly have reacted in such a manner this morning?

As Rosemary and she walked around, their strolling was punctuated by the pressure of a little hand enclosed in the mother's clasp or by covert pleading looks from the child.

They sat down on a mound of silver gravel.

'I'm sorry,' the mother and daughter said together.

Tears filled the child's eyes. The mother felt the tears sting but she blinked them back. She put an arm around her daughter and kissed her and tasted the salt of the tears that trickled down the smooth cheeks.

She said: 'I shouldn't have lost my temper. Did you ever see me lose it like that before?'

'No,' the child smiled through her tears.

The mother took out her handkerchief and gently dried the tears. 'That was something new then. Not very nice but I promise it will never happen again.'

They were silent for some moments. Pam would have liked to probe the circumstances that led to the incident in which Pat used that word to their daughter, but decided against it. Besides, the sooner Rosemary forgot about the whole thing the better. She would take it up with Pat when he returned home because this was something she would not tolerate. He might and did drag her down, but she was damned if either of their children was going to be dragged down with her.

Rosemary said: 'Hasn't everyone got a temper? A bad temper, I mean. Only you never show it. Robert and I have. Andrea's mother has. She's always flying off the handle with Andrea, only Andrea doesn't seem to mind. She says she's used to it.'

Children are wonderful in spite of us, Pam thought.

'Mummy, I'm sorry I called you that name this morning.'

It came out at last. Perhaps it was better that it should, the mother felt.

'It was terrible of me. Such a wicked thing to say. I don't even know what it means exactly but I think it has something to do with being untidy–I hope that's all it is. You see, I heard Daddy call you that name some time ago. It was very late and I had wakened with a pain in my tummy and I was going out to ask you something for the pain when I heard Daddy and you fighting. Daddy was shouting when he called you that name. I crept back to bed and put my head under the clothes.'

So the children do hear us fighting, Pam thought, greatly disturbed, but she remained silent while the child went on.

'I remember you said in the morning that I looked pale and I said I had a pain during the night, though I hadn't remembered much about it after I got back into bed, and you were upset that I hadn't told you. But you were so cheerful that I began to think that I had imagined it all except that word wouldn't go out of my mind. Now and again I was tempted to look in the dictionary to see what it meant but I was afraid it would mean something terrible and then I would say to myself, surely Daddy wouldn't say anything terrible to you no matter how cross he might be. So then I worked it out that it had something to do with clothes as he had been talking about a dress or something. Some words sound horrider than others though they don't mean anything bad. Isn't that right?'

Pam laughed. 'I know what you mean. But to get back to the word slut. First of all, you must know through reading and watching television that adults have arguments the same as children, sometimes over small things as well as big. In fact the smaller the cause the bigger the argument, as it sometimes happens. And adults can be just as childish as children. And that night, as far as I remember, your father was annoyed because he thought I didn't care what I wore. And a slut does mean an untidy slovenly woman. You see the word sounds worse than it means. Nor do I think I'm quite as bad as the word actually means. People say things in a temper which they would not normally say, so we'll forget about the whole thing, will we?'

Pam was looking through the children's wardrobes.

It was time to put away all winter garments. She smiled as she looked through the muddle of good clothes, worn-out clothes and outgrown clothes. Rosemary, she noticed, made some attempt to keep her room tidy and her clothes in some order but Robert hadn't an idea. She remembered checking Robert about the state of his room when he was about six and she would always remember his reaction. Thinking about it never failed to bring a smile. Toys, books all over the place. Pyjamas dropped on the floor where he had slipped out of them. Wardrobe door open, drawers pulled out. It wasn't as if she or Martha let him away with it. They helped him, urged him, encouraged him, got cross with him. She was really angry with him that time.

'Your room is a disgrace. Tidy it up at once. You can keep it neat if you want to.'

He had rushed into a wild scrimmage of picking up things off the floor, dropping half of them in his hurry at the first hint of anger in her voice, but it didn't prevent him from looking up at her from his crouched position on the floor on hearing the last sentence:

'But I don't want to,' he said in a quiet, reasonable tone of voice.

She heard the clatter the children made as they galloped upstairs.

'Mummy, where are you?

'In Robert's room.' They rushed in.

'Anyone would think there were a dozen children in the house, the noise you make.' She smiled. 'I want you to help me tidy up. I've been weeding out all the clothes you don't need. Later on we'll sort out those and give the best of them to the itinerant children. Then we'll do your room, Rosemary.'

They worked together, Robert doing his share. Then halfway through the work in Rosemary's room he left with the excuse that a friend was expecting him. Pam let it pass, but I'll have to keep an eye on him, she thought. Rosemary kept at the work until it was done. Then she suggested they go through her mother's clothes. Pam agreed. They went into the dressing room, spacious with walls lined with built-in white-lacquered presses and wardrobes. When the work was done they stood back and gazed at the greatly depleted wardrobes and drawers, laughing at the onslaught.

'They have a lonely look,' Rosemary said. She patted a wardrobe. 'Don't worry. We'll soon fill you up again with really nice things.'

Resting her chin on her hand she looked at her mother. 'What you want now is a lot of new clothes. All the latest.' Her eyes sparkled. 'Supposing you and I go into Dublin before Daddy comes back and buy some. That would give him a great surprise.'

The mother looked at the earnest little face and immediately agreed.

When they were shopping Pam found herself influenced by

Rosemary's opinion. Her daughter seemed to know exactly what suited her. While they were having lunch she told her it was one of the nicest mornings she had had for a long time. And it was true. She was tired but she felt young again, alive and vital.

She had planned that she and the children would dress up and meet Pat at the airport.

'We'll make a day of it', she told them.

But he arrived home a day early. It was mid-morning and only she and Martha were in the house as the children had gone out with friends for the day. Some of Pam's disappointment showed on her face at his sudden arrival. She had such hopes for this homecoming. After the ritual poking about in his study he came out to the breakfast room.

'What would you like to eat?' Pam asked.

'I'm not really hungry. I'll just have a cup of coffee,' he glanced at his watch, 'and then I'll be off.'

'But you must be worn out. Do you have to work today?'

'I have lots to catch up with. But I'll go to bed early tonight.'

So you will. So you always do when it suits you and you can stay up half the night when it suits you too, she wanted to say. *And all that work you have to catch up with could have waited over if you had remained the extra day.*

The children were disappointed when they heard their father had returned home without warning. Pam hid her own disappointment and explained: 'Your father is home and that's the important thing. He's brought us lovely presents so you see, no matter how busy he is, when he's away he never forgets us.'

There was nothing to stop her from accompanying him on these journeys. Money was not the obstacle and Martha could look after the children. But having gone with him on a few occasions the persona non grata feeling she always experienced, apart from the fact the invitations had to be dragged from him, put an end to what should have been a pleasure for the two of them. But she did get the usual symbolic token of his absence. Something to show their friends, followed by the usual remarks on Pat's thoughtfulness and good taste.

Several times in the next few days Pam was conscious of her daughter's gaze fixed on her. She could imagine what the child was thinking.

At length she came out with what was on her mind.

'There's nothing to stop you from dressing up in some of your new clothes and calling in to Daddy's office. Say nothing and give him a surprise.'

Pat's coolness after his arrival and his withdrawn manner dampened any enthusiasm she had for attracting his attention, but to please her daughter she agreed. Rosemary's hopes and hers were dissimilar but were aimed in the same direction. Each of them wanted so little. She knew what Rosemary wanted. She knew what she wanted. A look of recognition from her husband. If only she could remember the words of the marriage ceremony they might comfort her. Remind her she was not being selfish. 'To have and to hold. To love and to cherish.' Were these the words that Pat had once said? What had she said? She couldn't remember all, but love, honour and obey came into it. Obey?

She couldn't say she ever thought of herself as having to obey, but she could substitute the word 'agree', and that she did. For many years. Honour had become somewhat tarnished. A wife who carried on in front of others at parties and functions the way she did could hardly be said to bring honour to her husband. Yes. She was guilty there. Love? She did love him even if that love sometimes had to struggle with spells of hatred that came upon her at times. If she loved him less it would be easier on herself.

Chapter Four

Sally Griffin's work as legal adviser to a builder's consultants firm was absorbing and interesting, and more important to her than the good salary and the fact that the job had up to the time of her joining the firm been held by a man, was the scope it offered her for using her own initiative. Life was exciting. There was so much to do, see and enjoy that she felt there was never enough time for it all. Falling in love with Morrison had brought about no great change in her day-to-day living, but her love for him had brought her love for life and living into a more exciting focus.

Sometimes she thought of Pam, wondering at her silence. She, herself, was so happy and contented she found it hard to understand somebody who seemed just the opposite. Did Pam really want her friendship? Or was she, Sally Griffin, so full of herself that she expected people to like or wish for her company? She smiled at the idea of her thrusting herself on people thinking she was conferring a favour on them. But Pam had promised to phone her and she hadn't done so, or if she had, she hadn't left a message. She would ring Pam now while she thought of it.

Pat answered the phone.

'What are you doing at home at this hour of the day? Is there anything wrong? Is Pam ill?'

'There's nothing wrong.' She could hear the smile in Pat's voice. 'Can't a man come home any time he feels like it when he is his own boss? Pam is fine. She's out at the moment. On one of her works of mercy, I think.'

The conversation continued for a few minutes. Pat promised he would tell Pam she phoned but as Pam didn't ring she wondered if Pat had forgotten. A long-promised weekend with her Aunt Penny and Uncle Walter and their young children was coming up and she was looking forward to it.

From the time they got up on the Saturday neither she nor her aunt had a moment to themselves until the children had gone to bed. The house was now quiet. The irregular crack of a spade or the cheerful calls of Walter's neighbours over the garden wall told them that Walter was occupied in his garden, or as Penny said, looking after his favourite child. Penny was a youthful-looking mother, not much older than Sally. Two dimples showed at the slightest movement of her humorous, up-turned lips. No one could call her a beauty with her indifferent colouring and pale blue eyes, but she sparkled and glowed, and on the rare occasions that found her depressed or out of sorts it was as if a light had been switched off inside that alert and lively face. The two women regarded themselves more as sisters than aunt and niece. Sally, being the only girl in her family, would have liked to be able to see her aunt more often, but it was not always easy to manage.

The evening had turned chilly and the central heating had been turned off, Penny hoped, for the rest of the summer but there was a fire burning cheerfully in the grate. Its warm glow created an atmosphere for reminiscence. Sally recalled her meeting with Pam. She spoke of the children and the lovely home they had but confessed to being confused about the husband-wife relationship. They seemed to have everything going for them and yet nothing.

She said: 'Pam and Pat are such nice people really. Pam can be hard to get to know at first but Pat is very popular with everyone. Pam is really a nice person, quite different from the image she projects of herself in company. Not that I've seen her often in company. Only the one occasion. And she didn't seem popular with either the men or the women. Even Vienna, who is so easy to get on with, can barely tolerate her. But why am I talking about people whom you've never even met?'

She had been aware, as she talked, of Penny smiling now and again and nodding her head in agreement.

She said: 'I must be boring you. I wouldn't mind if you even knew Pam.'

'But I do know her.'

'But you couldn't. Pam McElroy? I've never heard you speak of her.'

'And I've never heard you speak of her,' Penny said laughing.

'But that's because I've only met her recently. It was Morrison who introduced Pat to me some time back.'

'Well, I can assure you I know Pam for very much longer. For years and years, except it has been some time since we've seen each other. I went to school with Pam.'

Sally sat up straight in her chair: 'You didn't!'

Penny laughed: 'Will you stop telling me what I didn't and couldn't do. The fact is I did go to school with Pam. Not only that but we were inseparable. Indeed we had the doubtful distinction of being known in the school as the Pat Penny Dreadful on account of all the scrapes we got into. I think the teachers as well as the girls enjoyed us. We were never discouraged anyway, and it was Pat who usually masterminded anything we got up to.'

'But Penny, are we talking about the same person? I don't think so. You said Pat just now.'

'So I did. It's hard to break the habit of a lifetime. Pat was the name Pam was known by at school. Pam isn't her real name, nor is it short for Pamela as most people think. Pam stands for Patricia Angela Mary. We all called her Pat until she became engaged to Pat, and so to avoid confusion with the two Pats she decided to change her name. But it's the same girl we're talking about, and yet,' her voice saddened, 'not the same girl.'

She gazed thoughtfully into the fire. 'She was such a lovely person. Generous, affectionate and kind.' She stopped.

Sally waited. If Penny wanted to tell her about the past she would do so. The sound of Walter's spade now going click-clack-click at a steady pace emphasized the peace and quiet. Sally heard the mouse-like pitter-patter of little feet across the landing. There was the faint drone of a lawn-mower in the distance.

Penny was sitting, her body tilted to one side in the chair, elbow resting on its arm, her cheek leaning heavily in her cupped hand. 'I never remember anyone saying a bad word about Pam even when she got into scrapes, because there was nothing ugly or nasty in what she did. As you know, Pam qualified as a doctor but she never practised after she got married. She had intended to specialise in paediatrics but when she met Pat he couldn't wait to get married. After she married she dropped the idea of specialising and instead hoped to set up a general practice near home when a suitable place became available. Then when she got rooms, Pat objected.'

'Why, for heaven's sake?'

'So well you may ask. All I know is that Pat seemed to think she wouldn't be able to keep up the work and have babies at the same time, and as she loved the idea of having children I think it didn't take much persuasion to put her off.'

'But she could have managed both. They have a housekeeper and they could afford somebody to look after the children.'

'Obviously that's not the way Pat's mind works. He believes mothers should look after their own children.'

'Which should have made him admire you.'

'Are you joking? Pat would see it as me having no option. But there's no doubt that they were crazy about each other, yet for some reason, even when they were engaged I couldn't help feeling uneasy about the two of them.'

'Why?'

'I don't know.' Penny took up the poker and pierced the glued black mass. Fresh flames leaped up and a shower of sparks flew up the chimney. She bent to put the brass poker in place, then said slowly: 'I don't know because they seemed to be the ideal couple. And yet … I wasn't the only one who had doubts. I think her mother felt a little uneasy because of something she let drop when a few of us were admiring the wedding presents. There were the usual remarks about how lucky Pam and Pat were. Then her mother said, "They have everything they need to make them happy. I only hope Pat doesn't try to dominate Pam too much." None of the others paid any attention to this remark as they were all so busy talking.'

Penny faced Sally. 'You see, Pam and Pat had two strong personalities, and unless there was give and take there were bound to be clashes of will which could cause trouble. But even at that stage I saw Pat getting his way all the time and Pam seeing nothing wrong about it. Of course there were only small things but it was a sign of future trouble as it turned out. After they were married we kept in contact for the first couple of years but there was one thing I couldn't help noticing. Pam was losing touch with her old friends. She had made lots of new friends but except for a few neighbours they were all Pat's friends. And she was popular with them, then anyway. But it wasn't like her to drop old friends and once when I asked half-jokingly when she was thinking of dropping me she burst into tears, which again was unlike her. I expected then she would open up and tell me what was wrong, but no, she just made some excuse and left it at that.'

'So when did the break happen?'

'Oh, there was a grand finale. It was heading that way for some time, but I never thought for one moment that our friendship would come to an end.'

She stared into the fire, her face thoughtful. It seemed she was hardly aware of the other woman's presence, and when she spoke it was if she were soliloquising rather than speaking directly to her. *It must be painful for her,* Sally thought.

'Walter and I lived only a short distance from Pam and Pat's place before we came to live here and Pam and I used to see a lot of each other. I became pregnant almost immediately after marriage, but even when the baby was born it didn't stop the two of us from meeting. There were great times. Pam was mad about our baby.'

She remembered how disappointed Pam had been that she could not be godmother as the christening had coincided with her being away with Pat on the Continent, and how she had promised she would let nothing come in the way of her being godmother for the next child.

'All along I had the feeling that Pat didn't care that much for me but I didn't let it worry me. I liked him in spite of this feeling and we got on well together. You see, Pat was and still is, I'm sure a likeable person and you find yourself drawn to him with or without encouragement. But there were times I felt Pam couldn't turn around without asking his permission first. I got mad with her once and asked had she not a mind of her own. She was very annoyed with me – at this stage we seemed to be getting on each other's nerves – and she said, "I think it's only a matter of courtesy for a wife to talk things over with her husband first."

'"Then," I said, "I must be the most discourteous wife in the world if that's so. But I know one thing for sure, if I had to discuss every little fiddle-faddle with Walter before I could do something he'd think, and rightly so, that he was married to a nit-wit."'

Pam had been married, she recalled for her quiet and deeply moved listener, about eighteen months when she lost her baby after five months' pregnancy. The desolation was absolute and she seemed to despair of becoming pregnant again. The odds were against her, she kept saying, she being an only child and Pat being one of two children.

Sally said, 'You'd think being a doctor she'd have more sense.'

Penny said, 'You couldn't reason with her. Even her own doctor made no headway with her. He kept telling her there was nothing wrong with her and that there was no reason why she shouldn't become pregnant again. But she wouldn't be comforted. Pat was very upset too and this made it all the harder for Pam. On top of all that her mother was ill with cancer.'

'Poor Pam.'

'Yes, it was terrible. She wouldn't allow her mother to go into hospital and she was just skin and bone when her mother died. She told me some time after that she believed if her baby had lived and her mother could have held her first grandchild in her arms it might have arrested the cancer, even if only for a year or two. For her mother to die so young was too much for her. She was only forty-eight. And then a few weeks after the death I had a phone-call from her to say she was calling around as she wanted my advice. But it wasn't advice she wanted. She had already made up her mind. What she wanted was for me to come with her and look at some rooms in the village which she thought would be suitable for her surgery. The funny thing was, she hadn't told Pat about it. I couldn't believe my ears. What had made her make this move, she said, was taking care of her mother. It would be a sin to sit idle and not do what she was qualified to do. I remember thinking to myself, that's the old Pam back again.'

A coal fell onto the hearth, splitting into particles, making a nest of ashes. Penny knelt and caught the coal by the tongs and dropped it back into the red heart of the fire. She swept the hearth and levered herself on the balls of her feet back to her chair. A strand of hair which had fallen over her eye was pushed back.

'It was too good to be true. A few days later I got a phonecall to say the whole thing was off. She said something about Pat saying she was in no condition to work, not so soon after her mother's death. I knew that was only another excuse of Pat's, this being the second time he had objected to her taking up work. As soon as I put down the phone I rushed to her place. I was furious. "That excuse isn't good enough," I said.

"'It's good enough for me," she said.

"'Whom are you trying to fool?" I said. And then I cooled down as I could see I was getting nowhere.'

Sally said, 'You must have been terribly disappointed.'

I was. I had been so sure that Pam had turned the corner of what I thought was a fairly rocky patch in their marriage. But no. Pat had the last word there as in everything, but I still wouldn't give up. I tried reasoning with her, pointing out why she should take up work, including the reasons she had given me herself. But nothing I said seemed to get through to her. Then I started giving out about Pat and that was a big mistake.'

'Gosh! I'd imagine so.'

'Yes, but I found her loyalty more disturbing than admirable. Finally, I lost my temper. I told her that Pat was destroying her and their marriage. That it was time she faced facts and stop pretending. But do you think I got any response? And that frightened me more than anything else.'

Sally knew now she had not imagined things when thinking about Pam and Pat over the weeks. Almost from the start she had known something was wrong and that it was not all Pam's fault. How could Vienna and the others not have seen it the way she saw it. They knew her for far longer. Hadn't Vienna said that Pam had always been the same? And Vienna would not exaggerate. The change must have come before the two women met and have gradually worsened over the years. She could see how upset Penny was, even at the memory. She would not ask her any more questions.

Penny looked pensively at her. 'It was the end of our friendship. I wrote shortly afterwards asking her to forgive me. She wrote a note by return saying there was nothing to forgive. That was all. No reference to the row or about seeing each other again. I got the message.'

'Why did you leave it at that? I'd have gone to see her.' Sally had said the words before she could stop herself.

'I wanted to see her, but then I remembered the strain between us in the recent past and the small rows – something that was new to both of us – and the dropping of other friends. And I thought then that the inevitable was only brought forward and there was nothing I could do. Then Walter was promoted and we moved here. I thought indeed when she'd see the announcement of the birth of our second child she might contact me.' Her voice broke.

'Don't upset yourself.' Sally leaned over and put a hand on her aunt's knee. 'You did all you could under the circumstances. There's no point in blaming yourself.'

'I do blame myself. I interfered. How would I like it if Pam attacked me or Walter? Would I like it if she told me how to run my marriage? And, as you said, why didn't I call to see her?'

'It's all right for me to talk. You were in a difficult position. So was Pam. Pam was being pressured to drop her own friends and because you saw what was coming you really had no choice in a way.'

Penny was silent for a long time. Sally looked at her aunt and saw the shadows of sadness under her eyes. She pretended not to see the tears that began to trickle unheeded down her cheeks. Her aunt was back in the past.

Penny got up from the chair suddenly, smudging away the tears with the back of her hand. 'Damn that fellow anyway.'

A long sigh escaped her.

'I suppose I'd better see what Walter is up to,' she said, making an effort to smile. 'I don't hear a sound in the garden. He must have fallen asleep over his spade.'

Chapter Five

Pam remained seated at the table after Pat had gone to work, smoking a cigarette and sipping coffee. The children had gone out. She had heard them say something about going over to Andrea's but that they would be back to look at her dressed in her new clothes. She contemplated the morning's plan and wondered was it worth going through with. What was the point? Another disappointment in store for her. Extra days taken from her life trying to get over the disappointment and the crushed, beaten feeling that had now become the hallmark of all her efforts to change things between her and Pat. She could already see the result of another wasted effort. And then she thought of Rosemary. The child could hardly be aware of what she was trying to do and yet, knowing her little daughter, she felt there was something stirring in that active little brain of hers. She gulped the remainder of her coffee and left the table.

She would not use the car today. This was a day to take things easy. She had no particular timetable to keep. She would walk the half-mile to the bus stop.

Martha sniffed the air when Pam came out of the bathroom. 'Something's going on here.' She steered the vacuum cleaner out of the bedroom. 'So I'd better leave you in peace till you're ready.'

'Give me a couple of hours at least,' Pam called out. She was once more bright and cheerful. Once more optimistic. 'I'll call you when I'm ready.'

She selected the outfit Rosemary was most enthusiastic about, then sat down at the dressing table and arranged all the cosmetics necessary for the transformation she hoped for. When she had finished she sprayed perfume on her wrists, her temple and at the base of her neck. Some of the spray that had escaped onto her hands she pressed against her cheeks. She smiled at her reflection: I'm definitely out to seduce. Her shining hair was brushed into wispy curls to frame her face and tiny pearl earrings completed the picture. Excitedly she lifted the two-piece from the chair and put the jacket to one side. The dress was a pale coral-pink with pale green neck trimming. The jacket was in the same shade of pale green linen with lining matching the colour of the dress. The outfit was just the thing for such a sunny day. She went into the dressing-room and slipped into a pair of pale green shoes, then stood back from the full-length mirror.

'Hello, stranger. Nice to see you around once more. I had forgotten how well you could look.'

If Rosemary could see her now, she thought, wouldn't she be proud of her mother. She should be back by now. Perhaps, Pat might take the rest of the day off and bring her out somewhere. It was unlikely but on a day like this anything could happen. She wouldn't think too far ahead.

'What's the verdict?' she asked as she posed for Martha.

'You look beautiful, but that's no bother to you. On my word, you're a real fashion model, that's what you are.'

The big woman took her in her arms and pressed her to her before letting her go for a final inspection.

'You know, ma'am, I don't think it'll be safe to be on your own. I suspect you're up to something but I suppose you're old enough to know what you're doing.'

'I hope Pat hasn't read his daily horoscope yet because I bet it says he's to meet a strange and beautiful woman who will change his whole life, and I want that to come as a surprise. I'll see you later, Martha. Tell the children I didn't want to disturb them, that I'll be wearing the same clothes later on in the day. Expect me when you see me, Martha.'

She looked at her watch as she walked down the drive. She had plenty of time. When the bus arrived at the stop nearest to Pat's office she decided to do the fifteen minute walk the rest of the way and enjoy the sunny day rather than take a taxi. She mingled with the crowd. Where did they all come from, she wondered idly and where were they all going to? Were they all just as free as she was this morning and bent only on enjoying themselves?

People were staring at her. She had forgotten what it was like to get admiring glances. Before crossing the road to her husband's office she stood and looked at the whole building. It was set back from the main road and fronted by a smooth green lawn. Shrubs and flowers were placed at focal points. Wrought-iron seats were fixed to the ground in the shelter of ancient trees and though the grounds were private there was no sign to indicate it and the public were free to use them. Two elderly people were seated having a quiet chat and smoke. It was too early to go to Pat and she sat down in the shade of a rhododendron.

The whole place was a far cry from the shabby and ugly mansion with its overgrown gardens that had been an eyesore for so long and which it had replaced. Pat's alert eye had been quick to evaluate the potential of the neglected property. All the offices had been booked before the building was completed and she knew the income from these offices was substantial. She also knew that Pat had been urged by his friends to invest in similar projects but he hadn't been interested. He was an architect, he said, not a property magnate.

The offices of Patrick McElroy and Associates were on the second floor and had a fine view of the People's Park and beyond it to the sweep of Dublin Bay. His clients constantly remarked on the view, some of them saying it was a pity to have this view lost on just an office-block. Wouldn't it have been perfect for a luxury hotel or even a hospital! What a view for patients to look out on! Pat made a habit of agreeing with his clients, occasionally dryly remarking there was nothing he could do about it now, adding it was an ill wind that blew nobody good, because sometimes by the contemplation of the view he got some of his inspirations for the design and planning of hospitals.

Pam looked at her watch. It was twenty minutes past twelve. A nice time to call on Pat.

It would give them a little time to chat before going somewhere to lunch. She was tired in spite of her rest as she had been doing more walking than she intended to in shoes that were never meant for walking. Tension and a mildly throbbing headache did not cause her to question why she should have either as she was used to both.

She had no idea how many people Pat had working for him but she knew one thing, all would, without exception, find him the kindest and fairest of employers. She would have liked to have worked for Pat. She thought of Betty Aherne, Pat's private secretary, a thirty-year-old widow whose surveyor husband had worked for Pat. Pat had taken over the responsibility of looking after her affairs after her husband's death and had given her the job when his secretary left. Even if that job hadn't been going Pat would have fixed her up in something suitable, she was sure. She had heard all this from Betty shortly after she joined the firm. Why didn't Pat think it worth his while to tell her that? She had no desire to pry into his business but Betty made no secret of Pat's goodness.

After a few words with Betty Aherne she opened the door of Pat's office and slipped inside. Her husband looked up momentarily from his work. She smiled and waited for his reaction.

'Well, what is it?' he asked, impatience in his voice. 'I'm busy.'

'Is that so?' Her spirits were too high to be deflated by the almost predictable attitude.

'Well, your secretary didn't seem to think so, and when it comes to a question of who's right or wrong between boss and secretary, the secretary is always right!'

'Huh!'

She leaned against the door. 'What do you think of the latest fashion? Rosemary helped me to choose this and a couple of other things when you were away.'

Why did she have to think it necessary to mention Rosemary at this stage? Was her feeling of inadequacy so great that she needed some kind of moral support? She saw her husband glance casually at the outfit.

He said: 'Rosemary has good taste.'

'You can do better than that.'

'I'm busy.'

'So that's all you have to say? Don't start reading while I'm talking to you. Look at me. I'm your wife. Not a piece of paper which you sign and put aside.'

It took her all her time to stop herself from going over and shaking him. In a quieter tone of voice she said, 'Rosemary suggested I call to see you in my new outfit to give you a surprise. She said, "Get Daddy to take you out to lunch." I was hoping perhaps you might even be able to take the rest of the day off and the four of us to go somewhere. We were to meet you at the airport the other day and then you arrived unexpectedly. Rosemary was so disappointed as she had selected these clothes specially for me to meet you in.'

'I'll tell her how nice it is.'

'But that's not enough. She wants us to have lunch together. And I would like that too. It's nearly one o'clock and if you could manage it maybe you might take the rest of the day off. You owe it to yourself. Remember, you came back from Italy a day sooner than you expected.'

Even as she was speaking she had the uneasy feeling she was making no impression on him, that he was only waiting for her to finish.

He said: 'What you seem to forget is, that this is a business, my business that takes up all my working day. I can't just drop everything at a whim and go here, there and everywhere. If I neglect my work I have nobody to blame but myself if things go wrong.'

'But what on earth could go wrong? You can run this place blindfolded. What's the point in having partners and staff if you have to keep an eye on everything? I know in a minute you'll tell me I know nothing about your business, neither do I,' she smiled, 'but it's near lunchtime and you have to eat.'

He looked at his watch. He shuffled through some papers, looked at his watch once more and then looked apologetically at her.

'I won't be going to lunch for another hour or so. I had hoped to get this finished,' he gestured at the papers, 'before midday, but I was held up.' He attempted a smile. 'Not that it was a waste of time. On the contrary it was very rewarding.'

He took up his pen and frowning at a fixed point on the desk he said, 'But if you don't mind waiting I'll be glad to take you out to lunch.'

If the note of condescension coupled with the scarcely concealed unwillingness to ask her out had not been so obvious she would have waited the hour, even two hours, all day if necessary, but she had put up with enough.

'I do mind waiting. I mind very much. Who do you think I am? There's nothing in the world to stop you from coming out now. It's just that you don't want to but you couldn't come straight out with that. It all boils down to the fact that you don't want me around. I wish I knew that thirteen years ago.'

'Meaning what?'

'You know well what I mean. You've heard it all before. Or do you like to hear me going on and on so that you can lash out that I'm emotionally unstable, etc., etc. Now I'll tell you something. You are nothing but a sanctimonious, self-righteous, smug, self-centred, pontificating bore. You haven't an ounce of charity in you.

Not what I'd call charity anyway. You have loads of pharisaical charity which must satisfy you and your admirers. I was too much in love with you to see you as you really are.'

'Lower your voice.'

'My voice is low enough. Anyway, why should you care who hears me, seeing that it hasn't bothered you up to now what people think of me. But don't worry. I have no intention of letting myself down anymore.'

'That will be a change.'

'And there's more coming. I used to let you down in front of people because it was the last weapon I was left with to make you notice me and if you noticed maybe you'd begin to wonder why I was doing it.'

'Well, your little trick didn't work, did it?'

"It's typical of you to call it a trick. My God, you have as much sensitivity as that … as that desk. It would never occur to you that there must be a reason for me to do such a thing. But then, why should it? All through the years you've never looked at our marriage and noticed what was happening. My letting you down in public was a final desperate effort made by a desperate woman to save a marriage. But it's not worth saving and you're not worth loving. You're not worth anything. You're nothing but a sham.' She got up from her chair. 'Do you know something? I'll never forgive you for what you've done to me in our marriage and I'll never forgive myself for allowing you to do what you've done. Go back to your work. Someday, not so far away, that's all you'll have to go back to.'

She smiled at Mrs Aherne as she said goodbye on her way out. Then her courage deserted her. Through a mist of tears she saw the ladies' room down the corridor. She went into one of the toilets and locked the door. She pressed her face against the hard surface of the door, her body shaking with sobs. She remained there not caring about anything or anyone. Neither did she care when a young girl employee gave her a curious glance as she came out of the toilet. She washed her hands and saw herself in the mirror. She looked a wreck. *But I'm not beaten yet,* she told the reflection. Slowly from the damaged pieces of herself she would build a new person. She would not allow Pat to destroy her.

She had repeated this so often in the past that there were times she despised herself for turning traitor. She dabbed her smudged face in furious repair work, examined the poor result and thought: this won't do. *This is where I take my first lesson in self-rehabilitation.* She poured fresh water into the washbasin and removed all traces of make-up. She dried her face and sat down at one of the dressing tables to apply her make-up. In spite of herself her eyes would fill with tears. Then she remembered she had a pair of sunglasses in her bag.

Forgetting the lift, she walked down the broad stairway, feeling weak. Once or twice she stumbled. Out in the brilliant sunshine she wondered what to do, where to go. She looked up and down the road: *I might as well go home. There's nothing for me to do here.*

She turned in the direction of the bus stop and stumbled once more. *If only my knees would stop buckling,* she thought. *Come on, get a bit of energy into your stride.* It was then out of the corner of her eye she saw a small child of four or five dart across the busy road. A single-decker bus was bearing down on him. She heard the screams of the passers-by. The child stopped halfway. She rushed across the road to pull him out of the way. There was a screech of brakes.

She lay on a blanket of pain. She tried to open her eyes. Tried to move. Impossible. She heard voices from far away. Words ebbed and flowed. Hysterical. Shouting. Whispers. She slipped into nothingness. She surfaced once more. 'What happened?'

'What child?'

'Does it matter? He's saved, but that woman has had it. Did anyone go for the doctor?'

'Yes, somebody went across the road for him. He's coming now. Oh, here's the husband.' Voices, voices. A cacophony of voices. Now she could hear Pat's voice.

'Oh my God! Pam! Pam! Can you hear me? You'll be all right. Everything will be all right. The doctor's here now.'

In spite of that other world of pain she was in she tried to concentrate on what was being said. She heard the word 'priest'. *I'm dying. Oh God, my children!* Voices. 'Yes. Very serious.'

'Will she live?' Was that Pat's voice? Again she tried to lift those heavy eyelids. But they would not budge.

More voices. 'Beautiful, isn't she? She looks like the Sleeping Princess.' That was a man's voice.

An answering murmur from a woman. 'She is beautiful. Beautiful and brave.'

Who are they? What are they talking about? What are they doing? Where am I? *I can hear you,* she wanted to tell them. Was it then or later she tried to open her eyes once more? At last she succeeded in lifting one heavy eyelid and saw a white-coated doctor at the side of the bed. The effort was too great to keep that eye open. She tried the other. A nurse was at the other side holding something. She held that eye open and tried the other again. It worked. She saw the two white figures, their gaze fixed intently on her. She tried to smile at them. The effort was too much.

It was on the tenth day after the accident that Pam remained fully conscious through part of the day. She remembered being fed, being examined by doctors, nurses attending her. Little by little she began to remember what led up to the accident. The small frightened child paralysed in his tracks, the bus bearing down on him, the words and phrases she was conscious of while lying on the roadside floating back to her, the voices she had recognised. She remembered as in a dream Pat sitting by the bed, yet everything in a way seemed as disconnected as if it were all happening to someone else. She was only a spectator. She was conscious of bandages, immobility, pain and a great weariness. A thought that had entered her mind early on in these first conscious hours now teased her but it was sometime before she could bring herself to ask the question. As two nurses set about making her more comfortable she thought, now is the time to ask and get it over with. It was still an effort for her to speak out but she managed to get out the words slowly, haltingly: 'Any limbs missing down there?'

The nurses had been busy chatting to each other, believing she was half asleep. She could not help being amused at their reaction. They stared at her, then looked at each other and laughed.

One of the nurses said: 'Sorry, Doctor McElroy, for laughing. But there we were, believing you were too sleepy to bother about anything and then you pop up with that question. But we wouldn't be laughing like that, I can tell you, if there were any limbs missing.'

The other nurse, a redhead, said: 'Your two beautiful legs are still there. Not even a toenail missing. They, the legs I mean, got a bit of a bashing and so did the rest of you, but it was your internal injuries we were most worried about. And you lost a great deal of blood but we fixed that up for you. So all that is needed is time and patience to make you right as rain again.'

Her relief almost overpowered her. 'Thank God for that.'

'In case you weren't quite with it, your husband has been here every day, three times a day most of the time. He was in a terrible state. Of course he had a reason to be as we were all worried about you, wondering if you'd make it. There's no harm in telling you that, now that the danger period is over. You were great though. You fought back every inch of the way. You know, you were the talk of the place. Your picture on television and everything. Well, if you weren't famous before, you are now.'

The room was massed with flowers and the two nurses were non-stop in comments as they added water to each vase or re-arranged the flowers. She closed her eyes. She was so tired. Rosemary and Robert? Were they in to see her? She hoped not. It would be terrible for them to see her like this. The redheaded nurse whom she had just heard being referred to by her companion as 'Reidy' must be psychic.

'Your two children are coming in to see you this afternoon. They were in one day with your husband but the visit upset them, so your husband thought it better that they shouldn't see you until you had improved a little.'

'Which was the right decision,' the other nurse said. 'They really broke down when they saw you.'

Nurse Reidy gave her a warning nudge. She had noticed the tears steal from the closed eyelids.

'That's only to be expected,' she interrupted in a comforting voice. 'They wouldn't be normal if they weren't upset.' She injected a cheerful note into her voice. 'But that's all in the past. Everything is going fine and you won't feel it until you're back home. It gives us a great kick when we see patients improving each day. It's the terminal cases that sadden us, only we can't afford to show it.'

She came over to the bedside and smiled down at the still figure. Pam opened her eyes and smiled through her tears. Nurse Reidy gave the pillow a comforting pat.

'Try and get as much sleep as you can before your husband and children call.'

She was lying awake, studying the cloud shapes when Nurse Reidy came in with a tray.

'Think you could manage soup and a little chicken?' She wasn't hungry but she must try and eat.

She was uncomfortable and in considerable pain. One of her shoulders was out of action and her other upper arm had a multiple fracture, but she was so grateful that no permanent injury had been done that she regarded everything else as a minor nuisance. After the nurse fed her the soup she forced down a small piece of chicken and mashed potato. After that all she wanted was to go back to sleep. Funny how she could sleep in spite of the pain and discomfort.

She was fully aware of her husband for the first time when he came to visit her later with the children. She gave him a quick glance. He smiled at her but she could not respond. As yet, what had happened immediately prior to the accident had not been re-awakened in her, but she knew something had happened.

Pat was pale and tired-looking, lines of suffering etched on his face. The children paused uncertainly for a moment beside the bed. She smiled at them. 'Ah, Mummy.' The pent-up longing for their mother was wrung from them and they knelt by the bed, one on each side, and covered her face with kisses.

'Mind! Mind!' their father warned them as he tried to intervene. 'Be careful or you'll hurt Mummy.'

They got up, excited and overjoyed at what they considered was a miracle. When they had first seen their mother they had gone home believing she was dying. That night they slept in the one bed crying and comforting each other until Rosemary was struck by a sudden thought: 'Why not pray for a miracle?' Now their miracle had happened. They told their mother how they had prayed for it, not saying how much they had cried. Soon it was time to leave, husband and wife having scarcely exchanged a word. Pam pointed to the locker when she saw the tears well up in the children's eyes.

'There are some chocolates there.' Pat got out one of the boxes.

'That will help dry those tears,' she said, kissing them. 'There are clothes-dryers and hair-dryers, but did you know that chocolates and sweets were tear-dryers invented long before any other dryer?'

When Pat McElroy called later that evening he was disturbed when told his wife was running a temperature. Although he was told she was put on antibiotics he worried as he watched her drift in and out of sleep. He remained silent most of the time, holding her hand which lay outside the coverlet.

His wife was aware at times of his kisses, of his face pressed gently against her hot hand, of the whispered words of endearment. She wished he would leave her. His presence upset her, his touch, the words of love irritated her. They meant nothing to her now, so why was he going on like that? She wanted to pretend he wasn't there but each time she drifted back from sleep he was there and still holding her hand. She found herself giving way to a feeling of panic. Go away! I hate you, she wanted to scream at him. She tried to move her hand away from his clasp. Her husband felt the flutter of her hand. He bent closer to her.

'What is it, darling? Am I keeping you awake?'

She nodded. He saw the almost transparent eyelids drop heavily. He kissed her and walked blindly towards the door, his eyes filling with tears.

He stopped the car on his way home close to the river. He got out and walked towards the bridge. This was a quiet spot of natural beauty, but largely ignored in favour of the attractions of the nearby beach. He leaned over the bridge and stared at the amber water, his mind recalling at once the past tragic days.

Someone, he could not remember whom, had rushed into his office that fatal day to tell him his wife had had an accident. As he raced down the road he visualised her mangled body. The crowd made way for him. The doctor looked up from attending his wife when he saw him. He knelt down. What had he done? Had he driven her to this? Blood seeped in slowly widening blots through the clothes she had worn specially to meet him. The sight of the blood made him sick to the stomach. It was everywhere. He was sure she was dead. Yet, he found himself praying, please let her live. The ambulance arrived.

He followed the still figure into the ambulance. The doors closed. He could have been in a tomb, so remote was he from life, so dead his body and mind.

At the hospital he did all he was asked to do. He remembered hearing as in a dream that Pam was being prepared for an emergency operation; there was internal haemorrhaging, multiple fractures of? They had all been repeated to him afterwards but even now he couldn't remember. He had been asked if he would like to remain in the waiting room.

A cup of tea was brought to him and automatically he drank, without pausing, the scalding liquid. Feeling slowly returned to his numbed body. Oh God, let her live. The words went on and on in his head like a litany. Oliver Gilligan, one of the surgeons, found him kneeling on the floor when he came with news of the operation and helped him to his feet. He had searched his friend's face for hope, the smallest sign, anything to hold on to. Oliver's face was enigmatic. He stated facts. Pam had lost a lot of blood.

He described the extent of her injuries. But why couldn't he be told in simple words, not have all this professional stuff thrown at him? But he mustn't be impatient. Oliver was doing the best he could.

'Will she live?' he asked.

'Honestly, I don't know, but if you have faith in prayer don't stop praying. Stay with her.'

So that was it. All he had left were those last unconscious moments. Oliver added: 'Or you could go home. We'll let you know immediately if there's a change.'

'You mean a change for the worse? When hope is gone? No thanks. I'm not going to be told that. I'll see for myself.'

'Do the children know?'

'I hope not. Not yet anyway.'

He wondered what he should do. 'I'll phone the housekeeper.'

Oh God, how am I going to face everything? If Pam were only here to help me. After he had spoken to Martha he phoned his mother. His mother said she would leave immediately for his place and the phone was placed in its cradle with the sound of her shocked, tearful voice in his ears. Why had Martha and his mother to break down like that? Couldn't they...? A nurse guided him silently to where Pam was. He felt death in the room as he knelt by her bed.

A breeze was tickling his neck with cool fingers. The evening was turning cold. He turned up the collar of his jacket and continued to stare at the now troubled waters. A drop of rain slanted off his hand, then another followed and another. The lowering skies threatened, but after a shower it stopped as suddenly as it began. The breeze faltered, then took itself off to other places.

What had he done when he was persuaded at last to go home and get some rest? He remembered Oliver returning and giving him a small envelope with sleeping tablets in it. He would be rung immediately if Pam showed signs of sinking. He accompanied him unresistingly to the car park. His car? Where was it? His mind was a blank and then it came to him where the car was. He remembered his journey in the ambulance. His car was still in the office car park. He refused Oliver's offer to drive him there. He wanted to be alone.

He remembered walking on and on, forgetting where he was, forgetting everything but the frighteningly still figure he had left in the hospital. He had taken the sea-road and turning up an avenue found himself unexpectedly facing the office. With a shock came the thought that the hospital might have been trying to contact him, might have been ringing his home to tell him the worst. With shaking fingers he inserted the key into the lock and raced upstairs. He dialled the number of the hospital. They hadn't rung him. There was no change. As long as there is life there is hope, he thought, as his lone footsteps made an eerie sound in the quiet building.

He drove home carefully in spite of his anxiety for a possible message. Pam would want him to take extra care; in spite of less traffic more alertness was required for late-night driving, she used to say. He wouldn't take the sleeping tablets. Not being used to taking them he might sleep through the call and Martha, at the other end of the house, would never hear the phone ringing. And he didn't want his mother, who would be worn out after her long journey, to be disturbed. He hoped neither of them had waited up for him. He had impressed on Martha that she and his mother were to go to bed.

All was quiet when he entered the house. He made coffee, brought it into the lounge and drank cup after cup as he paced restlessly up and down until he heard the first tentative twitter of the birds. Pam was still alive. He threw himself on the couch and was fast asleep in seconds.

It seemed now, he thought, as he stared bleakly into the still pools of water locked in by boulders, that he had gone and was still going through some horrible nightmare that had no ending. This evening he had got a fresh shock at the sudden change in Pam's condition. Her deathly pallor had been replaced by an unhealthy flush. He noticed the twitching in her face. There was a strange look in her eyes that contrasted painfully with the look that was there earlier in the evening when the children and he were with her.

Did Pam love him? When all was said and done nobody mattered but her. All the well-meaning sympathy and help from friends, his mother's worrying and Martha's devotion were nothing if Pam were not around. But why was he thinking like that? Pam was alive and he loved her. The past years of their married life coalesced and everything bitter and unpleasant was forgotten. Now, he only remembered the loving, good times.

Chapter Six

Friends rushed to help Pat McElroy. He declined most offers of help. His mother and Martha would be able to cope with everything. Pam's father and step-mother came for a visit. He saw their look of relief when told he could manage. He must be sure to let them know if he needed their help at any time. They would keep in touch. Their conscience was clear, Pat assumed, as he saw them off.

Pam recovered from her setback. Her children's visits had been postponed for a few days. On their first visit after their absence she saw they were paler than normal, a little more subdued in their manner. She supposed that was to be expected; they had gone through a rough time. Martha accompanied them most days. Sometimes Pat took them. With him they were more themselves. On one of the days she called Martha back as they were on their way out. Was there something wrong? They seemed to be so quiet. She was worried. Martha said they were perfectly normal until they arrived at the hospital. Then they sort of shrank into themselves. But leave it to her. She mustn't worry. It would probably all boil down to the fact that they missed her.

When the children arrived the following day with their father they were more cheerful, as always, in his company. Nevertheless, she decided to talk to them about what was on her mind.

'As you can see, I'm getting better every day so you're not to worry about me anymore. You're to have fun the same as if I were at home. Both of you will have to put on a little more weight if you want to beat me mountain-climbing. I'm doing my best to eat enough to get the energy I'll need. As a matter of fact, Rosemary, if I keep eating at the rate I am, by the time I leave hospital you and I will have to do more shopping because I won't be able to fit into those lovely clothes you helped me to choose.'

A sob burst from the child and she buried her face in her father's jacket.

I shouldn't have said that, she thought. *The memories I must have revived for my little girl.*

The mother watched unhappily as the father, holding his daughter closely, smoothed her hair and murmured words of comfort. The boy stood near her bed and Pam wanted to tell him to stop making those irritating noises with his feet.

She was not pretending to the children when she said she was better. If only she could sleep at night. She found no difficulty sleeping on and off during the day in spite of the pain and discomfort, but the nights, even aided by sleeping pills, stretched long and wearisome before her. She tried to keep from sleeping during the day, but when the time would come to settle down for the night she would be so overtired she wouldn't be able to relax at all. A change of sleeping pills did not bring much of an improvement. The nurses often remarked what a good patient she was, doctors and nurses generally making poor patients. They enjoyed being with her and she enjoyed their company, Nurse Reidy, the redheaded nurse, the best of all. Once Nurse Reidy had asked: 'Do you always put up with so much, no matter what happens?'

'When you're as old as I am you will come to the realisation that when the going gets tough and you can do nothing about it, the best thing to do is, do nothing about it.'

The nugget of truth disguised by her light-hearted reply was lost on the nurse.

'You're awfully lucky having that gorgeous husband,' said Nurse Pettit, a tall blonde girl with blue eyes. 'That's the kind of man I could fall for in a big way.'

'Better watch out, Doctor McElroy,' Nurse Reidy said laughing. 'I wouldn't trust her with my grandfather. I'll keep an eye on her, if you wish, when your husband is around.'

'Do, as I could never hope to compete with such sexy glamour.' Nurse Pettit treated her friend to a mock-haughty stare. 'Whatever else I may be I am not, repeat, not a husband stealer. But to be serious, I do think you're lucky. He's crazy about you and he's so attentive. He worries just the right amount about you.'

A giggle escaped from Nurse Reidy. 'What do you mean? He worries just the right amount about you? Whatever will you come out with next?'

Nurse Pettit said, 'I suppose you're thinking that I think Mr. McElroy carries a weighing scales around with him.'

The two nurses choked with laughter while their patient gasped with the agony of laughing under her straitened circumstances.

'You're not very understanding,' she complained, bringing her head forward to her arm to wipe away the tears of laughter.

Pam was not blind to the change in the attitude of her visitors. The accident, she felt, with the accompanying heroics, was sufficient to make them look at her with new eyes. How kind they are, she thought with some bitterness. There were times when her room with its flowers, cards and scattered wrappings looked more as if a party were in progress. She was bemused by the whole thing at first. As the novelty wore off she reverted sometimes to the less attractive self she had so often shown in the past where there was not a soul to whom she could turn, when even her father couldn't be bothered to keep in touch with her. She did all the writing, all the phoning, all the visiting except on the occasions when her father and step-mother needed a convenient home for their young offspring. How she had idolized her father.

She was an only child and she knew how difficult it must have been for her parents not to spoil her. Her father would have spoiled her, her mother confessed in later years, but he could always be won over to her way of thinking, and so no damage was done. How she had loved those two wonderful people. She had come closer to her mother, if that were indeed possible, as she looked after her during her last days; days she dreaded, because each one that ended brought closer the day her mother would steal away. At first she had been unable to accept the fact of her mother dying. The thought frightened her and yet she couldn't get rid of it. Her father had moved from their bedroom and a small bed had been placed at an angle where at any time during the night she could see how her mother was. Her mother worried about her as her days and nights were broken. She warned that her own health would break down if she kept up that pressure, and Pat had to be considered as well.

'Pat said to stay for as long as I'm needed and I'm taking him at his word. Besides, what have I to do except keep an eye on you and see that you're comfortable. So stop fussing and for once do what your doctor/daughter tells you.'

One night, instead of going to bed for a few hours as she normally did when her mother fell asleep, she sat at the bedside holding the frail white hand, looking at the face with its grey shadows more pronounced in sleep. She did not know how long she sat there, her mind refusing to accept that her mother's life was near its close, when her mother stirred uneasily in her sleep. She bent closer to her and it seemed just then that her mother had moved that much nearer to death. She released her clasp from her mother's hand and stumbling to her own bed she knelt beside it and wept despairingly into the pillow. Even in her distress she was careful to control herself and yet as she knelt there why did she feel as if there were watchful eyes fixed on her?

She got up from her knees and went over to her mother. She knelt down and took the outstretched hand in hers.

'You know, Mum. You knew all along.'

Her mother smiled and nodded her head. 'I'm glad for your sake you have come to terms with the inevitable. I have prayed.

77

How I have prayed. I didn't want to die. Not yet. I know what you've been going through. I'm not a mother for twenty-six years for nothing.'

They talked for a long time.

Her father was inconsolable at her mother's death. He had loved her dearly, she was certain. She had grown up in an atmosphere of love and contentment, and as she grew from girlhood to womanhood she was aware of the love that drew her parents so closely together and in whose secure circle of love she was firmly fixed.

Her confidence in her father's love for her mother was shaken, more than she admitted to herself, by the remarriage of her father before her mother was barely two years dead.

When she thought about it objectively she couldn't blame him. He was still comparatively young, handsome, well-off, but alone and lonely. Why shouldn't he remarry? He was entitled to companionship and love and yet, how ephemeral love was. Her mother was probably but a memory to her father, a thing of the past. She could have understood his marrying somebody nearer his own age, but a girl just a year older than herself! She was upset but it was her father's life and she wished him luck. She kept up her visits to her old home in the belief she was welcome, and also to show her father she loved him just as much as ever, and to build up a friendship with his wife Linda. Linda and she got on well together, yet why did she get the feeling she was wearing out her welcome? Eventually it dawned on her that it was her own joy and pleasure at seeing them that was hiding from her the reality of the situation. Her decision to make the intervals between visits longer and to cut short these visits confirmed her suspicions when there was no reaction from her father or Linda.

As she lay in bed day after day she often reflected that there was nothing like illness plus the ability to think, to force one to see life as it really was. She had the time now to sit back and look at herself objectively, to look at everyone she knew and examine them as they were, as well as in their relationship to herself. The picture was far from bright.

All she really had were her children and they were only on loan. She had neither husband nor friends. Friends, such as they were (and, was there really such a thing as a friend?), she could do without. If she were to survive she must set about on a course of self-rehabilitation. Had she not said this before? Once, or many times? No matter. She was sick of her weakness in failing to carry out what she set out to do. She must be a little ruthless from now on. But there were no known courses in the kind of self-rehabilitation she required. Under what heading then should she place herself? Widow? Deserted wife? Unmarried mother? She was none of these. So, there being no known courses of therapy for people like her she would have to think one up and have it prepared before she left hospital. If only she could have been a different person, happy in giving, not looking for a reward. But that was it. She had been happy in giving. Giving to Pat, joyfully, but it did not satisfy Pat. Not content with giving little, of which she wasn't fully aware till the crunch finally came, he tried to change her from the person she was and mould her into something that fitted his idea of how she should be. She tried hard at first to become this creature but she still didn't satisfy Pat.

As the days went by the steady flow of visitors thinned, which was a relief in a way to the patient. Now she was concerned about her children; their attitude perplexed her. If they weren't holding themselves back they were certainly not coming forward. Something was wrong and it upset her, because for the first time since she became a mother she didn't seem to be able to get at the root of what was causing it. She spoke to her husband about it. It was just that they missed her, he said, and that was understandable, but they were perfectly normal at home and he himself saw nothing to worry about in their manner in the hospital. They were children. Perhaps the atmosphere of the hospital subdued them a little. It could upset an adult, never mind two small children.

He took her hand. 'I think you have too much time to think and worry over nothing. Do you want us to give you something to worry about? Martha! There's someone to worry about. She's only a shadow of her old self, or did you not notice?'

A smile released the worried frown on his wife's face. She had heard all about the strict diet from Martha. Pat gave her his version of it. The children kept telling her she could be five pounds thinner if she wore a certain advertised girdle. If she did that, she could skip her dieting for a while and that would give her a chance to take a breath while she lost some breadth the easy way.

'So Martha's diet is the best thing that could happen because it helps to stop them worrying about you. What with the tape-measure out every day and each of them taking measurements of Martha's waistline and getting different results, the reason, Martha tells me, is that Rosemary tightens the tape-measure more than Robert does, so as to encourage her, so between everything they have enough to occupy their minds. By the way, you'll have to hurry up and put on some weight. You were thin enough before the accident. And worrying unnecessarily about the children isn't going to help.'

He waited for an answering smile. What was wrong with her? What was there to worry about? Hadn't he just put her mind at ease about the children? If she were worried about him…? But he mustn't fool himself. Pam wasn't concerned in the least about him. That much was obvious. If only she showed that she cared. He would be satisfied with the smallest show of interest in him, but he felt shut out. There was no room for him in her thoughts. The children were her whole life now, it seemed. Even Martha got more attention than he did. What was he talking about? Martha, on returning from each visit never stopped talking about what the missus said and did. She could talk non-stop to Martha. It wasn't for want of energy that made her conversation with him erratic or non-existent. Only that if he kept on talking he doubted if there would be any conversation at all on his visits. It was bad enough having to put up with this as well as what seemed bare tolerance of his company, but he had noticed at times a feeling almost of repugnance she had for him when he kissed her or touched her. But he would be patient. There was no alternative. But God, it was hard to put up with this coldness, this indifference. Time was his ally. Time, patience and love would win the day. Surely Pam loved him. Surely she found him loving and attractive. Perhaps she no longer found him attractive or loving. He hoped this wasn't the case. He loved her and he was proud of her, intensely proud of what she had done. It pleased him that his friends made much of her courageous action. Even complete strangers had come to him in the early days, had shaken hands with him.

The years had slipped by with things not going too well between Pam and himself. Why this should have happened he couldn't understand. He had done his best but she never seemed to be happy. What else was left that he could do? The memory of the many occasions he had been humiliated by her in front of his friends came to mind. Why had she behaved like that? What pleasure did she get from attempts to ridicule and hurt him in front of others? Sometimes he had overlooked these incidents, but there were times when his annoyance and chagrin had been the cause of one of those rip-roaring rows that had become all too frequent. Where had he gone wrong or was it that he was to blame? What was the answer? He knew many people envied him, his success and wealth, all achieved by brains and hard work, but he also knew some of his friends pitied him and this he found a bitter pill to swallow, because of the wife he had. He was well aware of what they said behind his back and one or two gave him a hint of their feelings and when they were pushed to it, Pam herself, got directly and indirectly something more than just a hint. But the odd thing was, she was far more able for their cracks than he was, and her reaction varied between bland ignoring of unpleasant remarks, or a curt or withering response.

Sometimes he hated her for being the way she was, but most of the time he was able to forget, absorbing himself in the work he enjoyed and loved so much. He and Pam had lost a great deal, but perhaps they could cut their losses and look to the future for a better life together. It was worth working for. Perhaps this accident, as terrible and near tragic as it was had had to happen to bring them together again. He would leave no stone unturned until they got back to their old relationship. The more patient he was and the less a patient Pam became, the more surely that day would come. He smiled at his choice of words. His sense of humour was coming back.

Pam looked at her diary. She would be nine weeks in hospital in two days' time. The summer would be over before she would be well enough to leave. She was being cheated of all the glorious long days of the best summer they had had for years. Just her luck. She longed to get out and about. To be with Rosemary and Robert. She had such plans for this summer. She had always been good at thinking up plans to make the most of the long days. If only she could be with her children. Did they miss her? She wanted them to miss her and yet not to miss her. Had Pat taken care of them, really taken care of them? She knew they were never at a loss for somewhere to go. They had plenty of friends, but that wasn't the same thing as having fun with their parents, at that age anyway. Or was it she only thought that?

They were staying with the Butlers in their summer cottage in Dingle and having a good time. She had postcards from them. She was glad they were happy and not missing her. Tears filled her eyes. She was not depressed, she told herself. It was only natural she should wish to be with her children. She loved to hear they were so happy and Sue Butler was very good to keep in touch with her. It would be great to see their suntanned little bodies on their return. Sue who was very careful about sunburn on account of their colouring said they were a lovely tan already. She wasn't to worry about them as they were no trouble; give them enough to eat and what with their days so full with all they found to do, that as soon as they went to bed they went out like a light! It was terribly nice of Sue to be so offhand about the responsibility of adding two healthy lively youngsters to her own four. I love them and I want to be with them so much. She covered her face with her hands and wept silently.

She was still feeling lonely and depressed when her husband called in to see her. She had tried to curtail his visits, partly for his own sake and partly because as far as she was concerned, they were a waste of time. She did not want his company, though she did not tell him in so many words but if he insisted on being a martyr then he was welcome to the role. She enquired about the children after she asked about himself. Had he further news of them? She showed him the cards she received from them that morning, told him of the plans she had made for their holidays and how everything had been upset because of her being in hospital.

Pat said he too missed Rosemary and Robert. Martha had taken her annual leave and gone off to Lourdes. It was useless telling her it was a bad time to go as the heat would be sweltering, but she would not change her mind. She was going specially for the missus, she told him. Now, he was alone in the house. The daily left him as soon as she had seen to his evening meal.

He said: 'I know you miss the children's visits but I think it was a good thing that the Butlers brought them on holidays.'

'It's not only the children, it's everything.'

'How do you mean, everything? The doctors tell me you're improving every day and you won't feel it before you're home. I've kept the papers with the report of the accident. You may like to read them –'

'I know what happened.'

'Come on, cheer up.'

'There's nothing to be cheerful about.'

'You're alive. Isn't that something to be cheerful about?'

'Is it?'

'Of course it is. All you have to do now is to be patient and–'

'I've spent my life being patient.'

He was tired trying to be cheerful. Did Pam give him a thought? As if she were the only one who was depressed. The only one who missed the children.

'So have I, for that matter. But let's not get into an argument about our virtues! Do you think it has been easy for me since your accident? I get depressed too, you know. I've to go home to an empty house this evening. At least, you've company here.'

'Do you want to change places?'

'I'm in no mood for that kind of thing. All I'm asking is for some kind of response from you. I come in here twice a day and what do we talk about? Nothing. You don't give me any news. It's up to me to keep the conversation going.'

'What do I have to talk about? Nurse comes in. Nurse goes out. Doctors come. Doctors go. That's about it.'

'You could tell me who calls to see you.'

'You wouldn't be interested.'

'Who said I wouldn't? Martha has come home full of news after her visits. The same with the children. And I've been here with other visitors and you're never stuck for a word to say. Don't I count?'

Where had she heard those pleadings before? Those accusations? She had said them all. Over and over till at times she sounded even to herself like a tiresome non-stop record. The sight of his tired face failed to move her. He didn't deserve pity and he wouldn't get it. He had reserves of pity and sympathy from his friends in the past. Let him look to those sources again.

Her eyes were devoid of feeling when she spoke: 'I don't believe you do count. Not anymore. The day I walked out of your office, I walked out of your life. What does it matter if I have to live in the same house as you for another few years for the children's sake and keep the peace, which I am determined to do. I have threatened to leave you before but you said if I did you'd see to it I would never get custody of the children, that you could prove in court I was an unfit mother. I suppose you could too. You proved I'm an unfit wife to yourself and to your friends.'

His mouth opened in astonishment. So this was what she was bottling up all those weeks. 'Will you, for God's sake, stop dragging up the past.'

'Why should I? Isn't it the past that has brought us to this present moment? But you wouldn't understand that. You have never tried to understand. Do you know the last time you were away, Rosemary, a gentle little girl of ten, called me a slut? And I slapped her on the face. Can you imagine that?'

'I can.'

'You would! And yet you know I have never lifted a hand to either child since they were born. And it was because of you I slapped her.'

'I like that! Blame me for everything.'

'Yes, you are to blame. Rosemary told me she had heard you call me a slut one night we had a row. God knows what else she heard.'

He was cold with anger. 'What else am I to blame for? You might as well continue as you're at it.'

'No, I'm not going to continue. But I'll just say this: as long as I live I shall never forget your attitude to me in your office that day.'

All the poignancy, all the heartbreak of those few minutes in his office, all the preparation that led to it, Rosemary's suggestion to get rid of her old clothes, the excitement of shopping, the first disappointment at not being able to meet her husband at the airport, then Rosemary's suggestion that she should dress up and call into the office, all those memories had come back slowly to her as the days went by. She had relived each moment, taking one scene out and dwelling on each detail of that scene, going over and over it, then another scene, not always in sequence. Then painfully slotting each scene into place so that the whole vivid picture was spread out before her, torturing her with the memory. She knew Pat would not understand what all this meant to her. It was too small and insignificant for him. But if he only knew that marriage is made up of little things; the word of appreciation, the patient moment or two given when least afforded, the realisation that it was love that should motivate everything. 'It's not what you said or did. God knows, it was nothing compared to what had happened a hundred times before. It was your utter refusal to understand the significance of my calling to you. Do you think I wanted to call? Begging you to take me out to lunch, seeing that for years I have never been near the place? All I was trying to do was to make you see that the children were beginning to notice how things were between us. I didn't tell you this, but the day Rosemary and I went shopping she said to me, "I think Daddy doesn't like you very much anymore. Why?" She said other things as well which made me realise that Robert and she weren't blind. Of course I tried to explain away her doubts and I think I succeeded. But what's the point in telling you all this? It won't make a bit of difference to you.'

'If I knew what you were getting at, it might.'

'That's the reply I expected. You see, what's wrong with you is that you look on things like that as being too small for you to bother about. But it's by taking care of the small things in life that success is achieved in work, and the same goes for marriage.'

His patience snapped. 'So you're still annoyed over that day in the office? Wouldn't you think you'd have more important things on your mind? So that's what all the coolness is about! Well, if you want to go on like that that's all right by me. But before I go there are a couple of things I'd like to tell you. You think you're the only one who suffers –'

'I'm only interested in me.'

'You can say that again. That's all you've ever done.'

'As usual you exaggerate. As usual you can't see any point of view but your own. But you should be flattered that I'm following your example: think of yourself first. If only you didn't think you were so blasted perfect there would be some hope for us. You know, it's hard to believe now, but you meant everything in the world to me. Not even the children could come between you and me. There was nothing I wouldn't have done for you, but what happens? One day I wake up to the fact that I'm just a nuisance in your life. Worse still, for most of the time I don't exist.'

'That's not true.'

'Good God, do you think I'm enjoying myself saying these things? And it could have been so different. You married a happy, affectionate woman that only wanted to do all that was best and good for you. What have you done to me?'

It was a cry of anguish but the man could only feel the ingratitude that had been shown to him for the weeks of hardship and suffering he had gone through.

He said: 'What have you done to yourself? Do you think I'm to blame for the way you've turned out? I didn't marry a child. For a while there after you recovered consciousness I thought you were changing for the better, more like the girl I used to be proud of.'

'So you were beginning to be proud of me? Why? Because I made the headlines! How you must have lapped up the attention, particularly when I wasn't around to share it! And what were you proud of anyway? Because I saved a child from being killed?'

'There's no heroism in doing something when you've no time to think. You jam the brakes in your car when somebody crosses the road in front of you. A purely automatic exercise. My so-called heroic act was equally automatic. So don't be proud of me.' Tears welled into her eyes, but she mustn't cry. Her husband used to accuse her of using tears so as to have her own way. She turned her head away.

Pat said: 'Is that an order?' He wondered what kind of stupidity it was that made him wait on, but he might as well stay for the full time.

She did not reply. Her mind was on the wasted years, years that could never be brought back, the heartache that was so much part of those years. She still had that heartache. It was too much to bear. If only there was someone she could talk to, who would understand. Who would see that she wasn't asking for the impossible. Her whole soul was in revolt. She could not, would not resign herself to what should not be. Her mouth trembled. Her heart ached with a heavy suffocating pain. This heartache is real, she realised, not just a fanciful affliction that frustrated lovers in novels are supposed to feel. *I have a heartache, a heavy aching sensation that is crushing my chest.* If Pat would only see, just once, that she was a person first of all, a human being with equal human rights as he had. Then she was his wife which should put her in a special place in his life. She had loved him as a friend, husband and companion. She had seen that as the perfect relationship. But it hadn't worked out. What had she been to Pat? A woman whose needs he fulfilled? In sex only? How could love survive neglect, the usage and abuse? Even the soil in the fields and gardens needed care and attention, needed nutrition, if they were to go on giving. It must have been hope that had made her love survive. Hope that someday, some time, things would change. Otherwise she could not have gone on, children or no children.

When she had gained her composure she turned to look at her husband. She could see that he had no desire to break the silence. She supposed he had put her back into the niche he had made for her. He must think of her once more as an exasperating, demanding, impossible-to-please woman.

She said: 'Don't let me keep you. I'm sure you've had a long and busy day. And from now on there's no need to call so often. Everybody here is impressed by your devotion, so give yourself a break and give a chance to visitors to come in at this hour. As you probably have noticed, most of them are inclined to give this time a miss knowing you are always by my sick bed.'

'As you wish.' He arose to go.

As he bent to kiss her she said: 'There's no need for that kiss when there's no one around to notice.'

Her eyes did not leave his face. She was searching, hoping for a change of expression, for a sign of regret, anything. I'm an idiot, she thought. *Will I ever learn? Pat's mind is probably miles away from me at this moment.*

Her husband raised his hand in formal salute at the door. She did not respond to the gesture. She was thinking, as he closed the door gently behind him, you might not be my husband, you might be nothing at all to me, and yet...

That's that, Pat thought, as he took the lift. *Nothing will ever change Pam.* He had thought he had got closer to her at times over the weeks; the accident seemed to have brought about changes he thought could never be. No such luck. It was asking for the impossible. Let Vienna, Sally and the rest of them take over. He didn't care. They will soon get their stomach-full, soon tire of her tantrums. That's her funeral.

Chapter Seven

The more Pam saw of Sally the more she liked her. What was it about Sally that made her so popular with men and women? Her sincerity? Her willingness to see the best in everyone, understanding that in common with herself people had their faults but that did not make them less a person? This willingness was plainly obvious to everyone, Pam thought. Then there was her kindness, her sympathy, her ability to laugh at herself. She had all these gifts. She enjoyed Sally's visits and she felt Sally enjoyed them too; that her visits were not made through a sense of duty, but because Sally also looked forward to their time together.

After her showdown with her husband Pam longed to confide in Sally, to release some of her pent-up emotion, but she was afraid she might put a strain on a friendship, which was still too young to share the burden of confidences so troubled and perplexing. She would wait. Sometimes, Morrison came with Sally. Occasionally Vienna, or Vienna and her husband were with her. But more often than not Sally came on her own.

Now that she had finally come to terms with her relationship with Pat, and she fervently hoped she had, she was able to give more of herself to others, to derive more pleasure from other people, other things. She liked to take a back seat when her visitors came and enjoyed the drama of ordinary living. She found Vienna more likeable than she had thought possible; perhaps being a friend of Sally helped. She had always regarded her as an affected blonde, full of herself, sure of herself, demanding attention and getting it. But now that she had the time and the inclination to get to know her better she found her sincere, almost too frank and completely herself.

When Vienna smiled her face softened into youthful and innocent beauty. Her face in repose had a touch of sadness, wistfulness replacing the devil-may-care look in the slanting green eyes. The affection and loyalty that existed between her and Sally, two personalities that seemed so totally opposite, was deep and lasting. Vienna treated her husband Michael with apparent nonchalance. She loved him but she was punishing him. What made her come to that conclusion? And then she remembered.

It had happened so long ago that she had forgotten about it and looking back now she thought that Michael and herself were the only two who shared the secret. But there must have been others who knew also. Who whispered. Who passed on confidences that weren't meant for other ears and were careless of the consequences. So that was why Michael seemed unsure of himself, always that bit apprehensive in Vienna's company. Perhaps I'm the only one who notices this, Pam reflected, but maybe that's because there's an affinity between me and Vienna. It seems mine is not the only marriage that is fighting for survival except that my battle is over. I suppose if I were to look around I'd find that instead of a marriage being a haven of love and peace it's more often a battleground.

Vienna. That name. Pam discovered she wasn't the only one who wondered about it, but she hadn't been taken in by Vienna's tongue-in-cheek explanation; her story being that her mother was convinced her first-born was conceived while on their honeymoon in Vienna and she had thought it was only right that her child should be called after that beautiful city.

'The unromantic explanation is,' she said to her on a later visit, 'that my name is Veronica. Tony, who's a year younger than I am, fiddled around with that name as a baby, getting, according to my mother, Vodka, very appropriate that, knowing my fondness for that beverage, then Venca, Venna and then Vienna, perhaps associating my name with a song my mother used to sing around the house: "I'm in love with Vienna," or whatever it's called. Anyway, the name stuck.'

Pam's chat with the nurses gave her pleasure; their eventual confiding of their joys and troubles to her, her attempts to sort out their love-lives being sometimes a cause for uproarious laughter. She found pleasure in the doctors' visits. She looked forward to the newspaperman who came and went with impressive regularity.

Sally Griffin watched Pam McElroy's progress with anxious eyes. There were days when her condition seemed static. It was obvious from her movements and the cloud of pain that shadowed her face from time to time as they talked that she was in distress. But there was something else. Something that puzzled her. Pat could not be the cause of this something. She had seen them together on his visits and she couldn't help being impressed by his affectionate devotion to her. Whatever harsh thoughts she had of him before the accident, and she did have a few, especially after Penny's disclosures, they were all gone.

Was it the children who troubled her? But when Pam talked about them she seemed happy. So what was it? If only she could get her to talk, not of other people and things, but about herself. To confide in her. She was afraid to probe, to delve too deeply into affairs that were not hers. Perhaps in time Pam would learn to trust her. Until that happened she would have to wait. Weeks went by and still Pam gave no indication that she wanted to talk to her, but then Pam might be one of those people who preferred to deal with her own problems or she might like to forget the past, whether it was their parentage, their background, their school, their religion or family quarrels. For someone to come along and remind them of the thing they wanted to forget was a risky step.

Could she take that step with Pam? And then her problem was solved in one of her visits to the hospital. Pam, in referring to the cards and letters she had received from people she thought had forgotten her, mentioned Penny. It was obvious she had been deeply moved by Penny's letter. Penny had explained that she couldn't visit her in hospital as she was threatened with a miscarriage. Pam told her she knew what Penny was going through, having had a miscarriage in the early days of her marriage.

'And I believe you are her niece,' she added almost immediately. 'What an extraordinary coincidence. No wonder I took to you!'

One night after a visit from Sally, Pam came to a decision. I'm going to have a talk about marriage with Sally. See what she expects from it. I bet I'm not all that different from other women, or is it that other wives are better than I am? Or have they got greater capacity for endurance than I have? Are they better at covering up than I am because they have more pride, more guts, or is it simply a matter of being able to adjust better to the role of wife?

She passed her hand wearily over her forehead. Would there ever be an end to this tortuous thinking? Hadn't she once and for all made it plain to Pat that from now on he meant nothing to her? He was a husband in name only. Couldn't she resign herself to this fact? Where was her courage, her consistency? This is where real courage is displayed. She mustn't be a victim to spur-of-the-moment notions. But her whole being rebelled at the thought of what was in front of her.

Pat, if only you were what I thought and believed you were when I married you. I know you didn't plan to hoodwink me, to fool me in any way, nor did I at any time feel that you were putting on an act for my benefit. I loved you because you were you, a wonderful person in so many ways. I remember one evening, when we were only about six months married, the two of us were sitting together in the lounge. You were reading. I had been reading too, but had closed my book and looked over at you sprawling in your armchair on the opposite side of the fire, the leg of your trousers hitched fairly high above your ankle, yet not showing any bare leg. That was typical of your neatness; you were always so immaculate-looking, yet so masculine in appearance. There you were, looking so handsome and attractive, absorbed in your book and I wanted to go over and kiss you there and then, but I wanted also to prolong the pleasure. So I continued to look at you, reminding myself how lucky I was to have such a husband, when suddenly you raised your eyes and looked over at me. I wonder now what kind of picture I presented to you then, but all you did was smile, such a gentle loving smile. I don't know if I smiled back but I remember saying to you: 'You know, darling, you're not perfect, but you are as perfect as I want you to be.' What was your reaction to my remark? I forget, but I don't forget that shortly afterwards you came over to me and made love to me.

Is this a dream? Were we really like that? That young husband and wife so wonderfully in love? It seems now that we travel on two separate roads, but the destination is the same – the end of our marriage.

Her thoughts returned to the first time she met Pat. She and some of her friends had gone to the closing night of a theatre seminar which had been taking place in Dublin where there was an open forum. First, they listened to a panel of experts giving their views on theatre and then the director of the seminar asked the audience for comments and questions.

After a slow start people started popping up to say their piece. Eugene had wanted to speak from the beginning but each time he had got up the director pointed to some other person and Eugene would sit down, impatient and frustrated. They sympathized with their hero but their sympathy didn't prevent them from breaking their hearts laughing and putting wild bets on his prospects of having his voice heard. Eventually Eugene sat back and decided to take things easy. He said he was getting cramps from all those unexpected limbering exercises. But the rest of them were not having this defeatist attitude. Eugene would speak for them and that was that.

When the next speaker sat down to a mild applause they

encouraged Eugene to rise once more through sheer manual pressure. He opened his mouth to speak, thinking he had got the go-ahead from the director, but it seemed the gesture was for someone behind him; Eugene, displaying great fortitude, flopped into his seat once more amid choked laughter. Then the voice of the speaker was pulling them from their distracted attention and they found themselves listening and being very impressed. They strained their necks to see who he was. He was about five rows behind, a tall attractive-looking man who spoke with humour and sense about everything from art to government subsidies.

When he had finished they stood up and applauded like mad. The rest of the audience followed their example, some craning their necks to see the man who had livened up a dull debate.

Myles said: 'We must meet that man.'

Audrey said: 'Yes. We'll have to talk to him.'

When it was all over the boys scrambled over chairs to catch up with him. The girls, keeping to the queue, heard Eugene shout: 'Over here. I've got him.'

They pushed their way through the crowd, shedding apologies to right and left, to where Eugene stood triumphantly holding their hero by the elbow.

He said: 'Let's take our breath of fresh air out with us. There's no room to introduce ourselves here.'

Outside the six of them crowded around the man and Eugene did the introductions. Moments later they were propelling him to one of their favourite haunts firing question after question at him as they walked, all six of them trying to get a word in, sometimes slipping onto the road as they tried to keep in line in case they'd miss anything.

They were lucky to get two tables close together. One of the tables was occupied by a young couple, but soon after the invasion they left and they pushed the tables closer and arranged the chairs. Pam sat opposite Pat. She listened to the conversation, contributing now and again, but she was happier just to sit and watch this exciting man.

What age was he? He looked older and more mature than her friends. He could be twenty-seven, twenty-eight years. He must be at least six feet tall. He had fair hair, dark brown eyes with long dark eyelashes and dark eyebrows, a straight nose, strong white teeth and pale perfectly-shaped lips. She was almost shocked with herself for thinking: *I would love to kiss that mouth.* He dressed well, his tie, shirt and suit in harmony. She noticed the gold cufflinks: *I wonder did he get those from a girlfriend. Or wife? He may be married. Oh, I hope not.*

The painful possibility jogged her out of her day-dreaming and she emerged from the haze that had enveloped her and prepared herself to hear the worst if and when it came. Suddenly she became aware that he was looking at her. It gave her a heady feeling to be looked at in that way. Her eyes met his. She was the first to remove her gaze, to look at some pamphlets that were being handed around, but she was conscious that Pat's eyes were still on her. The waitresses indicated that their night's work was done by making a great display of stripping the vacant tables. Finally they got up, Eugene and Damien trying to extract a promise from Pat to help with their own drama group. His help would be invaluable, they insisted. Pat's protests that he had no experience whatever of production or anything else fell on deaf ears. They insisted that he could meet them at least once to talk things over. Would he take one of their phone numbers? Any day that would suit him would be all right with them. If one or two couldn't make it at least the majority of them would.

Pat turned to Pam: 'I'll phone you if that's all right.'

'That's fine,' she said, speaking in a normal voice, but her heart was exploding. She felt sure he would ring. He wasn't the kind of person to break a promise. And she was right. The following Tuesday night at exactly nine o'clock – she was on duty as she told him she would be – she was called to the phone. Something in her bones told her this was his call.

'May I speak to Doctor Cronin?'

'Doctor Cronin speaking.'

His 'Hello, Pat. This is Pat,' sounded so funny that they burst out laughing. There and then she mentally decided that the name confusion must stop as from this point in her life everything for her had changed. Pat had come into her life and he was there to stay.

Pat said he would meet her friends if she would arrange a time and place that would be suitable. He gave her his phone number. He didn't delay on the phone but she was happy. She still had that lovely feeling that this was just the beginning. Now about the name business. She had it! She would call herself Pam from now on. P.A.M. The initials of her name. Patricia, Angela, Mary. One of these days when the time was right she would re-introduce herself to her friends and relations.

She gave Pat's message to the gang and it was settled they would hold a meeting in Eugene's place, as he was the only one of their crowd whose home was in Dublin and where meetings could take place without too much trouble. It was at this gathering that Pat explained he wasn't qualified to handle any dramatic society. He had no personal experience for one thing, apart from taking minor parts in college productions, and for another reason, his free time was fairly limited. They had managed fine up to this on their own and it would be a pity for an outsider who knew so little about theatre to come along and perhaps bungle things up for them, but if they thought he could give any advice or help for sets or anything like that, for what it was worth, it was theirs. They talked and argued good-humouredly late into the night.

'I suppose that means we won't be seeing you again', Audrey said.

'I don't remember saying that,' Pat said.

His eyes rested on Pam. 'I hope to see you all again and often.'

Eugene, on the alert, said: 'It seems not only have we not gained a Pat. But we have lost a Pat.'

As she instinctively felt how it would be for herself and Pat, so it was. They had fallen in love and wasted no time in admitting it. At the first opportune weekend she brought Pat home to meet her parents. They were to announce their engagement during the weekend. Not only that, Pat also intended to mention a date for an early marriage. She had suggested that meeting them for the first time and the excitement of their engagement would be enough for the weekend. What was wrong with combining the two of them, he had asked.

'Marriage usually follows an engagement and the fact that the interval between them is short is of little importance as we're fortunate to be able to get married any time we like, so the sooner the better. That's the way I feel anyway. Do I sound unreasonable?' She did not answer. She loved to listen to him, to see him act like a man deeply and responsibly in love, yet not beyond getting as excited as a schoolboy. When she queried the rush once more she knew what he would say. She had already heard the reason, yet their very repetition added to her intense joy and happiness. He would tell her parents he was twenty-nine, so it couldn't be said he was too young to make up his mind. He had a good profession, was a success at it and there was no indication that he wouldn't continue to be a success at it. And there was no problem where money was concerned. He had a ready-made house partly furnished for them to move into.

When he repeated the reasons he added: 'I'm in good health and,' winking at her, 'I'm not too unsightly-looking.'

He reached out his arms and drew her face close to his. 'Do you think you could stand the sight of me first thing in the morning when you open your beautiful sleepy eyes?'

Pat shouldn't say such things to her. It filled her with a terrible and uncontrolled longing for him, yet this feeling, strange and new as it was, was a wonderful kind of happiness. She took his face between her two hands and squeezed it hard. 'I've seen uglier faces and anyway they say ugliness grows on you.'

But he was so handsome, she told herself for the thousandth time. She loved to look at him, his dark eyes smouldering with love for her, the sweet smile that curved upwards. She longed to marry him. The sooner the better. She was twenty-three. She knew what it was to fall in love. She had fallen in and out of love regularly since she was sixteen.

Now she was sufficiently mature to realise that this love she had for Pat was the real thing. All the other experiences had led her to this and this was her final goal. It was unthinkable that there could be anyone else for her.

She hoped her father and mother would understand. She would finish her internship after her marriage. She must discuss that with Pat in case he had overlooked it. What seemed so important to her such a short while ago suddenly faded into insignificance. This is what being in love meant.

There was a great welcome for them from her father and mother. They took to Pat instantly as she was confident they would. After announcing their engagement Pat brought up the question of an early marriage. But being on the alert for the slightest sign of disappointment in her parents, she thought she noticed a change in their expressions before Pat had finished speaking. Her mother's dismay was more evident than her father's but his reply to Pat displayed a hesitancy not in keeping with his previous enthusiasm. The time they had known each other was short, he said, but they weren't children and he was confident they were doing the right thing. She saw her mother exchange glances with her father. It was obvious their pleasure at the engagement was dimmed a little by the hasty marriage plans, but they weren't going to spoil anything by expressing doubts. Their selflessness activated her into forgetting her own happiness and to giving some thought to her parents, who at all times in her life thought only of her.

'I like the way you two sit there without showing the slightest regret over the imminent loss of your daughter. You seem to be very anxious to get me off your hands. Well, I'm not budging yet. You see, I know what you two are thinking of. After all, I've known you all my life which is more than either of you can say about knowing me all your life.'

She was rewarded with smiles which quickly replaced the flickering doubts that had shown in their faces. She took hold of Pat's hand and held it tightly.

'I really feel I ought to finish my internship before I get married. Then after we're married I'll decide whether to specialise in paediatrics or take up general practice.' She squeezed Pat's hand for support of the sudden change. 'There's really no need to rush into marriage or plans for the future.'

As her eyes pleaded with him to see it her way, his disappointment melted and he kissed her to confirm his willingness to the change of plan.

This was the cue for her father to leap to his feet and get out the champagne. She managed to get home the following weekend to start on plans for her wedding. There was now plenty of time but she felt there was nothing like starting early for such a big event. She was bringing home samples of material for her wedding dress and the bridesmaids' dresses, she told Pat, and she wanted her mother to see them before deciding on anything. There were other things that could be started.

'All right. All right,' Pat said, giving her a quick hug. 'You don't have to explain. I can see you're losing interest already. Leaving me at the first opportunity. I can see what it's going to be like when we get married.'

'About the dresses,' he said to her before he said goodbye, 'don't decide on anything yet. I have one or two ideas which you might like.'

'What are they? Please tell me.' She was excited at the idea that he had given them any thought.

'Not now. Time enough to talk about such things when you come back. Go off and enjoy yourself. Remember I'll be thinking of you all the time.'

She was longing to hear once more what her father and mother thought of Pat. This was the main reason for her journey home though she couldn't very well say that to Pat or her parents. Her father was full of praise for Pat. She listened entranced as he enlarged on his good qualities. When she had her mother on her own she said: 'Now, Mum, what do you think? And I'm not fishing for more praise. It's just that men are inclined only to see the best in each other. They overlook faults which to a woman might appear as a disaster when she is faced with them or has to live with them. I'm not saying Daddy isn't a good judge of character, but mothers see things that fathers might be blind to and I just want to know if you have noticed anything I should know about. Do you think I'm odd going on like that? You see, I know one has to live with a person's faults, but sometimes love can blind people and they only see faults which they find almost unbearable to live with when it's too late.'

Her mother looked at her with searching eyes. 'You're quite right in going on like this, as you put it, and a person is obliged, I would put it as strongly as that, to make himself or herself aware of faults, and indeed it would be a good thing to discuss each other's faults. To go into marriage believing you've got the perfect partner is asking for trouble. Your father has more or less said everything about Pat that can be said. We have talked about him, naturally, and we do think he will make you a good husband and we're looking forward to having him as a son-in-law.'

When they were discussing the house Pat had built Pam saw her mother frowning.

'What is it, Mother? Anything on your mind?'

'Yes and no. It's not terribly important but perhaps I should mention it as it worries me a little. Pat seems to be in control of everything. I mean, he is such a competent person that he seems to take over everything and nobody else has a chance to share in what he does. I'm putting this rather badly I know, but take his house for instance. The whole thing was planned and finished before a future wife came on the scene, even down to landscaping the gardens and furnishing the house. Is that usual? It appears to me anyway that he had no intention of letting a wife share in this lovely experience. It just worries me a little. That's all.'

'Oh Mother, if that's all that's worrying you I'm relieved. First of all, as regards the furnishing of the house, well, it's only part-furnished so that I do have a chance to plan the rest. And as regards Pat building the house even though he had no immediate thoughts of marriage – what would you expect him to do? In his business it must be quite usual to hear of unusual sites for sale before most people, and when he saw this site he told me that was the place for him. The design of the house, the gardens took shape in his head before he had left and when he bought the site he was itching to get cracking on the job. And can you imagine the pleasure it gave him seeing his dream become a concrete reality. Excuse the pun! Seriously, though, the house is beautiful and I'm looking forward to making a home of it.'

'So you don't mind?'

'Oh Mother, even to think that way is nonsense. There are thousands of couples who have no choice whatever in the sight or design of their houses. I'm no architect and Pat is a brilliant one. Have I told you he does the most wonderful oil paintings. You don't know half of that man's talents.'

'I give up. You win!'

'It's not a question of my winning, Mum. I think you thought I was going into married life and without realising it, turn out to be a wife with no say in anything, that Pat would always be in control. Pat's not like that at all. Now, are you satisfied?'

Her mother smiled and the small frown that had bridged her eyebrows disappeared.

When they had settled down at the Aerie after the honeymoon they held parties for friends and relations. Pam's one regret was that neither of them had brothers or sisters who could come to visit them in their beautiful home. She would walk slowly through the rooms touching some piece of furniture, examining an ornament, lingering when her gaze was caught by a view from the windows or attracted by the colour harmony in a room.

There was the time when Pat brought her into the lounge to see a painting he had bought and had hung on the wall as a surprise for her. She couldn't take her eyes from the picture. It was a painting of a family picnic. Father, mother and four children. Two pups scampered around to the amusement of the children. The mother, her arm out, obviously trying to control one of the pups. Her face reproving until you noticed the twinkle in her eyes. The children's mouths opened wide in laughter. The father sat in the middle, alert and watchful, a protective hold on the picnic basket. Close by, a brown and white cow showed her head over a wooden gate, her unblinking brown gaze solemnly fixed on the scene.

It was an extraordinary life-like scene. Pam could almost hear the crackling laughter of the youngsters. She could almost hear the mother's appeal to the father to watch out for the picnic basket as she tried to control the antics of the pups. Was she regretting giving in to the children's plea to bring the pups?

Pat said he had picked up the picture at a sale of young artists' work. The young painter was someone to watch out for, he told Pam; his work was recognised by some of the critics to be far above the normal standard of his contemporaries and indeed some of the more widely known, long-established painters. Pam had no need to be told this. Even she could see that this was an artist who had already the touch of the master.

'Do you miss them?'

Pam gave a start. Pat was behind her looking over her shoulder. 'Them? Who? What?'

He drew her to him. 'I mean the brothers and sisters you never had. I've been watching you. You haven't taken your eye once off that picture.'

'I must admit I did feel a little pang of, I suppose you could call it loss, never having the joy of knowing or sharing the love of brothers and sisters.' She touched his face letting her fingers slide down the smoothly shaven skin. 'What about you?'

He pressed her closely to him. 'You're all I need.'

Isn't it wonderful, she thought, *to feel that all we really do need is each other.*

Chapter Eight

They were eighteen months married when she became pregnant. There had been moments of doubt and worry when she wondered would she have a baby, but these doubts were but small isolated prickles that appeared and disappeared rapidly in the glow of their early married life. And she was free. Really free for the first time in her life.

Free from study and exams. And she had achieved her two goals in life. One was to become a doctor, though she hadn't attained her real ambition which was to specialise in paediatrics, but this she could take up later on and this course was only moved to one side for the present, Pat expressing the wish that they should enjoy the freedom of their present life for as long as possible, and the other was to love some man in the way she loved Pat. Now, she had lovely months ahead in which to look forward to the birth of their first-born.

She was five months pregnant when she was threatened with a miscarriage and was advised by Ivan Thornton, her doctor, to take things easy and to rest as much as possible. Ivan was the father of her college friend Eugene. Eugene was following in his father's footsteps. He called to see her on one of the days she was in bed and he phoned her every day. He was a cheerful person and he made her laugh when she was feeling sorry for herself. She might have married Eugene had she not met Pat. She had never fallen in love with him but she loved him. He said to her once when she got engaged, 'You let me down, you know.' There was no smile in his voice, no twinkle in his eye. But he continues to keep in touch with her, making no demands on their friendship, but in a quiet, affectionate way letting her know he would always be her friend.

She teased him about girlfriends but he said he had no time now. Perhaps later. But there were times when she had caught him looking at her, his eyes thoughtful. He wasn't particularly good-looking but his soul looked out through his eyes. Dark blue eyes that lit up his face. Eyes that shone as he cracked jokes with patients. Eyes that softened in sympathy and kindness at some heartbroken elderly person whose one terrible fear was that he or she would die in hospital away from their own. Eyes buoyant with hope as he pepped up some borderline cases willing them to make a fight for it and more often than not succeeding. One couldn't help loving Eugene and she was sorry that Pat and he didn't take to each other more.

She supposed it was only natural for Pat to keep his old friends which he did, she saw with pride, than try and make new ones. There was less danger of letting people down. And Pat had some wonderful friends, people who would do anything for him and these feelings were reciprocated by him.

Following Ivan Thornton's advice wasn't too difficult. She had stayed in bed and relaxed as much as possible. She had no intention of losing her baby and her relaxed attitude seemed to have the desired result. Then early one morning she was wakened by pains. *I've had it,* was her first frightened reaction. And then her refusal to give up without a fight forced her to take a grip of herself. She would ignore the pains and go back to sleep. She was slipping into a dreamful sleep when she was thrust into sudden wakefulness by a sharp stab of pain. Another followed. They were coming regularly. *My God, I'm losing my baby,* she told herself. For one terrible moment she was crushed by the inevitable. *Then, I will not lose my baby,* she told herself. Her body would recharge to meet the demands that were being made on it.

She forced herself to ignore the pains. *Please, don't let it happen,* she prayed. She willed herself to be calm each time fresh waves of cold terror swept over her. She would not waken Pat. She turned her head to look at him. He was lying on his back, one arm flung across his pillow, his head resting on the other. *Oh Pat if you only knew what was happening,* she whispered. He stirred slightly, mumbling something in his sleep. The contractions were getting more pronounced. She switched on the light. Only five o'clock. Dawn would soon be here. She would let Pat sleep on for another while even though she longed for him to comfort her. She was so lonely. A little death was happening inside her and she was helpless to stop it. A tiny life was being inexorably pushed into the world and out of the world in one instant. Tears spilled down her cheeks. *Now I know what it must feel like to die. The terrible loneliness of it all. The knowing, if one is conscious, that one is so powerless to stop what is happening.*

She called Pat at half past five. He awoke with a start. She told him, dry-eyed and matter-of-fact, what was happening. There was no need to panic, she said.

'I'll make you some tea. But I'll phone the doctor first.'

'Time enough yet to phone. Let's wait for another while. His hours are bad enough as they are. But I would love a cup of tea.'

Already she felt better. Her main concern now was to calm Pat. In no time, it seemed, he was coming upstairs. She could hear the rattle of the tea things on the tray. He came into the room, face pale, unsteady hands holding the tray, and drowned her in a worried look. A lone cup of tea, some spilled on the saucer and on the large naked tray, was worriedly handed to her.

'Are you not having one yourself?' she asked. His pale face was pulling at her heart-strings.

'No. I don't feel like one at the moment. Is the tea all right?'

'Perfect. Good and strong with lots of sugar. Just what the doctor ordered.'

'Should we ring him now?' The urgency was crackling in his voice.

'No. Give him another while. Get into bed. You'll get a cold standing around like that.'

He climbed into bed, his dressing gown still on him. He lit a cigarette and smiled down at her.

She left her emptied cup on the tray. He removed the tray and placed it on the floor. He stubbed his cigarette after a few quick pulls and lowered his body further under the bedclothes. He put his arm around her and pressed his chin against the top of her head. They spoke little, the silence punctuated by the frequent pressure of his arm around her. She phoned Ivan Thornton at half past six. He prescribed pethidine tablets to help kill the pain. She was to contact him at any time during the day. There was nothing else that could be done for the moment. Pat looked at her, searching her face for some sign of hope, some kind of panacea resulting from the contact. She could not give him what he looked for. She had the miscarriage in less than two hours. The local doctor left the nurse with her until he contacted the agency for a special nurse.

Pat said he wasn't going into work. She told him there wasn't any need to stay back; she had the nurse with her. Privately, she couldn't bear to see the pain and worry in his eyes.

'I'll take you up on that offer of a day off when I'm up and about. So don't forget.'

'You won't have to remind me.'

Her cheerful attitude dispelled his doubts and though he left the house under a cloud of disappointment and sadness he was relieved all was so well with her.

While the nurse was in the kitchen having her breakfast an overwhelming feeling of despair suddenly took hold of her, followed by the sensation of being whirled around in a world of horrifying nothingness. She slapped her head, her face, to bring some feeling, even of physical pain, back into her. Then suddenly she was over the terrible ordeal, back to reality, surrounded by familiar things. The sound of the nurse's footsteps on the stairs did nothing to dispel the weakness she now felt. The nurse gave her a brief scrutiny as soon as she entered the room: 'My! You've been through the wars', she said, as busy efficient hands re-arranged pillows, pulled clothes tidily and comfortably into place. 'I think you could do with something to eat.'

At the thought of her recent ordeal a cold perspiration broke out and she began to tremble. The nurse noticed.

'You've had a shock, love. You'll feel better after a cup of tea.'

Was what she had just gone through the result of shock? She let herself be soothed by the nurse's calm presence and conversation.

From the moment she set herself the task of getting back to normal she tried to forget what had happened, forcing herself to live in the present and to look forward to the future. In her eagerness to have things just as they were before her miscarriage she tried too hard. Pat cautioned her. She was anxious to become pregnant again but as the empty months rolled by she began to lose confidence. Her visit to Ivan Thornton with his sterile words of nothing to worry about, everything was perfectly normal, left her flat and depressed. She hated doctors, then smiled, remembering she was one and that it was quite possible she would act much the same way as Ivan under similar circumstances. He had that amused look in his eyes as if to say, 'You of all people ought to know better.'

But why wasn't she becoming pregnant? In the limited number of cases she knew women became pregnant quickly following a miscarriage, as if nature were in a hurry to make good the loss. She confided her fears to Pat. Did he think they might not have another child, knowing their family histories? He laughed at her fears.

'If you want to start looking up family trees you don't have to search too far.

Remember my mother is one of seven children. That number should disturb you because that kind of thing skips a generation, so it's right into your basket.'

His cheerful optimism drove away her fears for the time being, but again and again she brooded over the possibility of remaining childless. When these dark moments came on her she found herself appealing to Pat for re-assurance more often than she knew was normal, but she could not help it. Sometimes she sensed his impatience, but she was too caught up in her own web of despair and depression to take much notice of his reaction. And there were times when she refused to be consoled or comforted. One night when they had made love and she lay in his arms she wondered out loud if they would be lucky this time.

'How do you mean lucky?' he asked sharply.

She reached up her hand to hold his face. 'I mean if I might conceive tonight.'

He pulled his face away from her clasp. 'Is that all you can think of? As far as I can see, that's all you ever think of lately. Is that all there is to our marriage? I thought there were at least two good reasons for marriage but you seem to have forgotten one of them.

I want a family just as much as you do. I also want you because I love you. Do you think I was thinking of you just as a child-bearer when I asked you to marry me? I love you with or without children. Is that plain? I'm getting fed up with this never-ending moan of yours. I can't help you any more than I'm doing. I love you. I make love to you, but am I wrong if I think you are only using me?'

His angry outburst shook her. It was uncalled for. She had been so happy and it was her great happiness that had prompted those words. How could he distort them? Turn them into something selfish and ugly. Yes, ugly. Her body shook with heavy sobs.

'This is great. That's all we need now. A big crying display. I'm getting tired of that kind of thing too. It's becoming too much of a habit for me to be impressed anymore. So give over.'

He pulled away his arms from around her, almost flinging her aside as he did so. He turned his back on her without kissing her goodnight. In a few minutes he was asleep. *How dare he! How dare he accuse me of crying as if I did nothing else but that. I've only cried twice in front of him. Little does he know how often I've cried to myself because I didn't want him to see me upset. It's unfair of him to exaggerate.*

Now she was angry too, but this mood did not last long. Soon it changed to one of sadness and regret. Regret for something that should never have happened.

Pat left a cool kiss on her lips before he left for work and she found herself receiving it with equal coolness. She stayed on in bed most mornings getting up shortly after he had left the house. He had decided this for her early on in their marriage. She could get up when she liked but not before he left for work. *So he's still peeved over last night,* she thought. *Well, let him.* She had been willing to forget his outburst and let bygones be bygones even before she had settled down to sleep. It wasn't she who had turned her back without kissing him goodnight. She could never see herself doing that. Very early in their marriage they had vowed that the sun wouldn't go down on their anger.

Although they had been serious they couldn't help laughing, thinking it inconceivable that such a thing would ever happen to make them feel that they had to have recourse to such a promise. And now, for the very first time when such a vow should be called to mind Pat had no qualms about breaking it. Not only that, but he was willing to extend the row into a new day. So much for vows!

Many times during the years that followed she often wondered when and where did the first crack begin in their marriage; when and where did the rot set in. The disintegration of all that was precious and beautiful in their relationship must have been a gradual, insidious thing. True, there were times when she had a premonition of what might happen if the relationship continued the way it was going, but never in her wildest dreams did she think she would ever be faced with the reality. Somehow, slowly but surely she was losing what she cherished most, but still she clung stubbornly to the bond that was supposed to hold them together, the bond of matrimonial love that included affection, consideration, tolerance, but it was almost more painful to see one's efforts dashed to pieces than to let things slide and face the consequences. The result would be the same eventually.

Whenever she tried to show Pat what was happening to them he took one of two courses: either it was her imagination, it's all in the mind being his favourite expression, or a battle of words followed, Pat usually emerging the victor. He had such a gift, or was it an evil genius for twisting her simplest statement into cock-eyed, semi-illiterate utterances. Her talk could start about some glaring wrong in their relationship but might end up with his referring to her inability to hold onto her friends and so, he would claim, she should be the last person to talk about relationships.

Now that she was alone, lying in hospital, temporarily cut off from home and family, with plenty of time to think and analyse, she hadn't the faintest doubt that the trouble in their marriage started with her miscarriage. If one could be objective about oneself she felt she had recovered quite well from that shock. Pat pointing out to her that millions of women went through similar experiences and put up with it served no purpose. What was the use of generalising like that and, what knowledge had he of those millions of women?

What Pat seemed to forget was that this was her particular sorrow and she alone bore it. She didn't suffer other women's sorrows though they would have her sympathy, nor did other women suffer hers. Surely this should be plain to him. Did he have any feelings about it at all? It would have been his child too. He might as well put forward the argument that because millions of women give birth to babies, why the fuss or display of any emotion by a mother over her newborn baby. But she could not get through to him. It was from that time it seemed that some kind of nebulous barrier had risen between them; sometimes it almost disappeared, at other times it became more intense depending on what caused it to appear. Even when she appealed to him to remove this barrier she knew what he was thinking: she was a woman, illogical, highly emotional, lacking depth and clarity of mind.

So according to his way of thinking the best way to deal with women was to dominate or ignore them. From the beginning of time, women had been used and abused: chattels for men's benefit. This is what the women of the world were slowly beginning to realise. There had been abortive movements by some brave men and women to right this wrong in the latter centuries, but those pioneers were often considered freaks or cranks by their peers, the saddest part being that most women failed to support their own sex, failed to see that they had any grievance.

The recognition of equality between the sexes was an urgent matter. There were reports of a Women's Liberation Movement being set up in the United States. Even rumblings of things happening in Britain. When would Irish women wake up to what was happening? So far there wasn't a peep out of them. She herself had tried to air the subject of liberation with other women but the strange looks she got, the embarrassed silence and the eagerness to change the subject told her she was only adding to her own private difficulties. She would not be an apostle for women.

And yet her mind dwelt on the subject, a subject which by its own momentum moved from the home to the outside world. If women had equal representation in government and in public life generally, the threat of wars between nations would lessen considerably, perhaps cease altogether. Women using the brains God gave them, and with their limitless capacity for patience, love and understanding, would make it possible to bring about those things. The continuance of wars was man's greatest and most enduring achievement. Because of wars men put their heads together to think up the most deadly instruments of murder, the most evil instruments of mental and physical torture. How hard it was too, to understand the attitude of grown men who squabbled over a peace conference – where would it be held? Who was to sit where? She sighed despairingly. How could there be peace in the world when men hadn't love and peace in their hearts? When homes were without love and peace?

She remembered reading somewhere what Abigail Adams wrote to her husband, the second president of the United States: 'Remember, all men would be tyrants if they could. If particular care is not paid to the ladies, we are determined to foment a rebellion.'

That rebellion had started publicly in the United States and was spreading. Her own rebellion had taken place quietly in her own heart, but getting nowhere. But, she thought, every cloud has a silver lining and her particular cloud had given her a deeper insight into the hearts and lives of women, to look beyond the brittle laughs, the care-worn or sullen faces, the apathetic attitudes; to have a greater sympathy and compassion for her sex and for their endurance of a life that shouldn't have to be endured.

Attending her dying mother had been a soul-searing but wonderful time for her. All the medical skill and knowledge she had put aside when she married was brought into use to alleviate those hours of suffering. Robin Patterson, the family doctor, was unsparing in his praise.

'You are what I would call a real doctor,' he commented in front of her father and mother. 'You have the talent and the heart for it. It's a great pity to let all that go to waste.' He smiled down at the wasted features of her mother. 'Have you any influence over that daughter of yours? Persuade her to go back to the work she was trained for. You know, there's a crying need for good doctors.'

Her mother had later backed up Robin's suggestion that she take up the job she was qualified for. She was amused that her mother brought up the subject. How active that brain was in spite of the suffering.

Her mother said: 'Robin Patterson is quite right. You have that special gift that goes to make a good doctor and it seems a pity to bury it; all that you sacrificed and worked so hard and long to achieve. Indeed you should specialise in paediatrics. Isn't that what you always intended to do? It would help take your mind off the worry of not starting a family, which isn't a good thing because it doesn't help to worry the way you do.'

She looked at her mother in amazement. 'Who told you I was worrying? Pat?'

'No one told me. A mother rarely needs to be told if anything is worrying her children. Some day you'll see that for yourself.'

Her mother didn't refer to the suggestion of her re-entrance into the medical world again. She was like that, but in the rare idle moments she found herself thinking more and more of it. She would give it more thought later. But when she told Pat about her plan his reaction shocked her.

He said: 'I knew you were unsettled all along. Almost from the day we married.' What a weakness Pat had for exaggerating, yet should she exaggerate he was down on her like a ton of bricks. 'I don't understand you. First it was paediatrics that occupied your mind. Now, you tell me you want to go into general practice.'

'That's because you were so dead against me going back to hospital work,' she interrupted.

'And if I were it's because you evidently hadn't given it any thought. Neither does it seem evident that you've given enough thought to what it means to be a general practitioner.' How dare he talk like that! What did he know about medicine! She was too furious to interrupt him. 'Being a G.P. is not just another hobby. Another of your works of mercy to take on or leave aside as the mood takes you. It's a serious matter.'

'Would you shut up for God's sake!' This time he had gone too far. 'You don't know what you're talking about. About medicine or about the voluntary work I do. As far as voluntary work is concerned I do not put it aside as the mood takes me and you'd have noticed that if you had the least interest in what I was doing. I take my voluntary work seriously and it's not a hobby, though you'd like to think so.'

He had been looking out the window while she was talking and she wondered had he been listening to her at all when he turned around and said: 'Being a general practitioner is a full-time job. What if children start to arrive? Have you thought of that?'

He looked at her as if he expected to see her suffering from some ailment. 'What's wrong with you? Why can't you settle down? Why has this thing become suddenly so important to you? It can't have been that important when you were so willing to give it up on marriage.'

She thought: 'You are the most cruel, most nasty-minded person I've ever known. You can't believe what you're saying. You're only saying that because you know it will hurt me or, that in your twisted way I'll begin to believe it's true. She did not voice her thoughts because she knew if she did the tension would only increase and would lead perhaps to more unforgivable things.

'Tell me something,' he said, looking at her coldly and almost with hatred, 'that is, if you can. Why have you changed your mind?'

'If I'm allowed to answer all your questions without interruption I'll do so.' She spoke quietly. 'First of all I'm not unsettled and never have been since we got married. Secondly, I underwent a certain amount of strain with the miscarriage.'

His eyes closed and his lips compressed in feigned suffering. 'Good God. Are we never to hear the end of that? How many more times is this going to be used as an excuse for every damned mood you're in?'

'I asked you not to interrupt, and before I go any further, losing our baby, meant and means too much to me for it to be bandied about, and I never have and do not wish to use it as an excuse for anything. In another few weeks it's quite possible you'll be saying the death of my mother is being used as an excuse for something or other. In future don't dare to mention either. If you can be so crude as to treat the subject of death so irreverently in an effort to bolster some stupid argument of yours, all I can say is God help you. If I can't have your sympathy and understanding I can do without your out-of-place and ill-timed sarcasm. Also, and this is for your own good, never ever talk about a subject which you know absolutely nothing about. Though you may be an expert in your own field it doesn't qualify you to speak on medicine or other professions as if you were infallible. Furthermore, it seems to me to be a waste of time discussing any plans with you as it's only too evident you don't wish me to go ahead for your own peculiar reasons . So forget I ever mentioned anything. I'll do as you wish.'

Her last words were spoken as she walked in the direction of the door. He took a quick step forward and grabbed her arm.

'I haven't finished at all yet–'

'That's just too bad because I have. Let go of me.'

She wrenched her arm free of his grasp and as she closed the door in his face she heard his raised voice coming after her as she raced upstairs: 'Go on! Run! That's all you ever do when things aren't going your way.'

It did not take her long to recover from this incident. Her husband made no attempt to make up the row but in those days she got over these things as quickly as she could. Somebody had to take the first step and it might as well be she. Soon they were back on the same loving relationship. There was no recriminatory post-mortem, no long arguments as to who was right or wrong. Much later she wondered if she had let Pat speak on when he wanted to, instead of running out on him as he had put it, would things have been different? Perhaps, he had only been warming up to the thought of her taking up her profession, and in getting used to the idea had to get rid of some settled notions. But then, if that were so, there had been plenty of opportunities for him to speak out in the following weeks and months.

She was only deluding herself, creating a false image of her husband. He had never intended to let her go out into the world of work. It might put the even tenor of his life off course and he couldn't risk that. She saw the way his mind worked: why would she want to take up an outside job? It wasn't as if she had to; as if they had a financial problem. And she kept herself occupied in various voluntary organizations; she wasn't bored for want of something to do. So why change things? *Jobs may come and go but housewives go on forever,* she thought.

Chapter Nine

They were sixteen months married when Rosemary was born. She came into the world without any fuss; a beautiful baby, alert and bright-eyed. The nurse who helped to look after Rosemary stayed with them for three months. Before she left she kissed Pam on both cheeks.

'Take it easy, ma'am,' she said. 'I'll be seeing you sooner than you think.'

Had her experienced eyes perceived more than Pam, herself suspected? Surely she couldn't be pregnant so soon again! In fact she felt she wouldn't have another baby. She would be a one-child mother like her own mother. But the thought didn't worry her. She was so delighted to have Rosemary.

The nurse was right. She was pregnant. 'It looks as if we may have a big family in spite of such a bad start,' she told a delighted Pat. 'I hope it will be a boy this time. After that they can come how they like.'

She felt rotten most of the time but her happiness bubbled over in spite of the bouts of sickness. Pat was upset.

'Is there anything that can be done to stop all this?' he asked, when for the first time he saw her getting sick. 'You don't look too well. Does Thornton know about this?'

She laughed even as she cooled her face and wiped the tears, caused by the strain of vomiting, from her eyes. 'Don't be daft! Have you ever heard of morning sickness? Well, this is it. I've been like this for a good while. Some women suffer from it and it's usually worse with the first baby. I wasn't like this with Rosemary but then I have to be different, don't I!'

Robert was a quiet baby with dark blue eyes that later changed to a glorious brown. Her heart used almost burst with happiness when she looked at her two beautiful babies. Pat loved his children and had the nursery furnished and decorated as only he could do it. Nothing was too much trouble for his children. Their future schools were taken care of. He wondered what special talents they would be gifted with. She was amused listening to him.

'Pat, will you have patience? Do you know whom you're talking about? Two babies of fourteen months and two months. Will you allow them to talk and walk before you marry them off on me?'

The sad and disappointing days were forgotten when such good days came along. Those were the times when they laughed a lot. Pat was a good conversationalist and she enjoyed listening to him. He made plans and decisions and she fell in with them for the good reason that they could not be bettered. She too had her own ideas but when they clashed with his he had a way of dismissing them which used to annoy her at times, but Pat was a brilliant man and he was usually so right. So what was wrong with being so right? She loved him and thought there was no one in the world like him.

His work necessitated their attending some social functions which she enjoyed. They gave parties and with Martha's almost total takeover in the preparation and serving at these parties, combined with the help of Mrs Henry, who was always ready to give a helping hand when needed she was able to devote most of her time to seeing that her guests enjoyed themselves and leaving her free to enjoy her own parties.

The first time she saw Pat in the kitchen giving instructions to the two women she was amused. The second time she was so absorbed in what she was doing she ignored it, but the third time she was annoyed. She manoeuvred him into the study on some pretext and closed the door.

'Pat, will you please allow me to be mistress in my own home? I'm quite capable of handling some situations and in the matter of party-giving I am not without experience.' When she was annoyed she found herself using words and expressing herself in a manner that wasn't normal to her in ordinary conversation.

'My mother gave me a good training and I was allowed a say in the planning of my own parties and also in the planning of my parents' parties. So will you please let me do things my way? I promise I won't let you down.'

She remembered another scene that showed symptoms of the breakdown of their marriage. At one of their parties there had been a discussion about a new play that was being shown in town. Believing she should give an honest opinion when asked she summed up her criticism of the whole production as rubbish.

'The easiest thing in the world is to condemn,' said Terence Boland, a zealous first-nighter who fancied himself as a patron of the arts and whose opinions were not to be lightly dismissed. 'But did you see it and if you did, give us your reasons for dismissing it so contemptuously.'

Finding his pomposity more amusing than irritating she decided to be frank even if it hurt, as in letting people such as Terence away with the belief that their opinions were the only ones worth considering or having, she was contributing to the present ground-swell of the sham and the shoddy. 'I did see it and it will give me the greatest pleasure to explain why I think it was, as I said, rubbish. Though I shouldn't feel pleasure in telling anyone why a play is rubbish, I would much rather tell how I enjoyed it, this play was a waste of an evening for me; when I go to the theatre I expect to get value for money. Or, is that too much to expect? Is the theatre world exempt from all attempts to give value for money, or does it think it's above that? And value means that I am entertained, whether what's on the stage is comedy or tragedy doesn't really matter. But what did I get the other night? I'll tell you. My ears were assaulted by filthy language, my eyes opened by obscene and unnecessary actions. It was a nightmare and in common with all nightmares it had neither beginning nor ending, plot nor plan. I've been wondering since why such a thing was written, but excusing the work of such a mind I can't excuse a director from putting such a thing on the stage.

'But this play is true to life,' Terence said testily. 'One can't be an ostrich and refuse to face facts.'

'True to life? Good Lord! As far as I was concerned the play was just an unwieldy number of episodes strung together without any connection with the express purpose to shock, without any regard for art or indeed the feelings of much of the audience the night I was there anyway, seeing as so many walked out. I know I left the theatre with a headache. Of course you'll say, if it were all that bad why didn't I walk out too? My answer is, you and people like you would say I wasn't in a position to pass any judgement on it. As it was I persevered to the bitter end and so am in a position to give a personal opinion, being as competent as any average theatre-goer or a recognised theatre critic!'

She had held the attention of her guests while she was speaking and most of them seemed to agree with her in the discussion that followed. She wasn't particularly worried about Terence and one or two more who seemed to be personally affronted by her remarks; they had no hesitation in shoving their opinions down her throat and those of her other guests, so why shouldn't she express her opinions; all the more because she was asked by Terence.

When the front door had been closed on the last guest Pat turned on her almost before the echo of his cheerful goodnight faded away.

'Did you have to make an exhibition of yourself tonight expounding on something you know nothing about?' His voice was hoarse with anger, his face red.

'What do you mean? An exhibition of myself. If you mean I don't have the same right as that self-righteous, pontificating

Terence Boland to express myself, I disagree. Anything I said most of our guests agreed with. Do you mean to say that they made a show of themselves too? Or are you annoyed that I had the nerve to cross that pompous ass just because he's a friend of yours? How dare he come here and shove his opinions down our throats!

'And that's exactly what he tried to do all evening and what he always tries to do. Why don't you turn on him sometimes when he makes an exhibition of himself the same as you've turned on me?'

She was too upset to say anymore. She turned on her heel and walked upstairs, tears blinding her eyes. The glasses and dishes that the two of them normally stacked tidily together to await the morning's washing were left as they were in all their disarray and grubbiness.

She would always remember one New Year's Eve. There were eight of them at the dance. Tony and Virginia, Teddy and Shirley, Tom and Clare and Pat and herself. All were enjoying themselves and during the night they had run into several parties of friends and people they knew. Jokes and drinks were passed around and the fun spilled over as did sometimes their drinks. Everything was going fine till it was noticed her glass was empty, and while her back was turned for a moment Teddy, she was almost sure it was him, saw to it that she had a refill – gin and orange, a drink she disliked. She looked at the glass knowing it wasn't just an orange drink and wondered what to do with it without creating a fuss, to find seven pairs of eyes resting on her.

She took a sip: 'Gin. And whom do I thank for this?' she asked, smiling, though inwardly she was a little annoyed because everyone at the table knew she didn't really care for alcohol. Why couldn't they respect her wishes? People should accept the fact that she didn't want to drink just as she accepted that they wanted to drink. How would they like it if she kept poking fun at them because of their fondness for drinking? But she wouldn't let them see she was upset. She pointed to the drink.

'What am I supposed to do with this?'

'Drink it of course,' came the chorus.

'I never saw a mineral doing anyone any harm,' Tom said.

'I expect you're right. But what about the gin that was already in the glass when it arrived at the table? As for a mineral not doing anyone any harm, I think your tummy would jump in fright if it came in contact with it.'

'Drink it. It will do you good,' Shirley said.

'Is that so? I thought I hadn't been doing too badly up to this. But if you say it will do me good who am I to disagree.'

She lifted the glass to her lips. A gentle hand-clapping teased her. She looked across the table at Pat. He smiled approvingly at her. As he danced with her later he said: 'You know there's no harm in a drink or two.'

'I've never said there was. Anyone would think the way people go on that I objected to drink; it's not true. It's just that I don't care for it very much. Supposing at the dinner tonight I said I preferred tea to coffee or refused either, would anyone have taken any notice? So what's so strange in substituting a non-alcoholic drink for an alcoholic one or, not having either if that's the way I felt?'

'Well, that's different.'

'How different?'

He laughed. 'Refusing an alcoholic drink focuses attention on you.'

'I see. I suppose it's as good an explanation as I'm likely to get from anyone.' Pat could have a disarming way of ignoring her annoyance or the cause of it. He tightened his arms around her, smiling coaxingly at her.

'Mind your step! No, no. That's not your bed, I assure you. That's the floor coming up to meet you.'

He could be so funny when he wanted that she couldn't help laughing even though she was still cross.

'Hold on to me, there's a good girl. I'll steer you through. Don't worry. You're doing fine. All you have to remember is that the place for your feet is on the floor, not in mid-air. Keep gazing into my eyes so that no one will notice your lovely blood-shot eyes. That's it. Here we are, safe and sound.'

And with exaggerated solicitude he pulled out a chair and guided her into it. She couldn't stop laughing. Pat was such fun to be with. When she was asked at the next round of drinks what she would have she said, 'Gin and tonic.'

'I'll have the same,' Tom said.

He was sitting beside her. She leaned towards him, their whispered conversation causing them to laugh a great deal. As the night wore on the merriment increased. She was enjoying herself immensely.

'See what a little gin-booster does for you,' Tony said as they all sat down breathless after a round on the dance-floor.

'Wouldn't it make you sad to think what you've been missing all those years,' Virginia said.

'It would indeed', Pam admitted. 'As the man said, "One becomes spiritless when one is spiritless".'

Tony said: 'What man?'

'I don't know,' shaking her head regretfully. 'He wouldn't give me his name.'

There were times during the remainder of the night when she found Pat's watchful eyes resting on her. She danced with him and said wickedly: 'How do you like the new me? Do you think they'll be calling me Pam Ginny McElroy from now on? Ginny for short?'

'Oh shut up. You're making a show of yourself.'

If he had slapped her on the face in front of everyone she couldn't have been more shocked. She stopped dancing.

'Come on,' he said. 'Don't be a fool.' He tried to persuade her into the steps once more.

'I don't want to dance,' she whispered fiercely. 'You can stand there if you want to.'

She walked blindly back to the table. Only Teddy and Shirley were there, having a quiet chat and smoke. They looked up, well-bred curiosity in control when they saw the look on her face.

'Tired?' Teddy asked.

'A little,' she said as she sat down.

She took a burnt-out match-stick and absently traced a design in the ashes, her mind a mixed bag of unhappiness, puzzlement and cold rage. She was aware of their eyes upon her but she could not bestir herself to hide her feelings or break the silence. Let them think what they like. Let the great almighty Pat come along and try and explain. She wasn't going to try. The embarrassment to him wasn't of her making.

She looked up and saw Pat talking to a small group of people not far from her table. As she watched he broke away from them leaving a happy explosion of laughter. He sat down beside her taking out his cigarettes and offering them around. She refused. He lit his cigarette. Elbow on the table, cheek resting on the palm of her hand, she watched his performance, mesmerized. She had the horrible urge to snatch the cigarette from those cool lips and throw it at his hypocritical face. Teddy smiled, winking at her. 'So our Pam was hitting the bottle too hard. Well,' he consoled her, 'it seems some people can take it and others can't.'

Because Teddy was trying to do something about the strained atmosphere she responded in the same jesting manner. 'I can take it all right, it's just that my legs won't co-operate with the rest of me.'

'For all you drank, why it wouldn't drown a fly,' Shirley said in a placating tone, sensing something had happened between her and Pat.

'Perhaps not, but as you see I'm drowning in sorrow and remorse, maudlin sorrow and remorse, maybe. The sad thing is, instead of getting drunk on what I should have drunk I got drunk on what I drank.'

She saw the mystified look on their faces. She got a gleeful satisfaction from seeing Pat squirm in embarrassment. When the others returned, the bantering and teasing really started and she played the part that was expected of her. She knew Pat was quietly furious but she didn't care. The silence in the car as he drove home with cautious speed was heavy and foreboding. She broke the silence when she got into the hallway.

'Would my dear abstemious husband keep an eye on me while I negotiate the stairs?' She climbed with exaggerated care all of the twenty steps. He followed her savagely and pushed her through their bedroom door. She stumbled and fell but was up on her feet immediately. She faced him angrily.

'How dare you push me?'

'How dare you behave the way you did, making an exhibition of yourself like some drunken...' He stopped.

'Go on. Say it. No one will hear you. The show is over. Say what you were going to say.'

His pride and rage must have hidden the obvious from him. She wasn't drunk any more than he was. All he had to do was listen. No slurring over words. She had picked herself up quickly from the floor. She was now standing in front of him perfectly steady.

'No. I'll not bring myself down to that level even though there is a word that describes you.'

'Why so fussy now? You Pharisee! God knows you have brought yourself down to that level, as you call it, often enough before.'

He remained silent.

She said: 'Do you know, I feel awfully sorry for you for having married me, knowing what you think of me.'

He was stung into reply. 'Huh! The drink talking still. You spent the night swilling it but I don't see why I should have to listen to the results. As you said yourself just now, the show is over. No wonder you're afraid to drink if that's the way it affects you. I'm sorry I was one of the people who encouraged you.'

'You encouraged me! You fool! So I spent the night drinking? How many drinks do you suppose I had?'

'I don't know. I stopped counting. I only know I counted four gins before I got so disgusted with your behaviour to care any longer.'

'What was so wrong with my behaviour? Because I was enjoying myself? Because I was told more than once during the night that I was the life and souls of the party? If you find that disgusting perhaps, after all, the rest of our crowd thought so too and I was being deluded. But then, it's such a comfort to know that I'm not the only one that's deluded. You, my self-righteous husband, are suffering from a delusion too.'

'What do you mean?'

'You'll find out in a minute. But first, let me ask you a question. How many gins do you think I had during the night?'

'I told you I stopped counting,' he said impatiently, beginning to undress.

She touched him on the shoulder. 'You will stop undressing and you will listen to me, because when I have finished with you, you will hate yourself for making such a fool of yourself.'

Something in her eyes caused him to stop. He stood in the middle of the room, jacket off and tie hanging from his hand, tired eyes fixed on her face.

'The one alcoholic drink I had for the night was the gin and orange you saw me drinking to a round of applause. Then when the next round came Tom and I ordered gin and tonic if you remember, and I whispered to Tom to ask the waiter to put as much tonic water in my glass as he would gin, and then bring the bottle of tonic to the table, and the waiter to do this for the rest of the night. Tom said he would do the same as he wasn't in form for drinking spirits. We were the only ones on gin and tonic which made it easier for us, and the two of us had a great time fooling you all. I had hoped to save all this up so that you and I could have a good laugh when we got home but...'

How she wanted to cry. The whole night was spoiled. She bent down to take off her shoes. Immediately he was down on his knees beside her, his arms around her.

'Forgive me, darling. Please. You're right. I am a fool.'

Though she had been so close to tears a moment before her eyes were now dry and quiet anger was the emotion that filled her. She could not forgive him so quickly. It was too soon to expect the raw blow he had given her to be healed. She moved from his arms and went into the dressing room. She took her time undressing, almost straining her neck to unzip her dress rather than ask him to undo it. She knew he was sitting on the bed waiting until she was ready. But she had nothing more to say to him. As she removed her make-up and brushed her teeth her mind went over the night's events. She was so mad she felt she hated him. She was about to pull down the bed-clothes when he reached across and arrested the action.

'Well,' he said with his little-boy smile.

'Well, what?' Her face was neutral, her voice calm. 'I don't know what you're expecting me to say, but I would like to ask you this: at what point do I cease to embarrass you? If don't drink I embarrass you and if I do drink I embarrass you.'

She did not wait for an answer. She got into bed, turned on her side away from his gaze and pulled the clothes over her head to discourage further conversation. Long after he had gone to sleep she lay awake.

Similar occurrences came unbidden to her mind. Many of these she had ignored or refused to treat seriously. Now she was beginning to wonder were they not part of a pattern of her husband's behaviour to which she had never given a great deal of thought.

Surely, when she came to think of it, he had always been like that. His insistence that she be subservient to his wishes, only that she had never seen it that way. She must be mistaken. One could not love a man who thought less of you as a woman and a wife if you were not always submissive and subdued. And she had loved her husband.

As well as that, she had never been the submissive type. Or had she, only that she never saw herself in such a role because love blinded all her actions. She must remember whenever she did cross him there was invariably a flare-up. But then she could be to blame; perhaps she might be in an irritable mood, tired or just plain crooked. Could that be true? If so, it could be true that she was always to blame. Was she the type of person who always reacted strongly when she was crossed, with other people, her parents, her childhood friends, her neighbours, the friends of her boarding-school and college days? Miserably she was forced to come to the conclusion that she wasn't.

Though she could never be called a weakling she wasn't the sort of person who felt she had to force her will on other people. Life was a matter of give and take and life had always been good to her. What kind of man was Pat? He must have loved her at one time. She remembered their first meeting; the wonderful days of their engagement when he could not bear to part with her; when the thought of postponing their wedding visibly affected him. How often had he drowned her in that adoring earnest gaze, his beautiful eyes burning with love for her; how often had he said: 'I love you till it hurts.' When was it he stopped carrying on an ordinary conversation with her try as she might to talk with him? At what point did Rosemary and Robert become their only link, their sole topic of conversation? Often she had tried to veer him away from talking about them, not that she didn't like talking about them, but she was resentful of using them as a sole conversation topic. Her brain was being slowly starved of intellectual stimulation, something she had enjoyed so much with Pat in their engagement days.

The few women friends that remained were not interested in anything unless it related to fashion, babies and holidays. What was happening to all of them? University graduated, highly intellectual women getting bogged down on whether green was the coming shade in clothes or, if putting baby onto solids too early was wise. All these things had their place, but why should they jockey every other subject of importance out of line. Nobody loved children more than she, nobody was more fashion-conscious, nobody took greater pride in her home than she did, but she was getting fed up with baby-talk, clothes-talk and holiday brochures. Once she tried to interest Vienna and some others in the plight of the itinerants, giving them some ideas of what she proposed to do to help them in a positive and constructive way, asking for co-operation. They shuddered at the mention of such propositions and weren't slow in saying so. They couldn't bear to go within smelling distance of them, as Margo put it. They were their own worst enemies, she said vehemently. She had tried to be nice to them when they came to her door. She gave them clothes and money and sometimes food, but they were never satisfied, and they always left the camp-site in a disgraceful condition. What really maddened her one time when she and Barry got out of their car to inspect the eyesore, was to find a good dress she had loved but had given to one of the women who called to her house, caught in a broken-down fence. She had taken the trouble to free the dress to see whether it was totally unwearable, to find it was still perfectly good except where a few threads had been pulled where it had got caught in the barbed wire.

'And did you bring it home?' Pam couldn't resist asking.

Margo took her seriously. 'Of course not. I wouldn't dream of wearing it after them.'

'A good washing and disinfectant would have given you back the dress you loved so much. A pity you didn't take the opportunity to recover it.'

'I didn't feel that badly about it,' Margo huffed.

She knew Margo was hurt but she couldn't say she was sorry because she wasn't. She supposed this was one of the reasons she didn't get on with Vienna and her crowd. These were all people she had become acquainted with in recent years and somehow she found herself more often than not completely out of tune with them. She stayed friendly with them because they and their husbands were originally friends of Pat, but she felt they just about tolerated her. How to make friends and influence people? She sure could do with some useful tips. She tried to show them that the poor people had no alternative but to leave clothes behind.

'You know, they're out in all weathers,' she said. 'So you see they have to leave wet clothes behind them when they move on whether they're good or not. What facilities have they for drying or airing clothes unless the weather is fine, or what room have they got in their caravans or carts for carrying bundles of wet clothing, not to speak of the discomfort and nuisance of such a thing? As it is, the poor things often have to wear damp clothes during the wet weather. No wonder so many of them die so young. How any of them reach middle-age at all is the miracle.'

She knew what she was talking about. She had taken a family under her wing and often she had to undress the little children, soak them in a hot bath and put on dry clothes belonging to Rosemary and Robert.

'How could you!' Vienna said. 'Your house must be full of lice.'

'Have you ever been bitten by one in our place?'

'No.'

'Of course not. What some of us forget is they are people with feelings too. Who said they could tolerate their bodies being plagued with lice anymore than we could? We may think they are always whining and begging for money and other things; that they are never satisfied with what they get. But are they any different from us really? We don't whine or beg, but are we ever satisfied with what we get or have? For example, look at what we were talking about before this subject cropped up.'

'You mean before you brought it up,' Vienna said.

'As you say. We were talking about clothes and the latest fashions. Not that we haven't got enough clothes, but like the itinerants we are never satisfied. And we have talked about these same things dozens of times before, and it could seem to an outsider listening that we had nothing else on our minds. These people have by necessity very little else on their minds but to whine and beg, cajole or even steal for a living. It's an actual way of life with them. They have no options. And here is where people like us can help. Give them options. Let us do our best for them, always remembering that they are people like you and me and, but for the grace of God, there could have been an exchange of places. They sitting down here whiling away an hour or so over coffee and cakes and we, that is I,' she couldn't help smiling, 'knocking at some wealthy person's door like Margo's, to wheedle a few things out of her.' She was sober for a moment. 'Imagine me now on my rounds begging for a coat for Robert and shoes for Rosemary.'

It was more a thought spoken aloud than directed at her friends, and though it momentarily had a subduing effect on all of them, further effort to rouse them to action failed. One way her talk did affect them, though not in the way she wanted, was that further communication with her became more erratic. She knew she wasn't the most popular person in the world with them, and her one-woman crusading lowered her in the popularity polls. She knew that it would be more sensible if she kept her ideas to herself. If she did this, at least she wouldn't be annoying people, upsetting them. Besides, it wasn't achieving anything except the doubtful distinction of her being regarded as a crank. Although she knew her husband wasn't interested she thought she would try once more to get him involved even if only with advice and moral support. But there was no reaction, only the feeling that as long as it didn't interfere with him she could do what she wanted. It was frustrating. She needed other people, their support, their co-operation. It was no good doing it alone.

She remained in touch with her poor family. She couldn't help feeling bitter towards Vienna and her friends. They had so much time on their hands, unlike Pat and their husbands. Not only time, but they would have ideas because they were all intelligent women, but because of their circumstances and background combined with an accursed tradition they felt they had no need or use for their brains. Her head was always buzzing with new ideas. If only she had Pat's moral support for some of them. True, he listened to her plans, but she wasn't blind to his painfully patient attention and the barely concealed sigh of relief when he thought her eloquence was on the wane. She thought ruefully of the reversal of their roles. It was he who had once been the non-stop talker, the intelligent conversationalist. Pat loved to talk. How could she forget that? He dominated every gathering and basked in the glow of the admiration and affection that surrounded him.

At parties she found herself reacting unhappily and awkwardly. She, who had been once the life and soul of the party was beginning to behave like a gauche schoolgirl, unsure of herself and unwittingly causing others to be unsure of her, some going out of their way to avoid her as much as possible.

Though Pat and herself seen together might present a good public image it was not helping their marriage. How did their friends think of them? The hard-working, brilliant architect having a millstone of a wife around his neck? The fact that she was a qualified doctor with exceptional exam results at every level, popular with patients and staff, counted as nothing with people because she wasn't on the job. It was possible that most of them had forgotten she was a qualified doctor because nobody ever alluded to it and Pat certainly never drew attention to this fact, much less to the reasons she wasn't a working doctor.

Whatever game Pat was playing, he was on the winning side. She fought hard. She thought up measures, some extreme, some moderate, to draw home to him what was happening. He listened, then went his way unchanged, or he listened and argued out of every situation, satisfying himself that she was to blame for everything. It was hopeless. If he could not change she must change. But to what extent could she change? Where was she at fault? Pat had pointed out her faults but they were not her faults. They were his and she couldn't get this through to him. Either he or she was mentally unbalanced when they couldn't sort out this confusion of thought. Why should she try to remedy faults that were not hers? It would be an act of madness, like trying to cure a disease that didn't exist. What did Pat take her to be? Was he trying to drive her out of her mind in a calculating, ruthless way? Her nerve was too strong for that, and then she remembered three women who had spent some time in and out of mental institutions. There had been whispers about all of them: 'It runs in the family... Always like that... Only now showing itself...' One thing these three women had in common – all three were married. One of the women whom she knew through her children going to the same school broke down one morning when she had invited her to have coffee after bringing the children to the school. At first the conversation covered the usual subjects and then the woman asked could she speak in confidence to her. At first she spoke calmly about her troubled marriage until she came to the part where her husband had her committed to a private psychiatric home, and what led up to it. Then she stopped, held her head in her hands while heartbreaking sobs shook her whole body. She let her cry her anguish out, then gave her some tissues and put her arms around her. After some time the woman turned around to look at her, face blotched with tears: 'I still love my husband but I'll never let him do that to me again.'

She tried to live her life independent of Pat. It would work for several days or even weeks and then the thought would hit her: 'I'm not a widow or single person. I'm a married woman with my husband living with me.' She craved for her husband's love. It was what made everything else worthwhile. Love did make the world go round. It made life worth living. But Pat didn't need her love. He needed to make love to her but he hadn't any need for the day-to-day interaction of love. This discovery caused her to lose interest in things, in people. Her friends of pre-marriage days had been dropped. The fault wasn't theirs but hers; there were so many of Pat's friends to be considered and whom he wished her to be friendly with that she hadn't got the time to keep up with them. Besides, it seemed Pat wasn't enamoured of any of them. He was always picking on some fault or other they had. But how she would have liked to contact one or two of them only she felt she would be using them to kill her own loneliness and despair.

It was hard to hide what was happening. Something had to give. The neglect of her appearance, her unpunctuality was demonstrated in public. It was a gradual process. Before long her name was anathema at most functions. She lost interest in having parties of her own. Her husband became used to booking a table at a hotel when the occasion demanded, and she offered no objection. She wasn't obliged to accompany him, but more often than not she roused herself sufficiently from her lethargy to make some attempt to do herself up and go with him. The more she thought he was happier by her absence the more dogged and determined she was to be there and if the chance arose, to make it as uncomfortable as possible for him.

But even this premeditated malice was seldom sufficiently strong enough to prod her into action, and she slumped back into the hopeless mess that life for her had become. It occurred to her that the more dreadful she looked, the more dreadful she behaved in public, the more gentle and considerate Pat showed himself to her in public. What an actor he was! The poor man to be so tolerant with that good-for-nothing bitch! She knew what was being said and inwardly she laughed derisively at it all, when she wasn't breaking her heart and beating her fists against an invisible wall at the unfair battle she had to fight.

She would try to look at her husband objectively while he solicitously attended her, to pierce the mask of make-believe, but when their eyes met she would only see in their depths indifference, if not cold hatred. Yes, he hated her. Perhaps not all the time, but the hatred was there, and it came to the surface when it became too difficult for concealment.

She had given up the impossible task of trying to understand him. He was three different people: one kind of person to the outside world, a different kind of person to her and a third personality emerged in front of the children. She was two people: the person she was to her husband in public and the person she was in her own home. With her children she found herself to be most like the person she once was, though there were times when to be good-humoured and cheerful was so much an effort she had to leave their presence hurriedly on some pretext, so as to regain some kind of composure before she returned to them. She knew that no one was in sympathy with her. Her own sex judged her more harshly than the men, though many of them had serious grievances, and the bitterness generated from hiding them sometimes broke through only to be hastily covered up once more. They were loyal to their husbands. What fine men they were, full of the joys of life. A contrast to their wives with their well-made-up faces concealing the shadows and lines; there was no cosmetic powerful enough to hide the strain from their faces or the pain from their eyes. Why did each one live and suffer, locked up in her own private world of privation and sorrow? Was it resignation, fatalism, pessimism or stupid pride that kept them from trying to rise above such treatment? She had hinted at this on more than one occasion, but it had brought no reaction from those present except a suspicious feeling that her listeners considered her slightly off-beam, or just a troublemaker. She gave up trying to rouse them and vowed never to try again, especially after one of the greatest wife-offenders attacked her and not one woman present spoke up to support her. So let them suffer. They enjoyed it. She would not fight their battles for them.

She supposed they thought of her as a discontented, spoiled and pampered wife with too much time on her hands to brood on imaginary injustices. She never went short of anything, nor did her husband physically assault her. But she went short of his love, she was starved of it if the truth were known, and she was mentally battered and beaten.

Only the will to live and be with her children kept her going, and she was deprived of his presence; when he was with her he really was not there. She had the sensation at times he was as substantial as a shadow. If only men had the courage and the wisdom to break with the tradition of centuries of women being their slaves in mind and body, how much better the world would be. What chance was there of peace and sanity becoming a norm in the world when private battles were fought continuously in the home, and families were divided by hatred and discord?

She looked around the hospital room and moved restlessly in the bed. She had to sort out her life. She could not continue the way she had. She must get away somewhere. From everyone she knew. The faces of her children swam before her eyes. Their smiling happy faces. They wouldn't need her now; they had moved away from her already. She had seen it coming. Pat was taking over where she had left off. Would they miss her? They would, for a short while. But children were wonderful; they adjusted themselves so quickly to change. But how she would miss them! Her heart would break and she would never recover, but it was either this or destroy them. Her mind would break down irrevocably, she felt, and the effect this might have on her innocent children was an evil she had in her power to avert. Let the break be quick, sudden and complete. Pat would be good to them. She was sure of that. Without the burden of her presence she could see Pat making an all-out effort to be a success with his extra parental responsibilities. And there was Martha, wonderful, motherly Martha. The two children would be well looked after by her. She had no worries there.

Yes, she was determined to break away, to begin a new life in another country. She would keep her plan a secret. Was she fooling herself? Was there anyone really interested enough in her to listen to it if she decided to confide in someone? There wasn't much time to lose. Though it was still early in the month and the doctors agreed she would be well enough to leave at the end of the month, there was a lot to be done and quickly if her plan was to run smoothly. But first she must try and get on her feet as soon as possible, because once she left the hospital she was on her own.

A shudder ran through her body at the thought but she forced herself to face the reality of the future. She took out her diary. She would go to London first. Stay a few days there to rest and make further plans before she made her next move. When she had recovered from that first step she would go to Spain or Greece for a long holiday after which she would return to London and take a job there.

Already the smell, the feeling, the atmosphere of future hospital life was beginning to infect her, something which even her prolonged stay in hospital had not been able to do to the same degree. She took a note of three hospitals she knew and thought a lot of. She would write to them and make appointments for interviews. She was getting excited at the prospect. Then, without warning, her children's glowing faces blocked out the vision. She could not leave them. They were probably playing at this moment, blissfully ignorant of a motherless future. No, no, no. She couldn't go through with her plan. She couldn't do this to her children. She wept until her eyelids, heavy and swollen with weeping, closed in tired sleep.

She was only awake a few minutes when a nurse put her head in the door to tell her Miss Griffin had called but found her asleep. She had left a message and a magazine on the locker. She read the brief note scribbled on the back of an envelope: 'Glad to find you looking so much better. Obvious even in your sleep! Hope to see you tomorrow. Love, Sally.' Sally! The one good thing that had happened to her recently. Suddenly she remembered the decision she had come to before she fell asleep. Her mind was a will-o'-the-wisp. Would she? Could she? Was she a fool? A fool preparing to disrupt four lives. She was wrong. So wrong. She could not, would not go through with it. She had told herself no one was interested in her but she had forgotten Sally. Sally, the thoughtful kind girl that she was could be her lifeline. She would surely help her if she asked her. Sally, because of her clear active brain and unprejudiced outlook would be the very person to give her advice. When Sally would call again and if they were alone for any length of time, she would discuss her problems with her. She shifted her pillows to make a more comfortable nest for her head and lay back, relieved that she had another twenty-four hours' respite before committing herself to plans for a future that would exclude all that was familiar and dear to her.

Chapter Ten

Sally Griffin arrived as Pam McElroy was halfway through her supper.

She said: 'Morrison phoned me just before I left. He's taking me out to dinner so I'll be able to stay until he calls for me. I hope no one else comes till then. Had you many visitors today?'

'No. You're the first. They're thinning out, but what would you expect. I'm here three months.'

It's a pity Sally is going to America, she thought. *I could do with someone like her and perhaps she might find in me the friend most people need.*

'A penny for them,' Sally said.

'I shall miss you when you go. It's a pity I didn't meet you sooner.'

Her voice trailed away, her thoughts hitching onto what might have been if Sally had come into her life earlier. Would it have helped her? Would this unspoiled person have helped her to see life differently? Or was it possible that in time she herself would be the destroyer of this friendship. Destruction seemed to be one of her greatest talents. Better for Sally to remember her as a friend.

'I'll miss you too, Pam.' Sally's words nudged the cloud of depression. 'I think we would have been good for each other.'

'You would have been good for me, whatever about me being good for you.'

'Didn't I tell you before to stop knocking yourself? You're a lovely person, Pam, and I mean that.'

Pam's eyes rimmed with tears and she turned her head away

from her visitor. 'It's so long since I heard anything like that. The children tell me what a nice mother I am, but outside that...'

Sally let her hand drop on Pam's wrist. 'Well, I believe in telling people the nice things about themselves. I wasn't always like that, I can tell you, but something Penny once said to me – I still can't get over the fact that you and Penny went to school together – anyway she said something that impressed me very much; I forget what we were talking about when she said, "It's funny how we're never stuck for words when somebody annoys or upsets us, but when someone does something good we're awfully slow to praise."'

'That's so like Penny. I'd love to see her. It's been so long.'

'As you know, she's having trouble with this pregnancy. It's going to be her last, she says. And about time too, I say. But when the baby is born she'll be free to come to see you. I don't know how she'll manage with so many children, but being Penny she will.'

'I'll probably be out of hospital by then. I was on the phone to her yesterday. It's great talking to her again, but if only I could see her, to sit down and talk... I'd love to be able to...' She'd better be careful or she'd let things slip she didn't want to let slip.

Sally said: 'Able to what?'

'Oh, nothing.'

'What is it? There's something on your mind. Isn't there?'

Pam laughed. 'No, nothing's on my mind. Tell me all the news. You won't feel it until you and Morrison are married.'

'Yes. And the latest news is that Morrison is off to the States next week due to a sudden change of plans, instead of the end of September, and I've given my notice.'

She gave details of her plans. Then: 'Aren't I terribly selfish? Talking about myself all this time. Now, what about you?' Now was the time to speak, to be advised. Sally was a good listener. Why was she stalling? She urged herself to talk out but found she was unable to unveil the picture of the misery of her married life. It was a mistake ever to have thought that she could do it. It would be a greater mistake to answer the question because no matter how sympathetic or understanding Sally was, she could never accept the painful facts of her married life. What then would she have achieved? Less than nothing. And as far as Sally was concerned it could be possible that she, Pam, might be responsible for shaking Sally's trusting belief in marriage and all that went with it. Sally had her own life to live. At all costs she mustn't let her unhappiness spill onto Sally's future.

She said: 'What about me? What do you mean? I've no plans apart from getting out of here as quickly as possible.'

She found Sally's eyes fixed on her. Could she suspect that her words and manner belied the truth? But of course she couldn't have the smallest suspicion. How could she? She had waited stupidly for Sally's visit to help her make up her mind, but it was foolish of her to expect anyone to advise her on a matter of such importance. It was her decision and her decision only.

It was morning once again, and as she lay awake, her thoughts churning to the background of hospital sounds, she knew, once and for all, that Pat could never change.

She couldn't change herself anymore for him and from now on she wasn't going to attempt the impossible. If that was marriage she wanted no part of it. How was it that Pat couldn't leave her alone? If she were content as she was last night Pat had to come along and put her under his own peculiar method of psychoanalysis, trying to discover why she could be happy with other people while he had to endure her moods of depression. In vain she pointed out to him that her good mood had remained with her when Sally and Morrison had gone.

He said: 'I hope it lasts.'

During the long hours of the sleepless night she realised that what had happened then had happened a thousand times before and would go on happening. When her accident and brush with death and the disruption of family life didn't change their relationship for the better, nothing ever would. Things would deteriorate. It was as inevitable as a fall down a mountainside. Helpless, slithering, scratched, bumps and bruises, till finally one or other of them or both, lay broken. What was the alternative? Separation. She had found herself last night on the point of blurting out her plans but stopped herself in time as she knew only too well what the outcome would be. And she had enough on her mind without engaging herself once more in a verbal battle. Pat, seeing that she was distracted, came to his own conclusion.

'I knew the good humour wouldn't last.'

'How could you know unless you were determined not to make it last?

'Why should I do a thing like that?'

'Exactly. That's what I've often asked myself.'

'Oh God, not another of those analysing sessions.'

'Do you hear who's talking? You've spent the last ten minutes putting me through one of your analysing sessions. Or am I not allowed to call them that?'

He was about to interrupt but she continued: 'Do you know something? For the first time in my life I'm beginning to feel sorry for you. You're a mixed-up man. I don't know why you treat me the way you do and I don't think you know either. If I'm in good humour you keep needling me until I get into bad humour. You seem to hate to see me having a friend of my own, and yet how often have you thrown it into my face that I cannot keep a friend. If I drink in company you call me a drunk and if I don't drink I'm calling attention to myself. When I was in the whole of my health many a time you told me to go to blazes, that you and the children need me like you need a hole in the head, yet I was told you panicked when you thought I wouldn't make it. To use your own vernacular, what the hell is wrong with you?'

'I'll tell you what's wrong with me. The fact that I ever listened to your never-ending diatribes. If only I had taken a record of them down through the years you'd never believe your ears if you heard them played over. What psychiatrists would give to have such records! Maybe after studying them they would find some clues as to why people like you behave the way they do.'

'Perhaps they'd discover why people like you behave the way you do. And now, I'd like to ask a few questions: why did you try to destroy the woman you fell in love with and married? Why did you stop me from practising as a doctor? After all, your own mother started a business after your father died and although she doesn't need the money now, she's still in business. What do you want from me? Tell me.'

'Would there be any point in telling you? All you want is to be the centre of attention and you'll go to any lengths to get it.'

'My God! You're sick!' How could he be so cruel? He was just as bad as ever he was. She thought that if he did not love her, at least he would leave her alone. Life could be tolerable if he hadn't such a cruel tongue. Her heart was pounding. Wearily she closed her eyes.

'It's you that's sick and I'm sick of you. I've had it right up to here with you. I'm tired of your tantrums and your moods. I never know where I am with you or in what mood I'm going to find you. Even your accident hasn't changed you.'

'And it hasn't changed you'. With eyes still closed she added, 'I don't suppose anything ever could. You're an impossible person to live with and the terrible part about the whole thing is that no one would ever believe me if I said that. You're so perfect in people's eyes. Your colleagues think the world of you. Everybody loves you and you love everybody. Except me.'

'So you're feeling sorry for yourself now?' She turned her back on him. He grabbed her by the shoulders. She winced with pain.

'You don't turn your back while I'm talking. That's an old trick of yours. Walking out the door when I'm talking is another. But you can't walk out now, can you?'

She opened her eyes to look at him. What a ruthless face he really had. And this man was her husband! But this man was also the father of their children, the benevolent employer of people, the good-humoured fellow who had innumerable friends. Had every person so many personalities? Was she so terribly wicked that she was the power that caused this ugly personality to emerge so often in her presence?

She said: 'You're hurting my shoulder.'

'You can't walk out now, can you?' He gave a harsh laugh; 'in that dignified way of yours. You don't even bang the door as normal people do when they're angry. You have to be different. That's right. You're not normal, only you don't know that.'

She sat bolt upright though the sudden movement gave her hell. It took him by surprise.

'I'm normal enough to ring the bell if you don't get out of here at once.' She grabbed hold of the bell.

He said: 'Leave that bell alone.'

'I haven't pressed it yet but I will if you don't get out.'

He tried to free her hand of the bell but she pressed it before she was forced to let it go.

'You idiot!' he shouted.

In the tussle that followed the chair was knocked on the floor. He had just put it into place when a nurse opened the door. The nurse's eyes travelled quickly from patient to visitor.

'You called, Doctor McElroy?'

'Yes,' smiling with a coolness she was far from feeling. She was ready with an instant excuse. Women must not only be good at acting, she thought, but should the occasions demand it be capable of improvisation as well. She looked at Pat still upset and uncomfortable. 'And I'm afraid my husband is annoyed with me for calling you. You see, he has a terrible headache and I want him to take something before he goes on to a meeting. Would you ever get him a couple of tablets, please? Anything to relieve it.'

She was conscious of Pat raising his head. She turned. He was staring at her in amazement. The whole thing could be funny were it not so deadly serious.

The nurse said: 'Sure. I'll bring your glass of milk as well. Would you like some milk, Mr McElroy or a cup of tea?'

Pat roused himself sufficiently to say: 'No... no, thanks. There's some water here. That will do fine.'

The nurse came over and examined the water. 'That must be nearly lukewarm. I'll bring you a fresh jug of water with some ice in it.'

Pam thought: if the nurse only knew what had gone on. No one did and no one ever would, not even when she left Pat. All the blame would be heaped on her.

But she mustn't go on thinking about last night's event. The time had come for action. She rang the bell for the phone to be brought in to her. There was one person who could be relied upon to help her now. Peter. When she left down the receiver after her conversation tears were stinging her eyes. How some men could be so nice, so gentle. She rarely saw Peter. How long was it since they first met?

Pat and she were returning from a visit to his mother. Robert was six weeks old at the time and Pat's mother had insisted she should come to her for a rest. To get away from the babies would do her good, she said. *The only good it will do me,* she thought, as she stared at the invitation, *is that when I return I'll appreciate home all the more.* She didn't look forward to her visit because she would be bored stiff in the palatial residence Pat's mother owned and which was situated some distance from the town where she had her fashion-house. She would have no one to talk to but the housekeeper and the gardener. She scarcely knew anyone around as Mrs McElroy did not encourage visitors to her home. Not that she was anti-social. She simply did not have the time to act the hostess as most of her waking-time was absorbed by her business.

She had a well-trained staff who could run the business in her absence, but Mrs McElroy was one of these women who was never really happy unless she was working. She had made her money and could retire on it, but the thought of retirement never entered her well-groomed head. Though she was a mother and grandmother, she was a business woman first. Pam was fond of her in a detached kind of way. She was not a woman she could warm to, but she could not help having admiration for such a self-made woman who was dealt a harsh blow by the death of her doctor-husband when Pat was only seven.

She wasn't with Pat's mother a week, when she phoned Pat to bring her home. She was lonely and she missed him and the babies. His mother was disappointed but her disappointment didn't last, Pam noticed.

She had dropped off to sleep on the way home but had wakened suddenly from a bad dream. She looked around confused and still half-asleep. Pat noticed she was awake and put his arm around her, drawing her close to him.

'Where are we?'

'We've about another five miles to go. Had you a good sleep?'

'I must have spent most of my time dreaming. A kind of nightmare. I was trying to drive along a narrow mountain road with the two outer wheels hanging over a ravine – Pat, look out!'

Pat withdrew his arm quickly, swerving the car violently to avoid what looked like a body halfway out on the road. He turned the car, drove slowly back to the spot until the lights found the crumpled form. They got out of the car.

She knelt on the ground. 'Get me the torch,' she said, as her fingers searched for a pulse.

There were tall hedges on each side of the road. The countryside was inky-black and but for the broad shaft of light from the car there was no sign of life. It was no comfort to know that around the corner were houses nor, that as soon as they reached the top of the next hill the lights of the city would remind her how close they were to home. There wasn't even the barking of a dog to break the silence.

Lying before her was a young man, not much more than a boy, curly hair matted with blood, face grey. Drops of congealed blood hung from his lashes. Her fingers touched a pool of blood on the roadside to the right of his head. She examined him as thoroughly as she could. She looked at Pat.

'He's frightfully injured. Get a doctor and an ambulance. Don't waste time trying to phone from a house. If they haven't a phone it's more precious time gone. It will be as quick to get the doctor, yourself.'

The urgency in her voice gave him no time to argue. No time to think about leaving her on the roadside. No time to warn her about the danger she was in from passing motorists. As soon as the sound of his car died away she pushed back the pall of loneliness that had suddenly enveloped her by seeing to whatever comfort she could give this poor creature. Pat had taken the rug from the car before he left, and before she had time to remonstrate with him he had taken off his jacket and put it around her shoulders. She doubled the rug over and wrapped it carefully around the boy. Then she placed Pat's jacket lengthways over that, not that she felt all this was going to help very much. She could barely feel a pulse. She had a horrible feeling it was too late for any help. Still, she could only wait, and hope and pray. She held one of his hands in hers. If he was anyway conscious at any time she wanted him to feel he wasn't alone.

A car drove up beside her with a screech of brakes. The window was pulled down and a head appeared.

'You're in trouble?'

'Yes.'

A man got out of the car: 'I nearly ran over you there.'

She looked at him but didn't see him. Afterwards she could

never remember what he was like, whether he was young, old, dark or fair. All she remembered was the comforting presence of this stranger of the night standing beside her. She told him how she and her husband had found the injured man lying on the road and how their car had to scrape the hedge to avoid passing over him.

'My husband has gone for help. We shouldn't have much longer to wait.'

How long was she here now? She beamed the torch on her watch. Ten minutes only. It seemed like a lifetime.

'Must be a hit-and-run,' the stranger said.

'Looks like it.'

'The bastard, begging your pardon, whoever did it.'

The stranger went to his car and took something from it. Then he came over to her.

'Here. Take a mouthful of this,' he said, unscrewing the cap from the bottle. 'It's brandy. It will do you good. I always keep some in the car. Just in case. And now it's come in handy.'

'If you don't mind, not now, please.'

He didn't press further. 'What about him, then? Do you think it will help?'

'I don't think so.'

'Are you a doctor by any chance?'

'Yes.'

'I thought as much. There's something about you that made me think you were. Not many women would stick around a strange corpse on the side of the road at this hour of the night, and all alone too. Come to think of it, not many men would either.'

'He's not a corpse yet.' She felt the cold wrist. There was life there still, but only just. Silence hung between them once more but it was not a frightening or cold silence. It was a silence that held them together, strangers whose paths crossing now might never cross again. They had a feeling for each other; he for the woman whose outline his car lights had found in the blackness of the night, she for his concern and kindness, both feelings joining, reaching out to touch a stranger.

'I could do with a drop myself.' He put the bottle to his lips and after a quick gulp screwed on the cap and slipped it into his pocket. 'That's better. And it wasn't for the cold I took it. I must say women are great.' She couldn't help smiling. 'I'd be no good for a thing like this. Now if your car had broken down I'd keep tinkering at it to see if I could get it going. But this is different entirely.'

'You tinker with cars and I tinker with people. That doesn't sound so good, does it? Better say, you mend cars and I try and mend people. Are you a motor-mechanic?'

'No. I'm a farmer but I'm good with cars.'

They heard the sound of a car in the distance. She hoped it was the help they needed so badly, but it turned out to be a young couple who drew alongside and made enquiries. They parked the car and came over offering help. The boy stood with his arm around the girl as she shivered with fright. They all stood close against the hedge, the flickering movement of the torch a will-o'-the-wisp in the inky blackness.

Then the ambulance came followed by Pat's car and a police car. The doctor examined the injured boy, then spoke in low tones to Pat and Pam. 'He might survive but I wouldn't hope too much.'

They waited until the ambulance bringing the doctor moved off first. While the police were questioning them three more cars pulled up at the fatal spot.

'They're like vultures when they smell blood,' Pat said as he turned the car in the direction of home. She was too numb with cold and weariness to say anything, but she didn't think that was true. People were basically kind and good-natured. Curiosity might drive them to a halt, but compassion made them linger.

The name of the boy was Peter Logan and his family lived in the country. As soon as he was well enough to receive visitors she called to see him. When she discovered how far away his family lived she promised she would visit him as often as possible. Pat showed no great enthusiasm for her frequent visits to the hospital.

He said: 'You've done enough for that lad. Can't you leave it at that?'

She would have liked if he had accompanied her on even one of these visits. Once when she had asked him he said he wouldn't like to interfere with the work of a Good Samaritan. But the visits gave her pleasure too: the atmosphere of the hospital with its antiseptic smells, its bustle and activity. *This is where I belong,* she thought, as she walked down the long corridors taking in as much as she could when doors were left open. But this mood invariably disappeared when she saw the faces of her children in the baby atmosphere of talcum and baby things. She could even be sentimental over the sour smell of expelled baby food. In the company of her babies she felt a different person.

She loved the innocence of it all.

One day she noticed something she should have noticed a long time before if she had been on the watch-out for it. Peter had a crush on her. At first it worried her and she wondered what to do about it. He didn't try to hide it but neither did he make it embarrassing for her. Should she mention it or ignore it? After thinking it over she decided to ignore it. She remembered most patients go through some kind of emotional but harmless experience like this.

She came on a last visit to him. He was due to go home the following day and she celebrated by making a longer visit than usual. She knew a lot about Peter at this stage. He was twenty-five, his father had a small farm and he was the eldest of six. He had been coming back from a weekend visit to his family when the accident happened. He had jumped at the chance of a lift home from someone he knew, and while at home he had heard that the manager of a roadside inn which was about a mile from the place where he had the accident, and who was a native of Peter's hometown, was returning on the Sunday. This man had wanted him to stay the night at the inn, but Peter said he would probably catch the last bus going into the city, and even if he had to walk, it was only a matter of about three or four miles to his digs.

'But you see where it landed me,' he said with a laugh.

She was now thinking, as she sat by his bed on her last visit, of all the 'ifs and onlys'. If only he had stayed overnight at the inn, or if only he had caught the last bus there would have been no accident. If Pat and she had not come on the scene, if they or some other passing motorist had run over him, if by some miracle he had escaped further mutilation but had died; but Peter was talking.

'You know, I'm not sorry I had that accident. Not one bit sorry.' The look in his eyes warned her to change the subject.

'What are your plans when you leave here?'

'Get back to the job as soon as I can, I suppose.' But there was no enthusiasm in his voice.

She said: 'But you like your work surely?'

'Of course.'

'Then what is it?' She knew there was something on his mind.

'It's just that I seem to have come to a dead end in my job, not that it didn't nearly come to that a few months back.' He laughed at his little joke.

You're a terrific person, she thought, looking at him, not to feel bitter about that hit-and-run driver. Apart from everything else there was the matter of compensation; no money would be coming to him.

He explained he was seven years in the travel agency business and his ambition was to open his own travel agency. He had the experience and the know-how but he hadn't the money to back up his venture. Of course he was still young and if he had the patience to wait which he hoped he had, he might see his dream come true. She could see that just by talking about it his natural optimism had overcome his initial despondency.

She had an idea. 'Where would you open your agency if you had the money?'

'I know the very place. The property is owned by a man who went to school with my father. The place became vacant a couple of years ago, but the fact that he and my father were schoolboys together didn't influence him to reduce the rent for me, so somebody else got the place. Anyway, I couldn't have afforded to open up even if he did reduce it. I'm in a better position now and with more experience, but I still haven't enough capital to get started properly. It's true when they say the only difference between success and failure is a matter of a few thousand pounds. I have some money saved. I would have more only that I've been helping out at home. I don't begrudge it. They need it more than I do. Still the bank manager isn't impressed by that kind of thing.' He smiled. 'But I must be boring you with all this.'

'On the contrary. Tell me, is the place you're talking about available now?'

'Yes. That's just it! The firm that rented it moved out about six weeks ago according to my friend, and he offered it to me. I told him I was grateful but I still wasn't in a position to accept his offer. I'm sure he was wondering what the dickens I had in mind two years ago. However, he said he would give me another while to think about it. But what's the point? They haven't found the person who drove into me.'

'Listen! I've a great idea. But first you must promise to keep this to yourself. I've some money of my own. Money which my mother left me and which Pat and I haven't needed to touch. And as it's not doing anything particularly useful you can have what you need as a loan, free of interest.'

Peter shot up in bed. 'I don't believe it! I just don't believe it!' His mouth remained open in astonishment. She reached over and placed her fingers gently under his chin and pressed his mouth closed.

'You'll catch cold if you leave your mouth open like that.'

Her offer and the touch of her fingers was too much for him. He took her hand and pressed it to his lips.

'I don't know what to say. It... you...'

He let go of her hand. Tears were in his eyes. He bent his head. She loved Peter. Did she love him as a brother? Or the way a woman loves a man, love, affection, desire all intermingled in one deep emotion? She didn't know. She only knew she had no feeling of guilt about it.

Peter raised his head. 'I love you, Pam. That's all I can say. I love you and I'll always love you. I would love to take you in my arms, to hold you close, to kiss you, but you wouldn't want that and I wouldn't want to upset you in any way.'

He did not rush into an apology for expressing his feelings nor did she remonstrate.

'Thank you, Peter. It gives me a warm feeling to know how you think of me. I trust you. It can't be easy for you but it proves one thing – you can be trusted with this loan. There'll be no legal document or signing anything. Take the money and use it. Return it when you can and I know you'll be a success.'

That was eight years ago.

Peter lived up to the trust she placed in him. She had told Pat of her little business venture with Peter when Peter had opened his own place and they had been invited to the celebration. It did her good to feel that outside her own family she was of use to someone. She felt a great pride in her protégé as he went from success to success. Her loan was returned to her much faster than she had expected accompanied by two holiday vouchers.

'What's that all about?' Pat asked when she showed him the vouchers.

'It's about eaten bread that's not soon forgotten.'

Peter arrived at the promised time. He bent down and kissed her, then sat beside her and took her hand.

'Now, what can I do for you? There's more to this than just some travelling arrangements.'

'Yes. But first of all may I have your word you won't tell anybody what I'm going to tell you. Not anyone. Not even your wife.'

'You have my word.'

He was worried.

She said: 'I'm leaving Pat. It's the only way out for me.'

Total shock was reflected in his face and in the silence that followed. After some moments he said: 'Tell me all, that is, if it will help.'

'It won't help but I'd like you to know something so as to give you an idea why I'm doing this.'

When she had finished he said: 'What about the children?'

'The children? Don't you think I've thought about them? Thought and thought until my head has nearly exploded. They're the only reasons I haven't left Pat long ago.

They're the only reasons I could stay with him now, but if I did they would eventually have an insane mother on their hands and what good would I be to them then?'

Peter did not know enough about her husband to condemn him, and the little he knew of him would never make him think he could be such a husband that Pam would have to leave or else be driven out of her mind. There was another alternative to Pam leaving the children: Pat to move out, leaving her and the children undisturbed in their home. It could take the form of a temporary separation with a possible coming together again. Anything was better than that other decision. He made his suggestion. She dropped her head wearily into her hands.

'Oh, if only I could do that.'

When she lifted her face again it was grey with anguish, hurt and despair. It broke his heart to see her like that.

'Peter, you don't know Pat. Pat wouldn't agree to such a separation. If anyone is to move out it's I. You see, he could never look people in the face again if it was so much as suspected that he might be to blame even in the smallest way. But if I were to walk out on him and the children, that's a different thing. That's a part he could take well enough. The wronged husband. And he would have plenty of evidence to prove that this was so and that he had a lot to contend with. His friends are not my friends, you know.' She drew up her knees under the bedclothes and let her face fall on them. Tears stung Peter's eyes. What a mess! What a hellish mess! He longed to take her in his arms, talk comforting words and kiss away the pain. But this was a time for silence. No words he could say could help.

She looked for her handkerchief and blew her nose.

'Well, that's that.' A wintry smile trembled on her face but was gone almost immediately. 'Believe me I would never involve you unless I had tried every avenue of hope first. I must get away. Book some place. I don't care where I go as long as it's reasonably quiet and warm. Money will be a bit of a complication but you'll be able to sort that out, I'm sure. I'll have to think of some way of getting Martha to bring in my passport without making her suspicious. I know I have it in an old handbag and I'll ask her to bring that in shortly before I'm due to go home.' She gave him a sad little smile.

'I never thought the day would come when I'd be asking you for the loan of money. I must have been hankering all those years to get my own back on you.'

'Don't, Pam. Don't.'

'Well, that's all Peter. I'm sorry to have to burden you with my troubles. It's something I hate doing and it does something terrible to my pride to let even such a dear person like you know anything about my marriage problems. Marriage is such a private affair.'

Her eyes had a faraway look. *What was she thinking of,* Peter wondered. The future or the past? Did she love Pat still in spite of everything? Love was like a beautiful painting. Then for some reason, perhaps due to the paints, the canvas, perhaps the environment, the painting began to deteriorate and where once there was beauty there was now an unrecognisable picture. Attempts to restore the original having failed the canvas is destroyed. Peter sighed deeply, wondering was his analogy making sense. But then how could anyone make sense of this unfolding tragedy.

Chapter Eleven

Pat McElroy was thinking of his wife's homecoming. It wouldn't be long now. Then everything would be back to normal or nearly normal. Naturally, it would take some time for Pam to be her old self again. He wouldn't be sorry to have her back. All those journeys to the hospital. It was no joke. You couldn't call a day your own. And then the house was so quiet and silent without her and the children. Should he leave the children where they were or have them home to welcome their mother? Perhaps it might be better for them to hang on for the remainder of the school holidays and give a chance to Pam to settle in before they returned home, as it was bound to take some re-adjustment for a person who had spent so long in hospital to get used to familiar sights and sounds. But he thought he should ask Pam first as to whether the children should stay with the Butlers, or whether he ought to bring them home.

He told Pam they weren't returning to school until the seventh of September and she should be ready to leave hospital a few days before that. Say, the twenty-seventh, he leafed through his diary, that would be on a Thursday, D-Day. Supposing the children remained on with the Butlers until the following Friday week; he could collect them – oh, he forgot. Sue said something about letting them wait on and she would bring them back at the end of the holiday. So better check with Sue and confirm the arrangement.

Pam watched his anxious sorting out of details in a detached kind of way. What was to be was to be, whether the children were at home or on holidays. Pat might as well get used to arranging these things. Responsibility for the children was all his now. She was handing it over to him though he was unaware of that as yet. Her quiet acceptance of his plans for the children puzzled him for a fleeting moment. He would have thought she would have urged that the children be brought home so that they would be there on her arrival; they meant so much to her. Either she wanted just the two of them together for a brief while – could that be possible? Or that she was prepared to let him make all the arrangements. For either reason the fact that his plans went off so smoothly was a good omen. He was in cheerful mood and his conversation ranged from his latest design for a church to his next trip to Spain.

Pam gave a start. 'When does that come off?'

'Oh don't worry. I'm not going away immediately if that's what you're thinking of. As a matter of fact I was hoping to take you with me, that is, if you would like to come.' He hesitated, remembering why those journeys on the Continent together had petered out.

He looked at her intently but her face gave nothing away. He went on: 'I'm spending a few days in North Africa also. You might like that. We'll probably be away three weeks altogether. You'll have to be much stronger of course because there'll be a lot of travelling involved, so it's just as well this doesn't come off until the fourteenth of November. That should see us home in nice time for Christmas.' He smiled. 'What do you say?'

Why did he have to be so nice and agreeable now, she thought, just when she had made her final decision? His smile twisted her heart. It was the memory of such a lovely smile that forced her to believe he loved her during the long lonely days. Its absence was made all the more painful when she realised that just by the merest quirk of those same firmly chiselled lips that smile could be replaced, as so often was the case, by a thin sneer, by a straight hard line of calculating cruelty, or by a tight-lipped silence. How often had she seen his smile, his face lit up with pleasure and affection, at so many of his friends and she had envied them the gift they treated so casually. Now that smile he gave her seemed to say, 'I love you.'

Could she trust it? And then, memories of the past and the recent past came to taunt her. There was no going back on her decision.

If she could only say to herself: there will be no raking up the past to stir up old bitterness, to open up old sores. But she couldn't say that. The past was inexorably bound up with the present and in her case was the foundation for the future. Why should she build her hopes on a rotten foundation? She had been given no signs of any kind that the future would be different from the past. There was nothing to indicate that Pat felt he had ever been in the wrong, was responsible in any way for the deterioration of their marriage. He never showed any sorrow, any regret or remorse. If only once, just once, Pat would say: 'Look, Pam, I've made mistakes. Plenty of them. So have you. I'm sorry. Let's make a fresh start.' That is all she would need. Even less. Just the words, 'I'm sorry.'

Was there something wrong with a person who couldn't admit to being ever wrong? Could never say, sorry? Friend said it to friend, stranger to stranger. Why was it so difficult then for a husband to say it to his wife? She had said it to Pat many, many times even when she knew she had done nothing to apologise about, she merely said it to keep the peace. And even then she did not feel it was any big deal.

Her eyes sought his in mute appeal; *Pat, I wouldn't force you to retract every cruel word or remind you of every cruel action. All I want is for you to remember you are just as human as the rest of us. As it is, I have forgiven you; it's just that I can't forget. And I would forget if only you gave me a chance to do so.*

He waited for an answer to his invitation while her eyes begged for a response to her mute appeal. She saw his smile slowly replaced by a look of irritability. How little he knew. How little contact he had with stark reality. Why was she such an idiot, pouncing on an infinitesimal glimmer of hope, to have that immediately quenched?

'Spain is an attractive country.' Her non-reply to his question seemed to satisfy him.

'That settles it then.' He remained silent for a moment. Then: 'Had you many visitors today?'

She gave him a desultory account of visitors and added that she had a letter from Penny. His curiosity was aroused. For years he had heard nothing about Penny and now, she was back in Pam's life once more. But he said nothing.

'Sally and Vienna are very good to visit you so often,' he said after a while. 'Vienna is a tough nut.'

His short laugh was faintly derisive. He liked Vienna but he regarded her as a tough nut. Perhaps that was the reason he liked her. But there was something else about her that attracted him to her. What it was he couldn't quite make out.

'Wouldn't she want to be!' Pam said.

'What do you mean?'

'Just that.'

It was obvious that Pam wasn't going to elaborate, yet he wondered why she made that comment. Did she know that story? He never told her and the few people who knew would have kept it to themselves. He was sure of that. Men were loyal to each other, especially in such circumstances. Anyway the whole thing happened such a long time ago. They had all forgotten about it. Anybody could slip off the straight and narrow. If Vienna had happened by any chance to hear all the facts then Michael would be paying for it ever since. Was he paying for it? Poor devil. Just over one brief love affair. It had blown over as suddenly as it started, with no harm done to anyone. His mind switched back to that particular period. Michael had spent a great deal of time in their house after that affair and he had encouraged his frequent visits, partly to get his mind off the sad business and partly because he suspected Vienna had smelled a rat and so, Michael was bearing the brunt of her wrath as her attitude to him was anything but wifely for some time after. For that matter, come to think of it, Vienna seemed to have changed quite a bit since that episode. Poor Michael remained the same decent chap; good-natured and crazy about Vienna and the children. He had availed of the permanent welcome that Pam and himself had for him, even when he had been away in Brazil around that time. Pam had remarked some time after his return that Michael had made a bit of a nuisance of himself. She had added: 'He has a wife and children. It's a pity he doesn't concentrate his attention on them instead of thinking he's a free agent.' He'd been annoyed at the remark and in no mood to listen.

Had Pam been trying to tell him something then? She couldn't have known about the Swedish affair. My God! If Michael could do something once there was nothing to stop him from doing it again. Could Michael have tried on something in his absence? Was Michael just one of these...? He couldn't face the thought. But he could know and did know that Pam would have no nonsense from Michael or from any other man for that matter. Perhaps Vienna wasn't to blame for her attitude after all, and who could blame her in a way? He would love to ask Pam more about the business but this wasn't the time, and the thought of probing into another man's private affairs was distasteful to him, but if it involved his own wife, well one had to swallow one's principles to get at the truth.

Was Pam reading his thoughts? That inscrutable face of hers unnerved him at times. She was saying: 'The important thing is that they love each other in spite of each other's weaknesses. If all married couples did that there would be less unhappy marriages.'

He was right. Pam had been reading his thoughts.

Pam had a good idea of what Pat was thinking. There were times when she felt she could read him like a book and this was one of them. She had seen the gradual dawning of suspicion on Pat's face. Pat was beginning to realise she had known about Michael's affair all along. Of course she knew, but only because Michael himself had told her when the affair seemed to have petered out and he had tried to enlist her sympathy by blaming the girl for the entanglement. He had said he had found it difficult to shake her off. All he was concerned with was what would happen if Vienna ever got to hear it.

'You know what these Swedish women can be like.'

'No, I don't,' she interrupted him. 'You tell me. But if you ask me what Irish husbands can be like I can be articulate fairly well on that subject.'

He gave her a quick startled look. Then a look of enlightenment spread over his astonished face. He burst out laughing.

'Don't tell me good old Pat has fallen by the wayside!' She was angry. Terribly angry. 'Good old Pat nothing.'

She would have slapped his face for his nasty insinuation only that without warning he had her in his arms and was crushing the breath out of her with his tight hold and his kisses. Her lips did not yield to his. There was no struggling, kicking or creating a scene. She was coolly and clearly thinking out a plan of action. Her lack of response soon brought him back to his senses, as she thought it would. In her heart she knew he wasn't such a bad fellow. Her anger melted as quickly as it flared up and she was glad she hadn't kicked up a fuss. He let her go suddenly, his face crestfallen. She poured out a drink and gave it to him, and poured out one for herself.

'Here's to all frustrated lovers,' she said, clinking her glass against his. It was the best antidote for the embarrassing scene, causing them to laugh, something that would have seemed incredible a moment or two before.

'I've been an awful idiot, haven't I?' he said. 'What with this just now and that affair with Ulla.'

'You're quite right. You have been an awful idiot.'

'Vienna would never forgive me if she found out I was going on like this.'

'Well, why do you go on like this, as you put it?'

'I don't know. Just a mad phase, I suppose. Anyway it's all over between me and Ulla. It has to be.'

'I should say so. Any regrets?'

'I can't afford to have them, can I? Not that I showed signs of it just now by making that assault on you.'

'Well, is that the end of your mad phase?'

'With you? Yes. No, I don't want to treat it as a joke,' as he saw the annoyed look on her face. 'I love Vienna too much to upset our marriage.'

'Well then, stop the nonsense.'

To soften the remark she said: 'If anyone had seen that last little scene they might have thought that it was I trying to seduce you.'

'No one could suspect you of a thing like that.'

'But to get back to you; you said just now that Vienna would never forgive you if she found out. I don't know Vienna that well but I'll say this, there is hardly a woman who doesn't know when her husband is misbehaving himself. People say the wife is always the last to find out, which I find hard to believe. A wife suspects and knows certain things but she blinds herself purposely to what's happening, hoping that it will go away or willing herself to believe that it's only her imagination, anything rather than face the truth she knows it is deep down. If she didn't do that how on earth do you think she could face each day, smiling at her neighbours and friends, though they all know and are feeling sorry for her, doing her work about the house, looking after her children, smiling, the hardest thing of all, at her unfaithful husband and acting as if nothing was wrong.

'Not every wife is able to act like this. Some of them fight it out with their husbands, inch by inch, and it can't be pleasant for either of them. The reason I've said all this is because I believe Vienna knows a good deal, or suspects a lot.'

'What do you think I should do?'

She stood up and took his empty glass. Automatically, he stood up and followed her out to the hall. She faced him as they neared the front door. 'Please don't ask me to solve your problems. I can't. And if I could offer a solution I wouldn't, because that would be the way my mind would work, not your mind. I'm not you. But one thing you could do is, be honest with yourself. Then be honest with Vienna.'

She had never asked Michael how things went and he, perhaps for reasons of his own, kept the sequel to himself. She respected him for that and somehow she felt that he had never repeated a similar mistake.

'You're very quiet tonight. Anything the matter?' Pat asked, as he rose to go.

He had spent the remainder of his visit chatting, giving bits of news he thought might interest her, exchanging the children's letters each had received. But he noticed that for most of the time Pam seemed to be miles away. At times she turned her face abruptly from his gaze but not before he noticed the tears welling in her eyes. He pretended not to notice. She would prefer it that way. Most likely she was suffering from a little reaction, the result of all she had gone through, so it was just as well for her to get these emotions over and done with.

He took her hand. 'Cheer up. In another couple of weeks you will be home. That's something to look forward to.' He bent down to kiss her. 'See you the same time tomorrow.'

Her eyelids dropped wearily on tired eyes before he reached the door. *I could cry an infinity of tears,* she thought, as the tears released themselves and trickled down her cheeks. But utter weariness and sorrow produced a sense of drowsiness, and she was in a deep sleep before the tears dried on her face.

The days passed by quickly. By not letting herself dwell on the past or think of the future, the present was tolerable. Peter made all the necessary arrangements. He had finally decided that his own villa in Benidorm would be ideal for Pam. It had a lovely view of sea and mountain. It could be quiet enough for Pam if that was what she wanted yet she was only a few minutes away from the centre of Benidorm. He had contacted Senora Camino, a childless widow who helped out when his wife and children took over during the summer, asking her to live-in while Pam stayed there. Though Pam would like to be alone, having no one around the villa might be just a little too much, especially for someone who was going through a crisis, and Senora Camino was the very person to take away that edge of loneliness and aloneness without being too obtrusive about it.

Seeing Pam so unswerving in her resolve was the only thing that kept him to his unhappy job. If he had found her at all unsure or confused, even saw her once breaking down unable to face the goal she set herself, he would have rushed in to smash down her remaining defences and destroy the terrible work in which he was such an unwilling participant. One thing he could not do for her, he told her, although he had already promised, and that was to accompany her to the airport. It wasn't that she was asking too much of him. It was just that he was asking too much of himself. She understood.

She had told Pat what clothes Martha was to pack for her. A sob caught in her throat when she saw the two-piece Rosemary had helped her to select. It was one of two they couldn't make up their minds about until Rosemary finally settled the matter by urging her to buy the two. The other one was... where was it now? She had worn it the day of the accident. But she mustn't let herself think.

Now, it was her last morning in hospital. How the last few hours had flown. She had willed them to go slowly, dragging out each hour, lying awake far into the night lest the precious time escape her in the extravagance of sleep. Even at this last hour she longed for a way out. But last night again there had been another row with Pat. She had been tense and on edge. And because he couldn't know the reason he had suddenly unleashed his anger and annoyance accusing her of total lack of interest in what he was trying to do for her. She was so caught up in herself and her own emotions using tears as she always did to get her own way – this accusation totally puzzled her as she had made no attempt to change his plans or interfere in any way; all she did was to remain quiet, though the tears did come into her eyes just once but she quickly brushed them away – while she listened to the worn-out, oft-repeated insults in silence. She would have been reduced to the humiliated and broken creature she had become so accustomed to being in the past or having the energy, would have retaliated, but the thought that as from tomorrow she would have branched out on her own, helped her to swallow the bitter recriminations, because even now, if she needed more proof, it was obvious that nothing had really changed between them or ever would.

How could he be so completely devoid of love for her? Even the newspaper man, noticing on one occasion her lying in an awkward position, had come shyly over to her bed and tried to re-arrange the pillows for her. Such gentleness and concern from a stranger! Was it too much to expect a small share of those feelings from her husband? Was it possible that she herself was one of those people who could show forbearance and patience to outsiders yet had little of those virtues to spare for her own? This was a question she had often pondered upon and to which she felt she gave a truthful answer now, as always. Her love for Pat had been so great in the past that the question of patience, endurance, forbearance were merely words in a dictionary. She had no use for them. Love smoothed every obstacle away. She had no need of any other virtue until in recent years she had to resort to patience and endurance.

She looked at herself in the mirror. She was plain. She was even ugly and she felt ugly. The two-piece still hung quite well on her in spite of the loss of weight. She checked once more all the essentials and then sat down to wait for the taxi. Her premature departure had been easily explained. She was going to surprise her husband by her arrival at his office.

She was all alone now in the room that had been her home for so many long weeks. The nurses had gone about their various duties. The doctors had come and gone. She could hear the rapid steps of a nurse pass her door, a voice on the intercom, bells ringing. She was surrounded by a world of living, dying and dead. Under what heading could she be classified? In any other circumstances she might have resented being deserted like this. There was a knock on the door. A nurse came in.

'The taxi.' She took the small bag.

'Are you all set?'

'As much as a jelly.'

'And I bet, almost as shaky.'

On her way out Pam handed a letter and some money to the porter: 'See that my husband gets this,' she whispered, thankful the nurse had gone ahead and was out of earshot.

Her last link with her husband was broken. She got into the taxi, refusing all help. She must get used to doing things on her own. Her physiotherapist had been excellent and she had carried out her instructions religiously, each day seeing an improvement in her mobility, her body responding positively to the exercises.

As soon as she made herself comfortable in the plane she relaxed. She wasn't as tired as she thought she would be. The road to full recovery would be quick, if the way she felt now was anything to go by. Things were going smoothly and her confidence increased. The worst was over. A short letter had been written to Pat. She recalled the words. How clearly they came to mind:

'Dear Pat, by the time you read this I'll have completed the first part of my journey out of your life. Please don't make a fuss, though knowing you as I do there's probably no need to warn you of this. I know what I'm doing and believe me, I've given a great deal of time and thought to the step I am now taking. All those weeks in hospital helped me to put into action what has been on my mind for several years. It has taken a great deal of courage to do this. To tell you the truth I didn't believe I would ever muster up the courage to go through with it. As you will realise, now that I've taken this final step there's no going back. I know you will suffer a certain amount of embarrassment but the sympathy you'll receive should help counteract to some extent this passing difficulty. I leave it to you to break the news to the children. You're good with them and they're very attached to you. They should recover fairly quickly. Children are good at adapting to various situations. They anchored me to you for years. I've broken away from that anchor, but the pain of this act will remain with me for the rest of my life. I love them – no one will ever know how much – but I will not have them destroyed by us and that is what we would do if we stayed together. You may say we could have talked this out, that there were alternatives. But do you remember how many times I spoke about the difficulties in our married life and what a destructive path we were taking? How many times did I bring up the subject of separation and you responded that if anyone was to leave the home it would be I, that you could prove in court what an unfit mother I was, so I've chosen the lesser of two evils. I think I've given our two children a good start in life. I trust you to follow it through. Pam.'

She thought of Rosemary and Robert. Every time she would see a child she knew she would suffer the agony of longing for them but she had emptied herself for them. There was nothing more to give.

She looked down at the clouds massed in luxurious softness. The sky was blue and without blemish. What perfection! Perfection? Was that what she always sought? Perfection in love? Perfection in marriage? How beautiful those clouds looked, showing a purity and softness that wasn't seen when viewed from below; those clouds meant different things to people who were living their lives way down below; a gloomy sign for the picnicker and the holiday-maker, a hopeful sign for the drought-scourged farmer. Down there, people sweated and worked, laughed and played. To them, a cloudy day was a cloudy day. Life was like that. Life meant working, playing, crying, laughing, putting up with people, putting up with things, trying to create while others tried to destroy; peace, war; living, dying.

Was she an escapist then? Clouds were only a temporary barrier to the warm sun's rays, a removable curtain separating sky and earth. The clouds would part, meet again to form strange and beautiful shapes, only to break away once more giving a glimpse of the blue backdrop. Having climbed above the clouds she had all this vast blueness to enjoy. How long before it would pall? One way or another there was no permanence for her. The plane would have to steer through those clouds to touch earth. If she were to come back to reality she must meet and pass through clouds of sadness and unhappiness. Was there never an end to it all?

She took hold of herself. This stupid introspection was all wrong. She must look forward, not backward. She wasn't a coward. She wasn't an escapist. She was a woman with a lot of living in front of her and living involved giving, and she meant to go on giving of herself now that she was free to do so. She could no more stop giving of herself than she could stop the flow of blood in her veins. Would it be too much to ask that someone, somewhere along the way would recognise this and show some small gratitude just now and again? She wouldn't ask for much, just a small recognition that she was human.

She glanced at her watch. Pat would have arrived at the hospital by now to pick her up. What would be his reaction? What would he make of her letter? The porter, who knew him well, would hand the letter to him. He would glance at it briefly, stuff it in his pocket while he strode to her room – the unexpected emptiness of the room, now bare of flowers. The freshly made-up bed silently awaiting its next occupant. The stillness. Where was he now? Making enquiries from some nurse? She would never know. She could only imagine what she would do, but that was no criterion for Pat's reaction.

Pat McElroy arrived at the hospital later than planned to take his wife home. He had been delayed over some business that had suddenly cropped up, but he had dealt with it there and then, and because of the rapidity with which he concluded the matter he told himself he deserved the rest of the day off. Pam would like that. It would be nice to have her home again. He had missed her. Guiltily, he remembered that treacherous moment when he saw her lying on the roadside with no sign of life in her, a moment so brief he had often wondered had it ever really been. Or was it something completely out of his control due perhaps to the effects of shock? A moment when he felt something very close to relief; now their troubled life together was over; no more arguments, no more shame. It was all finished.

But that moment went as suddenly as it came. The smooth death-like pallor of her face erased the troubled years and painfully and clearly revealed the lovely girl he had first met, the girl who stood out, sweet and gentle, smiling and humorous against the background of the theatre where the seminar had taken place, who shone more brightly in the attractive group of bright-eyed and intelligent boys and girls she mixed with. In a moment that seemed between time and eternity a ray of light had pierced the darkness that had come between them. This ray of light had brightened and dimmed as the weeks went by. There were times when, seeing in Pam much that had been desirable in the girl he loved and wanted very much to love, he found himself close to her. But there were times when something occurred between them, something he never seemed to be able to deal with and he was left confused and upset.

He took the lift to her room. She would be ready and waiting. He had forgotten the many times she had delayed him in the past when he was barely able to control his irritation at her maddeningly slow attempts to get ready for appointments, at her lack of enthusiasm, at her whole attitude to an evening's entertainment. He often got the impression she was doing him a favour and not willingly either. His memory leap frogged into the happy past when a joyous and delighted girl was always in happy anticipation of his arrival

A nurse greeted him. 'Your wife has already left.'

'Left? But I thought the arrangement was that I was to call for her?'

Could Pam not exercise a little patience? Just because he wasn't here on the dot. But the nurse was chatting away. 'It seems she wanted to surprise you. I think she couldn't bear to stay away another moment from you.'

She knew him sufficiently well to be able to talk freely with him, but he could not for the life of him put a name on her.

'Would she be at home by now, do you think? When did she leave?'

'But she was to call to your office. That's what she told us. Were you there all morning?'

'Yes. But at what time did she leave?'

'Oh, ages ago. About... well, I would say shortly after eleven. But perhaps I misunderstood her. She may have gone straight home or perhaps run into somebody and have gone off for a cup of coffee somewhere.'

He was annoyed. Pam was so irrational. A plain straightforward thing like calling for her to bring her home could not be done without all this confusion and nonsense. He felt a bloody fool. Couldn't she have rung him at least saying she had arrived home and so save him this unnecessary journey? And then he remembered how long he was on the phone. But Betty Aherne would have told him she was on another line. Oh hell!

'Did my wife leave anything behind? Anything for me to take home?'

'No. She brought all she wanted but she left some chocolates, fruit and flowers for patients.'

He smiled. 'Thank you, nurse.'

On his way out the front door, the porter caught up with him. What now? He was hanged if he was going to leave him another tip. He snatched the proffered letter and stuck it in his pocket, giving the porter a curt thanks. A receipt or something equally unimportant. He got into the car and turned the ignition key. Then something clicked. The echo of the porter's words: 'Your wife asked me to give you this.' What was she writing him a letter for? Wasn't she on her way home? Why was the nurse so sure at first that Pam was calling to his office? Feverishly he dug into his pockets. He had the crumpled letter in his hand. His trembling fingers tore open the envelope. He read quickly. What in the world had she done? The utter incredibility of the whole thing! It must be some kind of joke. It had to be. There had to be an explanation. He read the letter once more, this time more slowly. She must be out of her mind; even their two children or the thought of them hadn't been sufficient to dissuade her. Pam loved the children; she would rather die than hurt them. But the stark truth was, she had done just that.

He must get away from here. Away to somewhere he could think. He turned the car in the direction of the seafront and drove the few miles that separated him from peace and quiet. He parked the car facing it out to sea and turned off the engine. The calmness that stretched out before him did nothing to calm his nerves. How was he to face this catastrophe? Nothing mattered now. Not the children. Not the job. Not money or friends. *Oh Pam, why did you do this to me? How did I deserve it?*

He read the letter over and over, willing to see a reason, a hope, some simple explanation. Pam could not, would not leave the children. Not permanently. He knew Pam. She had done this to give him a fright, perhaps because of the row last night. Well, she had got her own back on him. He had got a fright. A damn good one at that. If she had left him she would be back. He was sure of that.

There was only one other explanation for her actions, and this he also held on to as it offered some comfort. Pam was suffering from shock, perhaps delayed shock, the result of all she had gone through. If that were so there was something he could do about it. He would get in touch immediately when he got home with Jimmy Doherty, a detective he knew. Perhaps, he should wait for a few days and see what would develop in the meantime. No point in bringing an outsider in on this yet, although he could rely on the discretion of Doherty. Pam might turn up at any time. He was sure she would. As for Martha, the only other person to whom it was essential to offer a plausible explanation, he could tell her his mother had been visiting the hospital and insisted on Pam going directly home to her place for a complete rest, and as she was returning immediately Pam decided to accompany her there and then. It sounded reasonable enough and it sounded like his good-natured but rather domineering mother. As for the question of a change of clothes, his mother could supply Pam with any outfit or garment from her own shop – indeed she would need a change of clothes as she had lost weight and was now only putting on a little in recent weeks. Martha, except for the initial disappointment at not seeing Pam, would accept his explanation without further questioning.

As for his mother, who would surely phone tonight to enquire about Pam, he would have to get there first and phone her. What the hell would he say? He dropped his head on the steering wheel and let the misery of it all submerge him. From the chaos that was now his mind an answer surfaced. He would tell his mother that he and Pam were going away for a few days. If she wanted to speak to Pam he would say she was asleep. Now his friends had to be dealt with. He would give them the same excuse as he had prepared for Martha. It would work for them too. For a little while anyway. He hoped it would only be for a little while. Thank God the children didn't have to be told anything yet. No wonder Pam offered no resistance when he had suggested they stay with the Butlers for the few extra days. He should have suspected something then. It wasn't like her not to want the children at home; she had been parted long enough from them.

Pam's death he would have accepted in time. He could never accept her desertion.

Why did she do it? Hadn't he given her everything? She hadn't married beneath her. He had given her a position in life most women would envy. He was a well-known personality. He was wealthy and he had never left her short of money. He had given her a lovely home and they had two beautiful children. What more could any woman want? He had asked for very little in return. He made no great demands on her time, on her energy or even on her love. His mind galloped over the passing years. Could it be possible that she had never really loved him?

And then the memory of those early days of their relationship tugged at his heart. Of course she had loved him. All through the years he had never doubted her love for him. It was as constant as – as the Sugar Loaf Mountain they both saw each day from their front windows. But when you live with something secure in the knowledge that it's always there, one can actually forget its presence. And this was how he felt now with Pam gone. Something terrible had happened to her to make her do this to him. Some mental aberration. Some kind of brainstorm. Nothing else could account for it. He was sure of that. He knew Pam. But, how much did he really know her, except that there were times she irritated him, annoyed him, maddened him; that away from her he felt more himself, more relaxed, more contented. But had he ever wondered why he felt that way? Was it normal for him to feel that way about his wife? Did he love her? Really love her? What kind of a husband was he? He gave a deep sigh. This was no time for self-analysis.

His thoughts swivelled to Pam, the girl who had laughed and sung through the early years, who had poked fun at herself and those she loved in the way that only she could. The girl who had all the gifts so desirable in a human being and so often lacking in people. Of course she wasn't perfect. She had a temper that flashed now and again over some blatant injustice perpetrated by a government or individual. He used to love to watch that sudden flash that lit those lovely eyes, to watch those amber sparks glowing.

He would sit back and smile delightedly at his not quite perfect creature, not listening to a word she was saying but enjoying the vivid and all-too-brief mood. And having delivered her tirade she would suddenly become aware of his lack of seriousness, stop dead, then plant herself on his knees and take his face in both her hands to shake it from side to side, the sparkle still alive in the glorious depths of her eyes, and demand what was so funny. His love for her used to be so intense then. When was it since he looked at her apart from those moments in hospital?

All those years now gone by in which he had forgotten what Pam really looked like. In which he had forgotten the meaning of love. True, he had felt the stirrings of his early love for Pam since the accident. She had been so gentle, so patient, so often good-humoured in spite of the pain. He had seen a ray of hope for their future. Pam was becoming more like the girl he had married. Or was it just wishful thinking on his part? He got a feeling of panic. What did he know of her? What did he know of himself?

How was he so blind as not to see what was coming? Not to have noticed something that must have been slowly but surely forming to lead up to this moment. If only he could talk to her now. Plead with her. Ask her where he had gone wrong, to help him correct the wrongs he had done.

For the first time in his life he found himself powerless to make a move. Where to start? How to go about it? If it were a plain and straightforward case of Pam just missing he could let the police handle it. But Pam was not missing. Pam did not want any public furore to be made about her leaving him. She had made that plain enough. But, supposing that message was merely a blind to put him and others off thinking of her real intention. Supposing she had intended to kill herself. She could be in that mood. No, no not that. Pam was not like that. He didn't know why the thought of Pam being mentally unbalanced kept recurring, unless his own crazed mind was pressuring him along those lines. Pam was as sound and as sane as he was, or as anybody could be in this mad world. A person didn't have to be of unsound mind to leave one's husband or wife or children. People around the world did it for different reasons. But why should this happen to him? 'Because you deserved it.' It took a shocked moment or two before he realised the voice was his own. He must get away from here. He would go home and see if there was any news. Perhaps Pam might have changed her mind, unable to go ahead with her plans and be already at home, there to greet him. Yes, that sounded more like Pam. They would put their arms around each other and maybe cry together, because that's what he felt like doing now. And after the tears there would be smiles of relief because they had found each other again.

This vision helped to cheer him up as he turned the key in the car. His sudden get-away startled the few parked motorists from their stolid gazing out to sea. He was unaware of curious eyes on him as the engine leapt into action, unaware that their ears were assaulted by the abuse he gave his car as he reversed rapidly and turned it for home. Let Pam be there, he prayed silently all the way home. Turning in the gateway he had an extraordinary feeling of certainty that his prayer would be answered. He drew the car to an abrupt halt outside the front door and bounced up the steps. The door was ajar. She was at home! She must be! Martha's solid sane figure was coming leisurely down the stairs as he dashed into the hall.

'Pam?'

His cry was a call of hope.

Martha's face was a picture of happy anticipation. She hurried down the last few steps.

'Where's my precious?'

He stood still unable to absorb the reality of the situation. Martha sensed something wrong. She clutched him by the elbow almost giving it a shake.

'The missus? Where is she? Has anything happened?'

Some of her anxiety seeped into his blurred consciousness. How could he keep it a secret from her? Her, of all people? He must tell someone. He couldn't take anymore. Unable to speak he put his arm around her and guided her into his study. He pulled her gently into a chair. Then he poured two brandies.

'Here.' He handed her one. 'You'll need it.'

She stared up at him with frightened eyes. 'Drink it,' he ordered.

She took one gulp and instantly spluttered into a bout of coughing. He took the glass from her and knelt down beside her patting her gently on the back. When she had recovered a little she looked at him, her face shattered by the experience.

'Excuse me, sir,' she gasped. 'I'm not used to that,' indicating the brandy.

He handed the glass back to her. 'Drink the rest. You won't find it too hard now.' Still kneeling, he finished his drink while he watched her sipping the remainder of the brandy. He put the two empty glasses aside and took her two hands in his. When he told her what had happened Martha did not break down or go to pieces as he had expected.

He was grateful for her calmness, her silence, broken only by sad comments: 'You poor man... My poor missus.'

When he had finished she put her arms around him and drew his face to her chest as she would a child. It was the last thing he wanted yet the one thing he needed most. The few remaining threads of stoicism which he had held onto broke under the love and compassion she gave him. He broke down and sobbed. He clung to Martha as a child would cling to its mother, and she patted him and held him until his tears were exhausted, her own silent anguish betrayed by the tears streaming down her face.

Chapter Twelve

After seven days with no word from his wife, Pat McElroy felt he could no longer keep up the pretence that she was due to return home shortly, either to himself, or to his friends.

It was farcical expecting his friends to believe that Pam should wish to convalesce with his mother rather than at home. And how long more must he pretend to be away to his mother, enjoying a few quiet uninterrupted days with Pam? He would have to face facts: get help in finding Pam. He was clinging more and more to the theory that Pam must be suffering from amnesia or a breakdown of some kind. She was not capable of doing this either to himself or to the children.

Granted, she did write the note stating her intentions, she did leave the hospital feeling she could no longer live with him, but having taken this first step, a step totally foreign and abhorrent as it must be to her nature, the enormity of her action would have become too much for her and by now she must need help. He had fooled himself into believing that help would not be necessary, that he would not have to resort to any publicity or exposure no matter how mild, as Pam would return. But hope, stubbornness and pride were of little value now. They had not helped to bring her back. For whatever reason, Pam was not coming back.

He was still loath to call on the police but he must look for help from someone. The first person that came to his mind was Tony, a barrister and a man with a lot of common sense. He would take him into his confidence. Tony would advise him what to do. He dialled his phone number. Virginia, his wife, answered. Tony was in Donegal but she expected him back tomorrow. Oh, she had almost forgotten, he wouldn't be coming straight home. He had promised to drop in on Michael and Vienna. They were giving a farewell party for Sally who was off to the States in a few days. He would see him there if he were going. She would be going with Margo and Barry.

'By the way, are you going?'

'I'd like to but I've a lot of work to catch up with, though I might drop in sometime late in the evening and see Tony for a few minutes.'

'Come as early as you can. It's a pity Pam can't be with you. How is she?'

'She's fine but I think she's getting restless.'

He was surprised at the glib way he could handle each sticky situation once he got over the initial shock that people were innocent of the nightmare he was going through. As he left down the receiver he wondered were people that gullible. Did they believe his excuse? Was it his fevered imagination that sometimes led him to read suspicion into every nuance and inflexion in people's voices? Or was it his own disbelief in the information he gave out that made him suspicious of everybody? There was something else; something if under ordinary circumstances he thought was true would have made him indignant, but under these extraordinary circumstances offered him a kind of cheerless comfort: people were not really that interested in you. When out of courtesy they asked questions about your health, your family's health or anything else connected with your well-being, most of them wouldn't really be listening to what you were saying, but waiting for you to finish so as to talk about themselves. Perhaps this is the way it is as regards the enquiries about Pam, apart from the fact that he knew she wasn't the most popular person among his friends and her heroic act had ceased to be a nine-days' wonder, but because his ears were attuned on account of the circumstances, what he had mistaken for suspicion was really a case of lack of interest. This construction, though it helped, pushed him back into the deep, dark ravine of loneliness that was so much part of his life just now. All around him were friends and how few there were to whom he could say:

'You understand. You know me. I need your help,' and be sure his appeal would be answered in the way he wanted. There was only one who could answer willingly and she wasn't there.

Pam McElroy had given a good deal of thought to where she would stay in London for the few days she needed before her holiday in Spain. The quiet of Mrs Howard's hotel, or accommodation in one of the more impersonal hotels she was familiar with? She had finally settled for Mrs Howard's place. Shortly before she had left hospital she had sent her a note telling her to expect her for a few days; not to bother about sending anyone to meet her. She knew her note would come as a surprise as correspondence between them had ceased except for the exchange of Christmas greetings. Nevertheless, she felt sure of a welcome and nothing surprised Mrs Howard any longer, or Auntie Kit as she called her. Would she have to tell her aunt anything? She thought not and she would prefer not. It was the feeling of confidence in the incurious nature of her old friend that finally decided her to seek her out. It would be a home away from home and the small hotel held many dear memories of her childhood for her. Mrs Howard was a distant relation of her father, a second cousin of his mother. She loved Auntie Kit and her husband Uncle Tom, the memory of whom represented happiness and security in a vast whirligig of a city. She had rarely seen their daughter Barbara who was married to an army officer stationed abroad. Howard's hotel played no small part in those far-off happy years, and she had continued to stay there on her visits to London as a young girl and after she had married. The Howards had been unable to come to her wedding as Uncle Tom had had a heart attack shortly before and was dead within a few days. Ken, her son-in-law, retired from the army some time later and he and Barbara helped to run the hotel. There were visits from Auntie Kit to the Aerie and she and Pat stayed with her when they visited London but Pat soon found excuses for not going there. He preferred the impersonal atmosphere of the more modern hotels and it wasn't as if they couldn't afford them. A lot of her enthusiasm for visiting London waned as a result and she stopped going.

Now she was here. Kevin and Barbara received her with open arms. They had got only the briefest reference to her accident in Mrs Howard's note and though Pam tried to enlarge on it she knew they could not absorb it because of the excitement of seeing her again. It acted like a tonic to feel such warmth and kindness surround her.

Barbara said: 'Mama will be so furious that she wasn't here to welcome you. She's out shopping for an autumn outfit.'

Pam was drinking a cup of tea when Mrs Howard showed up. She put out her arms and held her close. Her cheeks were wet.

'How thin you are.'

When she sat down she said: 'Tell me about yourself. About your accident. Everything. What happened?'

'If I had only known,' the old lady said, when Pam had finished, 'I would have gone to see you. Why weren't we told? Why didn't Pat write?'

'Pat didn't know whether he was coming or going he had so much on his mind.'

'Where is he now? Why didn't he come with you?'

The old lady sounded as cross as she allowed herself to be.

Pam laughed. 'It wasn't his idea that I came on my own.' How true that much was, she told herself. 'I wanted to come on my own to prove that I'm nearly back to my own self.' A long time was spent going over the happenings of the recent months. How the children took it? Martha? Was Pam fully recovered?

Pam said: 'Let's get off the subject of me and talk about you instead.'

When Ken and Barbara left to attend to their business Mrs Howard looked intently at her visitor.

'Any other news for your old auntie?'

'There's nothing more to tell.'

Pam knew her aunt was not just being curious. She must sense there was something wrong and in her gentle way was offering help. Mrs Howard did not pursue the question further. Her face relaxed and she smiled. That smile made Pam move the tea trolley out of the way to sit down on the floor beside her as she often did as a child, resting her two arms on her lap.

'I have left Pat.'

'And the children?'

'And the children.'

Mrs Howard's face betrayed no emotion. She sat still, her eyes staring into space. Pam waited. At last she could contain herself no longer.

'Why don't you ask me why?'

'There's no need to ask. I feel I know the answer.'

'You mean you're not surprised, horrified or something!'

Pam refused to accept that this terrible thing she had done should be taken so coolly as if it were a normal everyday occurrence.

'Surprised? No. Horrified? Yes. To think it should have come to this!'

'You couldn't know, I mean about Pat and me.'

'I didn't know, I certainly could not know that things had reached such a climax, but years ago I saw the direction you were both going.'

She placed her hands on Pam's shoulders. 'Do you know the kind of girl I once knew you to be? I watched you all through the years from babyhood to womanhood. You were like a daughter to me and I was as proud of you as any mother could be, but that didn't prevent me from seeing what was happening to you. I haven't spent almost eighty years in the world going around with my eyes closed.' She dropped her hands from Pam's shoulders. 'I wouldn't have this happen to you for all the world. You of all people.' She sighed. 'You and Pat seemed to have been made for each other. What went wrong? I'll tell you what. Pat couldn't leave you as you were, the girl he loved. He must bend you to his way even when it came to the smallest thing. You didn't see what was happening to yourself. You were being stripped of your own personality and, dammit, you didn't seem to mind. I wanted to shout at you at times to stand up for yourself. I tried to give you a hint now and again but I don't believe you even suspected what I was getting at. I went so far as to mention it casually to your father and mother. Your father laughed, said you were too high-spirited to allow that kind of thing to happen. Your mother didn't say much and that worried me because mothers don't miss much, and I bet she didn't either. The wise ones don't interfere and hope for the best; the foolish ones, and I'm afraid I was one of them at one particular time, would try and right things and aggravate matters, more than likely.'

She sighed deeply, her face clouded. She was silent for some moments, then she roused herself. 'You were such a happy person, full of the joys of life whenever I met you, so that I often said to myself my imagination must be playing tricks with me. I remember the occasion when quite a time had elapsed since our meeting each other and I thinking: "My God, what a change." You had become very quiet and though you still smiled and laughed there was no smile or laughter in your eyes. I travelled back with you to Ireland then and stayed a few days with you and it was during that time I saw the whole picture, and I couldn't hold my tongue any longer. Of course you never knew anything about this, and of course I shouldn't have interfered. But there are times I'm not one for taking my own good advice. I did poke my nose into affairs that weren't my business and I find it hard to forgive myself for that, but at that time I hoped I was doing it for the best and that some good would come of it. I didn't care two hoots what Pat would think of me. If we never saw each other again it would be worth it if I had succeeded in the smallest way in forestalling what I thought was inevitable.'

Pam was shaken. 'What did you say?'

'I don't want to go into the whole thing but I let him know what I saw was happening to you. I actually said that you were being stripped of your own attractive personality, that you seemed to have no will of your own, that his will was all that mattered to you, things like that; that what I was saying to him was not the result of some quick judgement but rather an observation that had been forming for some years. Things like that.'

'How did Pat react?'

'He took it very well. As a matter of fact he took it too well. Without saying much he more or less and very inoffensively, I must say, he put me firmly in my place. At the end of it all I was left with the distinct and uncomfortable feeling that I was just an old interfering woman who had more time on her hands than she knew what to do with.'

Pam said: 'Nobody could ever think that of you.'

'Ah, you could be prejudiced.'

'You know I'm not.'

Both women remained silent, each occupied with her own thoughts. Mrs Howard was the first to speak.

'The most insidious thing about your marriage, as I saw it, was that no one could point the finger and say: "Pat is a terrible man and Pam has an awful lot to put up with." What isn't seen in other marriages as well as yours, because your set-up is not unique, is the day-to-day wear and tear. What marriage can ask of a woman? Before marriage a woman has, as a rule, a career or job of some kind. She has money of her own, freedom to do what she likes with that money, a limited number of working hours, holidays with pay. She has time off to be sick, to be hospitalised if necessary. She has freedom to make up her own mind about things. People respect her opinions. In fact she is a person. Then she gets married. Now she has two roles to fill. She's still a person but now she's also a wife. She is free, or so she thinks, in the beginning. She accepts certain responsibilities and restrictions as she did without question in her job before marriage, except this time they are accepted with love and greater enthusiasm. Many women aren't even aware of such a thing as acceptance. It's part of their nature. Like a second skin. True, they have lost their earning power, but that's not even thought of until their moderate need of money is questioned by the loving husband whose marriage vows included, "With all my earthly goods I thee endow!" Then there's the third role: being a mother.

'Now, if a wife is to be the happy, well-adjusted person she should be, she must be allowed to live these three vital roles as fully as possible. And how often the three are constantly in conflict with each other. And how many times is that hoary old chestnut thrown up by the husband: "Everything was fine until the children came along. Then she had no time for me." Such humbug! I could write a book about that old excuse alone. What men forget is that as far as they're concerned marriage and children haven't interfered with their daily routine to any noticeable degree. They leave the house in the morning to do their day's work. They still earn their day's wages or salaries – they don't have to depend on their partners for that – and they may feel a greater sense of responsibility because now they have someone else besides themselves to look after.

'Granted, they share this income with another person or persons, but there again this can be done on the basis that favours are being granted or worse still, that money is being handed out with no visible return for it. So many husbands still live out their bachelor lives, nights out with the boys, plenty of spending money, few domestic worries. They have a good housekeeper, a faithful but unpaid mistress and someone to rear their children. Thank heavens there are men who are all that husbands should be, otherwise we women would begin to think we were aiming for the impossible. And the laughable part is, if men weren't so blind they'd see that if they acted more like husbands as the Lord intended husbands should act, they would be winners all the way in the happiness and contentment stakes, as a happy, loving, contented wife is worth more than her weight in gold.'

The younger woman couldn't help smiling. 'That sounds like something from one of the Psalms.'

'I wouldn't know. I'm not a reader of Psalms.' She pressed Pam's arm. 'Thank God you haven't lost your sense of humour. But to get back to you and Pat. As I've said, I saw trouble early on and I was hoping against hope it would pass.' She paused for a moment. 'Tell me something, Pam, something I don't understand. Why have you left the children? Surely you should be at home with them and Pat could go somewhere else to live. That would have solved a lot of problems.'

Pam told her Pat's reaction to the suggestion of separation and the ugliness that would result from it. For the children's sake it was the one thing she wanted to avoid.

'What do you think Pat will do now that you've left? Will he try to look for you? Or what do you hope from it?'

'What do I hope from it? I didn't go through all this just to hope. It's because I've lost all hope that I'm here. If I had any hope there would be a change for the better, even the tiniest sign, I would be at home with Pat right now. As for what Pat will do?' She passed a weary hand over her forehead. She was so tired. So terribly tired. 'I don't know what he'll do. I don't think I know Pat anymore.'

Mrs Howard saw the strain beginning to tell on the pale face. 'Look, I'm a stupid, thoughtless old woman. Here you are right out of hospital after a tiring journey, sitting on the floor instead of being up in your bed resting.'

She made to get up but the younger woman pressed her back into her chair. 'Auntie Kit, before I go tell me one thing. Have I done right? Deep down in my heart I know it's not the right thing to do, but under the circumstances, have I done right?'

The old lady pondered the question for some moments, head bent. At length she lifted her head and looked into the troubled amber eyes. What could she say? There was no answer.

'I'm not so sure that I'm gifted with wisdom as I am with length of years and it's not for me to advise you about your marriage. But since you ask, I believe if there was a way out you would have taken it rather than this final step.'

'Thank you.'

It helped Pam considerably to know there was at least one person in the world who understood, who realised in some way what forced her into making a decision of such gravity. She knew only too well how her action would be misconstrued by Pat, Pat's mother, Pat's friends. But that didn't matter now. She felt she had been condemned without trial a long time ago. To be condemned in her absence was of little importance. She went to bed. Later, when she awoke, though her body was still tired, her head was clear. She dressed and went downstairs. The rest of the evening was spent talking over old times. Pam was glad the talk centred around her own childhood and not around the children. Just now she didn't want to think about them or she would go out of her mind. She knew this forced respite could end at any time and when it did ...

Barbara and Ken talked amusingly about the running of the small hotel, the kindness and thoughtfulness of some of their guests, many of whom they regarded as old friends, and how they would be lost without their mother who looked after all the correspondence and was no end of help in seeing to the comfort of everybody.

Mrs Howard feigned complacency: 'I'm not such a bad old stick after all, Pam. I have my uses.'

They were nice people and she felt at ease with them. No

prying. No innuendoes. She was accepted as one of the family. Mrs Howard saw her to her bedroom.

Her room was not the one she had been used to. Alterations had been made. She remembered when she slept in a room with her parents – she must have been only four or five – they had been next door to one of the guests who snored. She had been wakened by it and not knowing what it was she had crept out of the bed and gone over to her father and mother who were asleep. She tugged at her father's shoulder.

'Daddy, I think there's a pig in the room.' Her mother was fully awake before her father eventually collected his wits. Since he was slow in doing something about it she squeezed in beside him. Her mother switched on the bedside lamp.

'A pig in the room?' her father said, blinking in the light.

'Yes, Daddy. Listen. He's over there,' and she pointed to a wardrobe in the furthest corner of the room.

She was more startled by her mother's sudden laughter than by the pig grunting. Then her father laughed and she looked bewildered from one to the other. Had they really got a pig hidden in the wardrobe? She didn't like pigs with their tiny eyes and ugly noses.

'The pig has stopped grunting,' she said, when her father and mother stopped laughing. They listened, but now she didn't care whether there was a pig in the room or not. She was safe and she couldn't keep awake. Next morning she heard her parents whispering about the snoring habits of the person next door.

She sighed. It seemed part of another world. Slowly she began to undress. She willed herself to control her thoughts; to let them wander unbridled was dangerous. She knelt down to say her prayers. *Oh, my babies!* Her arms dropped on the bed and she flung her head on them in agony. And then her resolution not to dwell on painful thoughts pushed through her distress; she levered herself from the bed and turned back the bedclothes.

She liked to snuggle well down under the clothes so that only the tip of her hair was seen. Once, a long time ago, Pat said how funny she looked. She was cut out to be a hibernating creature as she did such a thorough job of burying herself in preparation for sleep. *Oh God, I mustn't think like that.* She was grateful she was not sleeping in a double bed. *God, please help me to forget.*

There was a knock on the door. A maid came in with a tray followed by Mrs Howard. Mrs Howard drew back the curtains and looked down on the sleepy face.

'That's much better. You look as if you had a good night's sleep.' Pam slowly sat up in bed, rubbing the sleep from her eyes.

'Is it morning already? What time is it?'

'Just after ten.'

'Good heavens! I've slept twelve hours. That's disgraceful.'

Mrs Howard laughed. 'We wouldn't have wakened you, only we thought, being used to having an early breakfast in hospital, you might wake up with a headache if left too long without something in your tummy. That doesn't mean you get up after breakfast. Take it easy and if you don't take my advice I'll make it an order'.

There was an extra cup on the tray and Mrs Howard poured the tea for herself. She lit a cigarette and gave a satisfied puff.

'It's not often I indulge in these things,' she said as she examined the tip of her cigarette.

'But I like to be able to put my finger on one just in case.'

Breakfast was a lengthy affair. Mrs Howard rang for more tea. Under the motherly and understanding influence Pam found herself talking about her married life. The old lady listened without interruption while she unbottled accumulated troubles and sorrows. For the younger woman it was an unburdening of a weight that had become too heavy for her to carry alone.

She shuddered.

'Are you cold?' Mrs Howard asked.

'No. Must be someone walking over my grave.'

When Mrs Howard left the room the maid came with the

morning papers and removed the tray. She looked disinterestedly at the headlines. She yawned and lay back, pulling the clothes over her, and slept.

After lunch she said to Mrs Howard: 'Tomorrow you and I must go shopping. Everything is too loose for me and I was hoping to buy a few smart things while in London. Not too many. Just enough to tide me over until I regain my normal weight.' Her eyes travelled down the dress from the two-piece she had travelled in.

Mrs Howard directed a mock-reproachful glance at her daughter: 'It seems there's one person at least around here who appreciates my fashion sense.'

She gazed at the thin pale face. 'But surely you won't be able for any kind of shopping. Remember, you've been immobilised for months.'

'Not quite. The therapist has been working on me and I feel, if not exactly as fit as a fiddle, I feel fit enough for a harmless bit of shopping. This isn't going to be a mad shopping spree.'

Mrs Howard shook her head doubtfully. 'We'll see what you'll be like in the morning.'

'Oh, I'll be fine. And we'll take it easy of course.'

She was looking forward to the shopping expedition. As she made up her face she realised how quickly she tired and she must remember, as her Aunt Kit had reminded her, that she had only come out of hospital.

Her aunt knew all the right places and some of the staff. As she followed her around she couldn't help admiring her energy and verve. Even to think of her as old seemed out of place. She was small and slender and had a well-proportioned figure. No wonder she still got satisfaction in wearing stylish clothes. Her skin looked neither shrivelled nor aged and her grey eyes looked out mischievously from underneath her dark eyebrows. Pam said, looking at the dark eyebrows and grey hair, 'I wonder how many people think your eyebrows are dyed,' as they waited for an assistant to attend them. 'Barbara hasn't got your eyes.'

'No, she has her father's kind eyes.'

Pam felt young and free except when her mind wandered to her last shopping expedition. Each time the face of her little daughter kept thrusting itself between her and Mrs Howard, each time the echo of her chuckle or remark drowned what her aunt or the assistant was saying she pushed the scene away. Only by instantly recalling the different pictures of Pat could the double exposure blur the imprint of painful thoughts.

Left alone in the fitting room as Mrs Howard and the assistant searched the rails for what they wanted, she pinned her mind down to practical things such as her immediate plans. She was due to go to Spain on Thursday but in the meantime she had an appointment at St. James's Hospital for Tuesday and another at Radcliffe's on Wednesday. Each of them had an excellent paediatric unit, the only thing against her was her long lay-off from work, but she had never allowed herself to be out of touch with modern medicine. The main thing was to get established. She shivered. *Somebody's walking over my grave again,* she thought.

Pam had a restless night. She woke up once sobbing and calling out something, she could not remember what. Her words came with strange strangling sounds, slurring and slipping away from her. She had been walking over her own freshly made grave. She was buried underneath and yet she or her spirit was pacing up and down the mound of gluey brown earth, her feet getting heavier and heavier as more and more soil clung to them in an adhesive mass. She must walk endlessly up and down this tiny space. She supposed she would eventually be covered by the clinging, sticky earth. The weight of it was too much for her. She was so tired. The mass of earth adhering to her was pulling her down but she was too terrified to sit down and rest. Then to her horror, her foot slipped through a hole that had not been there before. She tried to pull it back but another hole appeared. Crouching sideways she peered into this hole. There, a few inches from the surface was the sea, curling, greedy, licking. Licking away at the sticky brown soil, drawing it into its frothy depths. The hole was getting wider and wider. Her whole leg had now gone through the first hole. She struggled hard to escape. She tried to call for help but her voice would not come. Her cheeks were puffed out forcing her frozen lips apart. Then her mouth was open and strange sounds escaped.

She was still sobbing as she sat up in bed looking around her trying to place where she was. She looked for the familiar shape under the bedclothes.

'Pat, it was awful.'

Then she realised she was sleeping alone. She turned her head and saw the outline of the other bed and gradually it came to her where she was. The terror of her dream lingered. She switched on the light and lit a cigarette. As she stubbed it she glanced at her watch. Only half past one. A long sleepless night was in front of her. She switched off the light and lowered herself under the blankets. She fell asleep but woke again and again, nightmare succeeding nightmare until she reached the point where she was afraid to close her eyes lest she should sleep and be subjected to another terrifying dream.

Mrs Howard opened the door of Pam's bedroom and walked noiselessly over to the bed. Pam was lying on her back, her face knotted in troubled sleep, the bedclothes rumpled. She was about to turn away and let her sleep on when Pam opened her eyes.

'I see you've had a great night of it', Mrs Howard said as she bent down to kiss her. She set about re-arranging the clothes.

'You can say that again. Don't bother about the bed. I'll be getting up soon.'

'That remains to be seen', Mrs Howard said, continuing to put sheets and blankets into place. 'I over-tired you yesterday. I can't think how I could be so stupid.'

'I'm perfectly all right.'

'You're going to spend all day in bed to undo the damage of yesterday. Your meals will be sent up to you and I'll get one of the staff to bring you the television from my room.' She noticed her visitor didn't look at all well. As she left the room the idea she would not have entertained up to now struck her as being the only sensible course of action to take: get in touch with Pat. Let him take the next plane, not tell Pam and take her by surprise. If this were done it might be the means of sorting out the whole sorry mess. Whatever feelings Pat had for Pam, she sensed that in spite of all that had happened, Pam still loved Pat. All she needed was a sign of some sort that things could change for the better. Supposing her disappearance had shocked Pat into thinking: that was something he must never have done or things would never have come to such a pass. If only there was a solution. How terrible to see two people drawn to each other originally by love now driven apart through lack of love. Was it possible they meant nothing to each other? Parting as battle-scarred foes, the marriage wars now over.

On second thoughts she rejected the notion she had of contacting Pat. She must remind herself that Pam was her first consideration. She had come to them looking to their friendship and love, the peace and security of their home as a kind of limbo, and she could stay for as long as she wanted.

Mrs Howard sighed. Life could be so complicated. Two intelligent, educated people travelling on two separate roads when they were meant to travel on the one road. She looked out the window of their sitting room. Such a lovely world this Sunday, here in the heart of London. Who would think in this quiet moment plucked from a restless, never ceasing world, that hearts were breaking, minds were bending or disintegrating and bodies were abused or cruelly used. Wounds and bruises everywhere. Sometimes masked or so well hidden as to be almost invisible. Her thoughts saddened her but she shook them off. But there was no avoiding the fact that many marriages were breaking down and Pam and Pat were only two more casualties. Not every marriage would end in the divorce courts, but divorce was there in the homes.

If married couples could only live as harmoniously as so many people did in religious communities. People from all walks of life, sometimes of a different race who couldn't possibly find each other's company constantly congenial, were able to live peacefully together. But then these men and women were given adequate preparation for the religious life. Six, seven or more years of concentrated preparation. What sort of preparation was given to prospective married couples? Was falling in love and enough money for a down-payment on a flat or house sufficient preparation? Was preparation for marriage, preparation for life on the school curricula? How much attention did the churches pay to the need for marriage preparation? Then there were the people with the clever answers: the home was the place where people learned about life; the home was the place from which one got all the guidelines necessary for the preparation of marriage. But in many families it wasn't possible to pass on what was never there. Had the overcrowded classrooms with their surplus of unrealistic subjects, time or facilities for imparting knowledge on the most important subject of all – family life? Mrs Howard fixed an angry eye on a policeman passing by.

She walked over to the other window which looked out onto her garden. She drew back the curtains to take in the beauty of her own little corner of the world. She liked to look out there. On the other side of the main entrance were the hotel dining room and lounge quarters. The dining room's extension was mostly glass and looked out onto the garden she had wrested from the cobblestones and stark surrounding walls. There wasn't a grey piece of wall to be seen anywhere. When she had first come to the place a sycamore tree had taken up most of the space. She had no regrets over its removal especially when she saw what results were achieved. More light in all the back rooms and a place for herself in the sun. She had asked the workmen to leave the tree stump; she had plans for that unlovely object. She would have no more trees. She concentrated on climbing and wall plants. A pergola of climbing roses with purple clematis made a focal point. She had clematis clothing her walls in pink and lavender blossoms, in white and brilliant red. She used as hosts for her clematis evergreen ceanothus, pyracantha and escallonia, so that winter or summer she never felt shut in by the sight of grey walls.

There were boxes and tubs of plants, some of them spilling their contents over the edges. In spring those containers were filled with daffodils and crocuses, tulips and hyacinths. She had trailing flowers over the sycamore stump. Here in this tiny corner of the world she found peace and tranquillity. Here was beauty wrested from a patch of what seemed a hard and unyielding piece of ground. Though it was a small thing to have done, still it hadn't been done by just sitting and staring at it, willing it into existence.

She had worked hard at it and now she enjoyed the results. But that didn't mean that all work could stop. She still had to care for it and tend it. A little consistent attention paid rewarding dividends. 'Consistent' was the operative word. Wasn't it the operative word if one wanted to achieve rewarding results in any walk of life? Hadn't one to work consistently to make a marriage happy? There she was back on the same theme again. But then, would there ever be a time in the future when her mind wouldn't dwell on it?

Pam ate most of her breakfast but without enthusiasm. She pushed the tray away and lit a cigarette. But even that too was distasteful and after two or three pulls she stubbed it out. She felt weak and depressed by the nothingness of her life and the bleakness of the future. Her mind searched a reason for living. Where were Rosemary and Robert now? They were becoming shadowy creatures, no longer any part of her. She could feel no love for them, could scarcely recall the image of their faces, the sound of their voices, the ring of their laughter. She tried to summon up some emotion but she was in a vacuum.

As in a dream she remembered something like this happening to her before. How did she get over it? Panic took over. She beat her head ceaselessly on the pillow, against the headboard, willing to feel at least some physical sensation. Was she dying? She sat up in bed to try her strength. It must be something worse than dying. She must be going out of her mind. She thought of the sleeping pills in her bag but there weren't enough of them to finish her off. If she jumped out of the window? She was on the second floor and might live after the fall. She tumbled out of bed and dragged herself half-fainting to the door, but before she reached it, it was opened and Sandra, one of the staff coming in with the papers, collided with her. The girl shrieked as Pam collapsed at her feet.

Pam opened her eyes and looked around.

Mrs Howard said: 'Don't worry. You only fainted.' She forced the concern from her face and smiled. 'Just the result of overdoing it yesterday, but we're getting the doctor to look in on you just to make sure everything is all right.'

Pam nodded. She lay, eyes closed, suspended in a world of mist and buzzing sound, aware of the presence of Mrs Howard and Ken but unable to wonder or care why they were there. Mrs Howard noticed her attempts to moisten her lips.

'Ken, we all could do with a cup of tea,' she said, trying not to sound as alarmed as she felt.

After Pam had taken the tea she said: 'I'm beginning to think I'm not able for a London holiday. So if you don't mind I'll go home, perhaps on Thursday. In the meantime I promise I'll give you no more frights.'

What had she said? She wasn't going home. She meant to say she was going to Spain. She had an idea. She would work on it later. For the present she would go along with what she had said.

Mrs Howard's happiness at the extraordinary turn events had taken without any help or interference from her was concealed under a cloak of practicality.

'You're quite right, Pam. London is no place for a restful holiday especially a convalescing one and to be quite frank, I'm not the best sort of company for you in the present circumstances. I'm too restless. Always on the go. Perhaps my extreme youth is to blame.'

'Isn't that what I'm always telling you? Barbara and I can't keep up with you,' Ken said, slapping her on the shoulder.

'All the same, go easy with those hearty slaps, fella. Well, that's that. Home is the place for you, Pam.'

When the doctor had gone, having prescribed rest and confirming Mrs Howard's diagnosis that she had fainted, Pam said when they were alone: 'Auntie Kit, you know what I said about going home, I meant of course...' She stopped. She couldn't say it. How could she disappoint someone who loved her, as she once said, as if she were her own daughter? She would have to think of something between this and Thursday. In the meantime what was the harm in a little deception?

'I meant it.'

'Thank God for that.'

Pam lay back in bed after Mrs Howard had gone and looked at the patch of blue sky that squeezed itself between the maze of buildings. Was it her subconscious, she wondered, that had made her say what she had said about going home. To hell with Pat. To hell with what he thought or would think, how he treated her in the past or how he would treat her in the future. She wouldn't sacrifice her two children for a harem of husbands, if there was such a thing. What if he thought of her disappearance as melodramatic, as no doubt he would? What if he thought it typical and in keeping with her so-called instability? He wouldn't be surprised that she had taken such a step and he knew she would be back; she wouldn't have the guts to stay away. How easily his words came to mind. He despised her for hanging on and he would despise her for crawling back.

Was she really the person that Pat made her out to be? From the depths of her mind she dredged something she had wanted to forget. A scene with Penny. Penny had accused her of running to Pat for permission before doing anything; she had said things that had hurt her, that she thought were untrue. Later, she realised how true they were. How revolting she must have seemed to people. Sliding downhill can be remarkably trouble free. It was on climbing up that one expended so much energy and willpower, clawing at reasons why it was so necessary to keep going, hanging onto the rightness of her purpose, slipping back when the will was weakening and no ledge of salvation offered itself on which she could pause and take breath, and to wonder was it worth all the effort.

How could she have possibly conceived that in wanting to be herself, so much would have been involved? If she had foreseen the consequences it would have been better if her eyes had never been opened.

But now there was a decision to be made: to return home or continue with her plans.

Her new found courage was aborted by the dark memories of the past. It was easier to go ahead than to go back. For the moment she saw no way out of the dilemma with her Aunt Kit. And she was too tired to think of a solution.

Mrs Howard, Barbara and Ken were watching a television programme when she came downstairs to join them for a short period before settling down for the night. They moved to make a place for her as Ken turned off the set. It was Barbara who brought up the subject of her impending departure. She was taken off guard when it was suggested by her that Ken accompany her home. Seeing the look in Pam's eyes she added quickly:

'But perhaps Pat will want to come for you.'

Inspiration came: 'I'd prefer to go home without fuss as if I asked Pat to come for me he would think the worst and would you blame him? I was able to travel here on my own but couldn't make it back.' She saw she had dispelled her aunt's fears of a change of heart. She put her hand on Ken's knee. 'Thank you, Ken. Some other time I'd love you to come with me.'

Before she went to sleep she went over her plans. First, she would keep her appointment with the two hospitals. Her aunt would understand her interest in visiting such top hospitals though she might warn her about overtiring herself. Then there was the problem of easing herself out of Thursday's predicament. She'd have to pretend to make arrangements for a flight back to Dublin. When the time came she would take a taxi to the airport. Her aunt had a great dislike for airports and terminals of any kind and only tolerated them when she was travelling, so there would be little difficulty in putting her off from accompanying her and, as for Ken who would be sure to offer his company, she had no doubt she could handle him too. He was a person who took you at your word. Barbara would be kept busy that particular day having to cope with an American extended family who were staying in London for a few days.

Instead of taking the plane to Dublin she would have her lunch at the airport and wait for her flight to Malaga.

Chapter Thirteen

It was Thursday morning and Pat McElroy was fully awake after another restless night. He looked at his watch. Almost half past six. A week had gone by since Pam disappeared. A week in which he had heard nothing from her. It was incredible. His attitude was just as incredible. He had let seven days go by without doing anything because, he had argued to himself, his hands were tied. Now, he could no longer afford to delay. It had been up to him all along to make a move in spite of Pam's protestations to the opposite. Why had he stalled? Pam had never stopped him from doing anything he wanted to do. Why was it so important that he acceded to her wishes at this time above all others? He hunched himself under the bedclothes. If he were to be honest it was because he hoped she would come back without him having to take any messy or disagreeable steps for her return.

If it were only a simple straightforward case of missing persons there would be, comparatively speaking, no problem, though at all times he would class it as a nuisance; something that should never have happened. But Pam being Pam had to do things the awkward way. She had been such a cause of worry and trouble to him in the past days he wasn't quite sure whether the strange emotion he felt was one of love or hate, whether he wanted her back or not. The only thing he knew at this moment was that he must do something to bring things to a head or he would go crazy. But how to go about it? Had it not been for the children returning home tomorrow he might have been tempted, in spite of his newfound determination, to delay another day or two.

He would have to see Tony tonight. Virginia had said he would break his journey home to go to the party. Perhaps tomorrow Tony would be impossible to track down and further delay at this juncture was unthinkable. He would face the party tonight. He would make it halfway through and hope that Tony would be there before him. He would ring Vienna and tell her he was able to go after all but pressure of work might leave him a little late in arriving. After a decent interval he would try and catch Tony's attention and see if he could get him to his place without attracting too much notice. What if his friends there suspected something? The truth would be out sooner or later, perhaps the sooner the better. It would end too some of the suspense and strain he was under. Besides, he realised they were no fools. They must have come to their own conclusions already. He had nothing to be ashamed of. Or, had he?

His thoughts came to an abrupt halt as they always did when he attempted to delve into motives or actions he wasn't quite comfortable with. He smiled grimly to himself. She had done him wrong. These weren't quite the words but they suited the occasion. He found himself ludicrously trying to memorise the old song. He had done her wrong.

That was it! He stopped short. Was he going crazy mouthing the words of a stupid song at this hour of the morning? He sat up in bed and impatiently swept back the bedclothes. He sat still for a moment, then swung his legs onto the floor. He went through the motions of shaving, taking a shower and dressing. He scarcely touched breakfast and left the house without bidding goodbye to a disturbed and greatly worried Martha.

There was a busy schedule ahead and he wouldn't have the time to indulge in the luxury of self-pity. His work was one of his chief pleasures in life. Was there anything else to compete with it? Anything else that gave him such complete joy and satisfaction? The thrill of seeing the creations of his brain on paper and then in concrete and steel; it was creativity and progress. None of the children of his brain thwarted or worried him to any great extent. He loved his work and that love infused his work, giving it a vibrant and appealing freshness which, combined with a quality of beauty, made him, he knew, outstanding as an architect and designer.

He sat at his desk in a more relaxed frame of mind. But while he worked or talked with his colleagues that silly phrase kept jingling in his ears. He had done her wrong. He worked doggedly on but it was no good. All the pleasure he got from work had gone. He felt suddenly dry, withered. He could not go on. But that is exactly what he must do. Where had he read that when you feel like giving up that is the time when you must keep going? It was his day for recalling quotations or stupid songs. With a diligence he never had to exercise before he once more dug into work. A short while later he threw aside his papers in despair. His eyes followed the route his pen made as it rolled to the edge of the desk to drop onto the carpet. He leaned his elbows on the desk and supported his tired heavy head with his hands. He had done her wrong. The phrase jingled-jangled on and on until he thought his head would explode with its insistent clamour. It's all my fault. His hands dropped onto the desk and lay motionless, fingers curved limply. It's all my fault. Oh Pam, what have I done to you?

He rested his head on the desk feeling its hard surface against his hot sticky forehead. The padlocked gates of his tidy, ordered past were opened. He was sickened at what he saw. Was he really as bad as all that? His feelings of disgust grew stronger than his feelings of despair. *Pam, if you ever come back to me, if you want to come back, if I ever can get you to come back...* None of it seemed real. He stood up. He was feeling claustrophobic. He must get out.

He walked down the road and turned left. Then his eye caught the pub on the comer. He was thirsty and could do with a drink. He ordered a glass of lager. As he drank the last mouthful he thought it might not be a bad idea to include a sandwich with his next order. Just then he became aware of a pair of eyes covertly watching him:

'You don't come here often?'

'No, not often.' He looked the other way. He tried to catch the attention of the barman.

'Great sandwiches, eh?' his neighbour said, a sliver of fat dribbling from the corner of his mouth.

He got up hastily from his stool and left the pub. He walked aimlessly on, hands thrust deep in trouser pockets. He passed a boys' school. The children were streaming through the open gates, shouting, laughing, arguing, pushing. He leaned against the sea-wall and watched them. Some of them on bicycles swung dangerously onto the road. The traffic warden shook his fist at them and they saluted mockingly in return. He saw a small boy of about ten thumping another boy at the bus stop as the bus was coming up the road. Then all was forgotten as they moved with the others to get into the bus. The bus moved slowly and his eyes followed it until it turned the corner. He felt more desolate than ever. He was about to retrace his steps when he noticed the school chapel. Would he be regarded as a trespasser if he called in for a visit? Nobody accosted him as he walked up the driveway. As he ran up the few steps to the chapel door a cleric came out of the chapel and gave a half-smile in response to his salute. He walked down the aisle and knelt in the front seat before the altar. He leaned his elbows on the back support and bent his head. He could not pray. He let the tiredness and weariness drain from his mind and body. It felt good to be here with no distraction. There was time for reflection.

In his office he had been sickened as he looked into the past. In the quiet of the chapel, slowly and hesitatingly and for the first time he confessed to faults. He did not know all his faults; he might never know all and perhaps it might be just as well. He had enough to correct as it was. What he had confessed in the past had been slotted into the religious section of his life. Faults that could change or destroy himself or another person were in another area of his life that up to now had not been charted. And if he had known they were there would he have seen them as grave transgressions? He had always believed in God and performed his religious duties faithfully if automatically, but he never felt the need of God. God was pushed to the background of his life. Now he prayed with a simplicity that was strange to him.

As Pat McElroy drove the lengthy driveway that led to Vienna's house the reluctance he felt at exposing his private affairs struggled with the immediate sense of urgency to get working at once on his wife's disappearance. He stopped the car under the shade of a tree. What had seemed a fairly simple and practical procedure when he left the chapel, what seemed fairly straightforward as he lay in bed that morning, now appeared unreal and distasteful. Was it necessary to get help yet, to confide his troubles to anyone, to confess his failure as a husband? Because that is what it would amount to. Could he endure the humiliation of the whole thing? Confess that his wife had left him? Would some of them think she left him because she couldn't bear to live with him any longer? Some of his friends would take his side regardless of their ignorance of the total circumstances that had led up to Pam's sudden departure. Some of them quite openly barely tolerated her. Few would blame him as much as he now blamed himself for what happened. But there must be others who would ask questions, who would surmise, who would derive certain satisfaction from hints and rumours and jumping to conclusions. But why the devil was he so concerned about what people thought? It was what he thought of himself and that was pretty low at the moment and what Pam thought, which must be lower still, that counted. But he must be careful for himself and for Pam. See that Pam and he suffer as little as possible. And if anyone were to be the butt of criticism let it be he; Pam had gone through enough. Yet he cringed at the thought of it all. But he must act. He hoped to heaven Tony would be at the party.

He knew Pam wasn't with her father or with any of her relations;

they would have been too obvious a choice. At the same time he took no chances and on one pretext or another had phoned them. Then it dawned on him that she could have left the country; something he hadn't reckoned with Pam doing anything more imaginative than looking for a quiet spot in some part of the country. The other thought which he had originally harboured, even though only for a brief moment or two, he had dismissed as evil and not to be entertained on any account. This evening he had found out that Pam had taken a plane to London the day she left hospital. That was something to start with. But after that it was like looking for a needle in a haystack. That fellow who booked the flight, Peter Hogan, might know something. It was a stroke of luck that he remembered he had a travel agency. He had been a hit-and-run victim whom Pam had attended on the roadside and she visited him in the hospital for a while, but as far as he was aware there had been no communication between Pam and him for years. Unfortunately Hogan was away but would be returning tomorrow. He would phone him in the hope that he might be able to get more detailed information from him. It was a slim hope but one worth looking into. He dwelt on that slender hope, wanting to use it to avoid going any further with what he had planned, but he was catapulted into action when, by accident, his elbow came crashing down on the horn. He put his foot on the accelerator and slowly drove the rest of the way to the house. He rang the doorbell and after a few seconds a small pyjama-clad figure opened the door and peeped out.

'Hello, David. What on earth are you doing up at this hour?'

'I couldn't sleep with all the noise.'

'That's too bad,' Pat said with a sympathetic smile.

The boy closed the door but appeared in no hurry to leave the visitor. 'But what really kept me awake was something else.'

'And what was that?'

'Well I was thinking – it's a favourite daydream of mine – I would love if Mummy would let me use the basement. It would be like another house with my own bathroom and bedroom and things, where I can bring my friends.'

'Isn't that an awful lot to ask for a small fellow like you?'

The crestfallen face told him that the boy, who was ten, did not consider himself small.

'What I mean is, would you be willing to look after it?'

'I would have a go if Mummy would let me.'

'Does she think you're able?'

'She's always saying I don't know the meaning of the word tidiness.'

'And do you?'

'I guess I do, but I suppose I don't bother very much.'

'Well, there's your answer. Try to bother and she'll get the message.'

The boy looked thoughtful. 'I'll do that.'

He continued talking about his daydream as he led the way to where the party was. He knocked at the door. Without waiting for a reply he opened it and cleared his throat as he stood a little to one side.

'Ah – Mr Patrick McElroy.'

The sudden silence was followed by shouts of laughter. The two were immediately surrounded by a group of people. Pat looked down with affection at the boy who had eased an awkward moment for him. David was looking at his father and mother. Some of those grouped around them gradually moved away.

Pat said: 'About this idea of David's, his plans for the basement?'

Vienna said: 'So that's his little game. He has roped you in on it. I'll hand it to our first-born, he gets full marks for trying.'

David remained silent. He would let Mr McElroy do the work for him.

When the boy left he took with him Pat's brief respite from his trouble. Vienna noticed the change in him. She drew him aside and Michael left them.

'There's something worrying you, Pat. What is it?'

He had not been prepared for such an overture, yet he did not rebuff her. Vienna could be blunt but no one could doubt her sincerity. He looked around. There was nobody near enough to hear.

'Pam has left me. You know that?' His query was a statement of fact.

'I think we've all been suspecting something was wrong.'

For Vienna everything connected with Pam's departure from the hospital had an air of suspicion about it. Pat's secretive manner, his sudden withdrawal from their society, his lack of enthusiasm when asked how Pam was getting on pointed to something that was strange and unfamiliar to his close friends. There was only one explanation – Pam had made a move from one hospital to another, a psychiatric hospital. So what about it? That seemed inevitable too. Vienna's thoughts had gone off on a tangent. She could not grasp that Pam would or could leave Pat. Lethargic, irritating Pam doing anything so astonishing or indeed foolhardy as leaving her husband. But then, Pat had just said that. She said: 'Has she left you or have you agreed to separate?'

'She's left me. Had I known Pam was thinking that way I might have been able – I hope we would have been able – to talk it over and not have allowed things to go so far.'

'Do you know where she's gone to? Has she taken the children with her or are they still with the Butlers?'

He looked around. 'Do you mind if we go somewhere else to talk?'

'Not at all.'

She guided him by the elbow to the library.

'I feel lousy taking you away from your guests.'

'Don't worry. They won't miss me as long as the drink holds out.'

They stood facing each other in the middle of the room, awkward-looking yet with no hint of awkwardness between them.

Pat said: 'I notice Tony's here.'

He did not explain to her why he singled out Tony from the other guests but Virginia had already told her that Pat wanted to see him.

He said: 'The children are still with the Butlers but they're due home tomorrow.' He paused, his face a mask of bewilderment. 'How could Pam leave them? She idolises them.' He gave a deep sigh. 'She left me a letter.'

His hand probed an inside pocket and from a packet of letters he picked out the note that from wear and tear of constant handling was in a state of near disintegration. He handed it to Vienna. She read it quickly, then very slowly she read it once more. It was simply written. No wild accusations, no recriminations, no promises of revenge. Just a statement as to why she was leaving Pat. A gust of anger shook Vienna. Who doesn't feel at times like leaving one's marriage partner but why the hell had she to go through with it? Why didn't she talk it over with Pat first? If things came to such a head between Michael and herself she would have fought tooth and nail every inch of the way, and if it were a case of anyone packing a bag and leaving it would be Michael. Why should she uproot herself and leave Michael to the comforts of home and to the sympathy and support of his defenders? And then the children? That was the last straw. The idiot! To do such a thing! She looked up at Pat.

'She seems to mean what she says.'

'Pam always means what she says. She's an honest person.' Vienna stared at him. She did not expect that remark.

'I tried to tell myself she couldn't mean what she said in the letter. She would be back. I mean, you hear it happening to other people but you never dream it's going to happen to you.'

'Did she ever bring this up before? About leaving you?'

'Oh, she did. Once or twice. But who takes a threat like that seriously?'

'What I can't understand, Pat, is why didn't she look for a

separation if things were that bad and arrange things so that she could have the children?'

He remained silent. Pam had asked him several times, he painfully admitted to himself and, how had he reacted? He remembered now all too plainly what he had said, what threats he had made. Vienna saw his distress and, guessing inaccurately, what caused it let the question hang. She had never much time for Pam and she knew Pam didn't care for her, but that wasn't important now. What was important was to try and find a way out of this whole rotten business. The children were coming home tomorrow.

'Can I be frank, Pat?'

'I've never known you to be anything else.'

'I thought I noticed something strange about Pam's manner during her last few weeks in hospital. Did you?'

'I did.' His sombre eyes met hers.

'And I wasn't the only person to notice either. Sally, Margo, most of the others saw the change too.' She gave him a level gaze. 'It's difficult to put a finger on anything significant. I thought Pam was just being her old self again. Sally disagreed. According to Sally, whenever she went to see her on her own Pam was always in a good mood. It was only when some of the rest of us were around that she noticed a change; Sally put it down to tiredness or convalescing. But Pam had been so different in the earlier part of her time in hospital that I was beginning to get fond of her. Excuse me for saying that but I'm sure you noticed that Pam and I didn't exactly hit it off with each other. Then, the next thing, she's behaving erratically, charming one minute, then going off into one of her silent moods. It was a bit confusing too. At least with the old Pam you knew where you were. We think Pam may have been heading for a nervous breakdown. It even crossed our minds.'

She could not go on.

'What were you going to say?'

'Well... it seems horrible putting it like this... but when Pam didn't come straight home Margo and I decided we would phone the hospital to ask for Pam. We were told she had gone home. When we asked when, that we were friends of hers, we were given the information and that she went home by taxi. You had told us that your mother had called for her at the hospital and that she was going to stay with her for a while to rest. So we knew that something wasn't quite right.' The last few words were scarcely above a whisper.

He was shocked. That people, his friends, could do a thing like that. He stared at Vienna. She looked ill at ease. One thing he could say about her though, she was nothing if not honest. She didn't have to tell him.

He gave her an encouraging smile. Vienna took a deep breath. She wondered what Pat thought of her. She knew what she thought of herself – the lowest form of life.

She continued: 'Then as the days passed and seeing you so reticent and keeping yourself to yourself, we even jumped to one awful conclusion, but at the same time we couldn't help wondering about you, why you weren't doing something about – '

'Doing something about what?'

It was hideous enough discussing a certain possibility between friends who shared a common compassion and curiosity, but to come out with their suspicions to somebody so intimately connected with the subject was unthinkable. She closed her eyes and then she felt Pat's hand on her shoulder.

'It's all right. I'll say it for you. You thought Pam might have taken her own life and that it was only a matter of time before the truth was out. I thought of that too, but only for an instant. Nevertheless, the thought was there. In times like these all sorts of terrible things come into your mind. But Pam isn't the sort of person to do a thing like that. She's much too level-headed.'

For the second time Vienna was nonplussed by Pat's unpredictable remarks about his wife. He went towards the door. As he opened it he said: 'You're a good friend, Vienna. I hope I haven't spoiled the evening for you. I believe Sally is off one of these days. I haven't given her a wedding present yet though Pam reminded me several times and told me what to get, but I'll send it on to her. I hope she won't mind.'

'Indeed she won't. Besides, wouldn't it be better to wait until you and Pam choose it together.'

'Thanks for saying that. It's the most heartening thing I've heard for days.'

The noise of conversation reduced considerably as they entered the room. The music was still playing but nobody was dancing. Vienna was dismayed as she saw her guests dotted in small groups about the room with Sally sitting alone and strangely apart. Sally couldn't possibly be feeling neglected, surely; she wasn't that long out of the room. Probably, she was missing Morrison and feeling lonely at the break-up of the old life. She would go over to her as soon as she could and cheer her up. She threw Sally an encouraging smile and Sally responded.

Now, to liven things up a little. This was a party, she thought, not a blinking wake.

Things had slackened since Pat arrived. Not that she blamed poor Pat for that.

Sally couldn't help smiling as she saw how Vienna handled her guests. She moved among them, chatting, laughing, handing out drinks, changing the record, calling out to Michael, to attend to a guest. She found herself taking part in the fun, yet some part of her remained withdrawn, meditative. Almost reproachful.

Later, Sally's imminent departure set the tone for nostalgia and sentiment. The old crowd was beginning to break up.

'What with Morrison gone and Sally joining him soon; and now, there's Pam gone.' There was a small stunned silence as Margo, who had spoken, stopped suddenly.

No man is an island yet I feel like one now, Pat thought. *I am an island in this room among my friends. Tony knows I want him because Virginia will have told him that and yet I haven't been able to have a minute with him.* The others know the truth or near enough to it anyway but they don't want to get involved, at least not tonight. They're too busy enjoying themselves. Why should they want somebody depressing them with his personal problems? Perhaps tomorrow they may be willing to do something but, tonight? For tonight we'll merry, merry be. He was becoming more and more bitter, the more he thought about it. What was the point in hanging on? He would get no good out of Tony tonight. He might as well go home. But home to what? And now, Margo's faux-pas. Only that she had stopped so suddenly he would never have noticed anything, as most of the conversation before that had passed over his head. So they all knew. Well, it came as no surprise to him. He was aware in a detached way of Margo's scarlet face and veiled, accusing looks sent in her direction as he decided to bring to life her half strangled remarks.

'Yes, Pam is gone. There's no point in further pretence. And I don't know where she is.'

Thank God I don't have to pretend anymore, he thought. His eyes travelled around the immediate circle of friends. They too were visibly relieved. They too did not have to pretend any longer.

'To tell you the truth I had hoped that Pam would return home before this, that she would have changed her mind, but it doesn't seem so.'

He was oblivious of the silence that followed his remarks. His thoughts were with his wife. Where was she? Where could she possibly be out of all the possible and impossible places? Where would he start? And if he found her would she want to come home? Slowly he raised his head.

'I hope you'll forgive me, especially Sally in whose honour this party is held, if I can't enter into the spirit of the party. I'm afraid I only came here to track Tony down.' Tony gave a guilty start. 'You see, the children are coming home tomorrow and I don't know what to do or how to explain to them about their mother not coming back. I want Pam back. The children... I had thought she would surely be back in time for their return, but she hasn't even sent them a card.'

Sally's eyes were focused, as were all the others, on Pat, but unlike the others pity and sympathy did not flow out from her in his direction. Here was this man posing as the wronged husband, a forgiving husband, a more than generous husband willing to go to the trouble to look for a silly, useless woman whom everybody knew he would be better off without. She would have to hand it to him, he was a clever man. He attracted the right kind of attention in good times and in bad. He knew what to say. Saying little and saying it well. No display of justifiable anger, annoyance or ill-feeling towards that unfortunate, totally incompetent woman who was his wife. He looked the picture of utter sadness and weariness. What a part he was playing. Sally's eye glinted with anger.

The nerve to come here in the first place. What callousness to use this party as a backdrop to play out his private grief. He had apologised for putting a damper on her party. That it was her party was of no importance. What was important was that Pat had a whole week in which to do something about Pam's disappearance and by his own admission he hadn't done a thing, simply because he had hoped he would be saved the trouble. Pam, his good-for-nothing wife, without a mind of her own, would be lost in a world without him and when this was driven home to her she would, like Mary's little lamb, come trotting home carrying her tail behind her. Home to what? To somebody who now held the whip-hand and who would use it to advantage in the future. *Good for you, Pam! Out of all this tragedy I see at least one ray of comfort. You have brought him to his knees, because in spite of the impression he's making he hates it like hell; what he had to confess, what he's going through and what he will have to go through.* His pride had taken a heck of a wallop.

Her thoughts flew to Pam. She was alive, of course, in spite of a vague suspicion that had gone the rounds. Her friends had been quite blunt. Nothing that Pam would do would surprise them.

Tonight, Virginia had started the ball rolling by announcing that Pat had been on the phone to tell her he would be calling around, but she had not mentioned why. And Sally's reaction on hearing this had been: how dare he come here to enjoy himself not knowing where Pam is. Or did he know and not care? At least, now she knew he had come for a definite purpose and that was something in his favour. The guests were not really over-troubled or upset about Pam. They speculated, conjectured, which she had found disturbing. But what she had found more disturbing was the fact there hadn't been one person to say a good word about her. *It's true*, she thought, *when you're down you're down.*

But the most damning thing of all was that of all the women present there wasn't one except herself to speak up for Pam. When she had said it takes two to make or break a marriage there was a chorus of: not in this case. After some argument she had said: 'I'll admit that one partner can be doing most of the giving and the other taking; that can happen.' And now the more she thought about this the more she realised that this must be a common state of affairs in some marriages. 'So now I'm convinced that not only did Pam do her share in trying to make the marriage work, but that she did most of the giving.'

There had been more interruptions and though she continued to expand on this statement no one took her seriously and she shut up when Vienna said: 'That's my Sally. Always champion of the underdog.'

She found it impossible to talk to them. Instead she had listened and her heart had swelled with indignation, pity, sympathy, chagrin in turn as the conversation ebbed and flowed. Poor Pam. What chance had she ever got with Pat? What chance had she now with all these people eagerly batting for her husband? She thought of the two lovely children, innocent and unaware of the tragedy that was taking place in their absence. The whole thing would explode in their faces tomorrow causing who-knows-what damage unless Pat could handle the situation properly, but no matter how well he managed it, it was inevitable that damage would be done to them.

It was at this point she became confused. How could Pam do this to the children? How could any mother in her right mind desert her children no matter what the pressures were? She couldn't believe that Pam could do this thing, was capable of doing it. And if she did, it was because she wasn't responsible, not sane, as was the general opinion or, that she had no intention of leaving the children permanently. That must be the answer. She had almost forgotten that Pam was a doctor – Pam never alluded to her qualification – that she could walk into a job as soon as she was ready and strong enough to take up work. Perhaps that was what was in her mind all along. But why on earth couldn't she have waited? Convalesce at home. Look for a job and somewhere to live and then take herself off with the children. If she had done it the simpler way the children would be better protected from unnecessary suffering and distress, and she would have saved herself as well from considerable suffering. Besides, people would look upon it as a more rational move. Oh, to blazes with people! Let them think what they like, because that's what they were going to do anyway no matter what was involved.

Now Pat was here and he was at the receiving end of support, of advice and he was absorbing it all. She smiled grimly to herself. She took no part in the conversation. She looked at her friends, all impatiently waiting to get in their little piece. No one noticed her silence nor would she care if they did. She was fed up with this spectacle. She never thought she would be glad to get away, away from these people who were her friends.

How relieved she would be to see Morrison. If Morrison were here how would he react? Would he be the same as the others? No, not Morrison.

And then, insidiously, they crept into her mind, the remarks made by him. Casually, almost innocently, in reference to Pam and Pat. Pam didn't come off too well in them. Of course her name was rarely brought up by him which could be said about any of the men she knew. Pam was really of no interest to him. And why was she torturing herself about Pam? What good was it doing her or Pam? After all it wasn't her business and she was in no way responsible for it. She hadn't known Pam long enough to have contributed to her misfortune. She had never felt anything but liking for her. She believed, had the time been theirs, a good and lasting friendship would have grown between them. There was something about Pam that attracted her. But why this oppressive feeling? She wasn't guilty of anything.

That time when she first visited Pam's home; had Pam been trying to tell her anything then, confide in her? Surely not. One does not open up to a complete stranger and she didn't believe Pam was the type of person to confide very much in anybody. Her thoughts skimmed over other conversations; chats on the phone, visits to the hospital. Was there any one time when Pam was looking for help from her? When she had been alone with Pam, Pam spent most of the time asking her about her wedding preparations, the world outside; she was a good listener and seemed to enjoy all the news and gossip. She was quite sure Pam hadn't tried to confide in her at any time. She probably felt, and rightly so, that this was something she must do alone. But the pity of it all was that she didn't confide in her. If she had suspected for one moment that this was the way Pam's mind was working, she would have used every ounce of persuasion to stop her.

There had been alternatives and she would have forced her, if necessary, to see them. The truth was Pam didn't regard her as a friend. Pam had no friends, it seemed. Just then she felt like crying on someone's shoulder. If only Morrison were here. How she loved that man. How kind and gentle he was. How strong and dependable. For the second time tonight she wished she were out of here, safe in his arms, surrounded by the security of his love and friendship. And then she was stabbed by the thought that that was how Pam must have felt about Pat at one time in their lives. To love so much, to want to give so much was almost unbearable to contemplate, and Pat must have loved her as much in return. How could such love and goodness turn into such a nightmare? How long did it take for that to happen? How could such love, the love she and Morrison had for each other right now be so destroyed? And yet, such a change must have taken place between Pam and Pat.

And Pam's situation was not unique. Marriages did break up for various reasons. Luckily, not in any great numbers. Imagine somewhere in the distant future she walking out on Morrison or he walking out on her; it took her all her time to control her emotions. She was brought back to reality by the movement of chairs.

Pat was leaving: 'I'm afraid I have to be going, but don't let me break up the party. I know that you'll understand that Tony, by kind permission of Virginia,' he smiled at Virginia, 'and I have to discuss certain things before we start the ball rolling tomorrow. Tony is coming over to my place. I hope you don't mind, but you see, every minute counts from now on.'

'Why should it? Why should every minute count and be so important now, when days, weeks and even years didn't count when you had Pam with you, safe and sound?'

If Sally Griffin had held up a stick of gelignite and threatened to blow them to pieces they could not have been more shocked or horrified than they were by the words just spoken. Sally's apparently calm expression belied her own sense of shock as she unexpectedly heard herself speak.

But once her feelings were released in speech she found herself suddenly relaxing. The rest was easy. She looked coolly at the stunned faces and then let her gaze hover over Pat's pale and haggard face. She let it rest there. At the shock of hearing her, Pat had dropped back into his chair and remained seated.

'So you're shocked, Pat, at what I've said. But if you're shocked, so am I, but for a different reason. I'm shocked at the pantomime that's being created around Pam's disappearance. Whether she comes back to you or not is surely up to herself, and no amount of blame or discrediting her will undo what has already been done. We are all horrified and intrigued by the scandal of it and, with the exception of you, Pat, there is even quite an amount of morbid satisfaction to be derived from it, but it must be consoling to know you have so many friends in your hour of trial and that they all stand by you.' She was vaguely aware of Vienna, who stood slightly behind Pat, holding up her hand in a warning gesture but she ignored it. 'And although Pam isn't here to realise this, though wherever she is she's probably aware of it, it's obvious how many friends she has here.'

She looked from Pat to each separate face. Seated on the high red velvet stool she looked like an angry goddess. 'The truth is, Pam has no friends. Not me. Not you, Pat. You especially. If you had been her friend do you think for one moment she would have walked out on you? Were you so blind that the obvious wasn't obvious any longer? You were her husband too. Remember? How could your relationship with her have come to such a pass? Tell me that. But I bet you can't. Was Pam such a cold-blooded, selfish person that she just upped and left without giving a thought to you and the children? Is she really that kind of person? You should know the answer, that is, if you know your wife at all. From the little I know of her, and I know least of all of you, such behaviour is in total contradiction to the kind of person I know her to be. So what drove her to do such a thing?'

She looked accusingly at Pat. 'Only you know the answer. There is something else I noticed this evening, and indeed, for the last few days. You're all talking about Pam in the past tense, as if she were dead, as if, to put it as some of you did, that she had done away with herself.'

There was a chorus of 'That's not fair,' 'That's not true.'

'Oh, it was said. What's the point in denying it? Of course it does sound crude when it's said out in the open, but it sounded fairly credible when heads were locked together and it was all hush-hush.'

'Give over, Sally,' Michael said, his face dark with controlled anger. 'This is getting us nowhere.'

'On the contrary I think it's getting us somewhere. I think it's getting us back to ourselves. To see ourselves as we really are and if we achieve that we might have a chance to see Pam for the person she really is. And if we get to know more about her we might learn what drove her to such an act. Who are we? We are a crowd of unctuous hypocrites. I'm sick to death of all the rubbish I've been listening to in the last few days. I'm heartily sick of myself for listening. I'm sick of you, Pat, coming here and for all we know the cause of all this, not only getting away with it but getting support and sympathy as well, while Pam – you know damn well what your friends think of your wife. You've known all along but it didn't upset you. You stood out all the finer person in contrast. And you've been such a brave person in these last few days. Bearing up manfully and courageously.' She was getting angry again but she didn't care any longer. She saw Pat opening his mouth once or twice as if to speak, then deciding against it. 'It's time we all knew the truth and faced a few facts. There's a pretence of interest in Pam for Pat's sake anyway. Seeing no one scarcely knows anything about her in spite of years of acquaintanceship I'll give you the little knowledge I have of her.'

She noticed Michael rousing himself to hand around cigarettes and Tony giving him a nudge. As cigarettes were lit an air of quiet expectation settled upon their faces, mingled with some surreptitious smiles.

'This isn't meant to be an entertainment,' she burst out.

'Nor a lecture either, I hope,' Tony said.

The incongruity of the remark made her annoyance vanish leaving her only sad and depressed.

'Heaven forbid.' She hesitated, wondering whether to go on or not. Was she a one woman-crusader fighting for a lost cause, making herself ridiculous into the bargain? What right had she to be a self-appointed spokesman for Pam? What right had she to judge or denounce? She was completely out of order especially in someone else's house, creating a scene among people who were, after all, her friends. She had chosen them as friends. If they were not what she had expected them to be, then the same thing could be said of her. But Pam was her friend too. She had to stand up for Pam's sake.

'I thought Pam was a charming, sensitive, intelligent person with an unexpected sense of humour and a great deal of real charity. This seems to come as a surprise to you.

'Well, it may also come as a surprise that I found her loving, kind and affectionate and she wasn't putting on an act for me. I saw her in the presence of her children and the housekeeper who has been with her for a long time. You learn a lot about people when children are present and you don't fool a middle-aged housekeeper. Pam was good to me. Then the way she took all that pain and discomfort in her stride after the accident. Although she was a qualified doctor and kept up to date with modem medicine, though not practising she didn't throw her weight about while a patient and it was obvious the nurses loved her and enjoyed her company.'

She spoke directly to Pat. 'She loved you, Pat. I know she did. What she feels for you now is another matter. But she must have loved you very much to have gone to the stage of nearly destroying herself for you.' Pat looked up at her, mingled wonder and disbelief on his face. 'And I don't mean an attempt at suicide.'

She saw by the expression on his face that he didn't think she meant that and she was unaccountably grateful for that.

'She sacrificed a talent for you but it seems she didn't give it a thought because it was her nature to give. How do I know that? Pam didn't tell me but I found that out from Pam's closest friend or who used to be her closest friend. So Pam couldn't even hold on to her closest friend. Is that what you're all thinking now? But that's another story and one which doesn't reflect very much credit on you, Pat, and it's unnecessary to go into at this stage. Pam not only sacrificed her career, but she offered herself up on your sacrificial altar, and after that there wasn't much left of the original person she had been. Her friends who had not seen her for some time were puzzled and astonished at the change in her. Why did she let it happen? I suppose if you love as much as she must have loved, you don't realise you're doing anything out of the ordinary. If cheerfulness, willingness and a generous heart are taken for granted and you give and keep on giving, why should it occur to you that someday you might wake up and see yourself as an empty thing? You're empty because all through the years you have been giving and somebody else has been taking without giving anything in return. I suppose, in Pam's case it happened that at some time or other her eyes were opened and she found herself repelled by the picture she had of herself and revolted.'

'I have two pictures of Pam: the one I've just described and the other, an unpunctual, unpopular person, prone to sardonic remarks or zones of silence, which is how people saw her and how she seemed to me the first day we met. If marriage can do that to a person I feel like opting out while there is still time.'

She could not remember when she felt so depressed. It was useless consoling herself with the thought that marriage could not change her for the worse. It could, and it could happen to anybody. But how was she to act? If one did one's best and this was the result, what was the point in doing one's best? If Pam were to start married life all over again she wouldn't act any differently.

Morrison and I are on the threshold of marriage; we both will do our best to make our married life as happy as possible. But don't all married couples start out with the same intention, and see what happens? She had only to look around her. She doubted if any one couple could say with truth: ours is a wonderful marriage. And that wouldn't mean just that it was devoid of pain, ill-health, money troubles. Marriage could be wonderful even with all of these. She knew some of the private sorrows of the lives of her friends. Even Vienna had not been immune. Vienna could never allow herself to forget Michael's infidelity; once her simple trust in him was shattered she felt she had nothing on which to build a future relationship. She had assured Vienna over and over that she had no reason to doubt Michael's loyalty to her; what was past was past and should be forgotten. But it was all very well for her to talk like that. She wasn't the one who had been hurt.

She knew her glamorous friend suffered pangs of pain and suspicion. Vienna seemed to need those moments when she could have a shoulder to cry on and be told that her suspicions were unfounded. Thank heavens, those bouts were few and far between as Vienna was basically a cheerful person, but it was a pity that her life should have been scarred by such unhappiness. And there was Margo, who never took her eyes off Barry in company for the reason Barry could never take his eyes off other women, and the younger and prettier the women, the more his eyes roved. Maybe it was all harmless stuff but she didn't think Margo saw it that way.

She could go right through her list of friends and see now with a clear eye faults that would greatly disturb her if they were to crop up in her marriage at any time: the meanness of one husband, the alcoholic tendency of another. There was Tom, a gynaecologist/obstetrician who admitted he should never have got married as he rarely saw his wife and children because he was kept so busy. He had given an example this evening. Clare, his wife, had laughed with him as he recalled the instance: he came home on Monday night about eleven, was gone from the house the following morning before she got up and he didn't see her again until lunchtime today. It seemed funny at the time but was it really so funny for Clare, married to a man whose first love was his work?

Sally herself didn't believe that Tom had to take all that work upon himself, but the truth was Tom found complete fulfilment in his work. His happy cheerful face confirmed this, but Clare's tired, strained appearance didn't seem to spell out unequivocal acceptance of this arrangement.

She could go on and on and still be only scratching the surface. How could she possibly have any inkling of their lives? Of husbands' private lives? Could a man cry on a male friend's shoulder as women could with their female friends? Could a man confide his marital problems to a woman friend? *I'm sure he could* she thought, *if he hadn't another angle for the confidence. I'm getting cynical now and that's not good. But shouldn't all these thoughts of mine make me stop and think twice before committing myself to marriage? I had been perfectly happy before I met Morrison. Why put such a life in jeopardy? Am I being unduly pessimistic? Couples jogged along pretty well contented with themselves. If that be so, would I be happy just jogging along too?*

Vienna was saying: 'Sally, I think you've said enough, in fact more than enough. We all know marriage isn't always a bed of roses, but we don't have to go around carrying banners to let the world know about it.'

'A pity people don't,' Sally said. 'If there is trouble in any other walk of life whether through conditions of work, a matter of wage increase or even if union members think one of them has been unfairly treated, we hear all about it whether we like it or not. The media give it full exposure and it doesn't matter two hoots how much the public is put out by strikes and walk-outs. So it wouldn't be a bad idea if women banded together and told the world the true state of what marriage is or can be like. But here I am talking about marriage with not even the ring on my finger. But what has happened lately has set me thinking. Women are afraid to expose their grievances, afraid they'll be thought discontented, disloyal, even troublemakers. Their attitude seems to be on the whole: we can't change anything so let's make the best of it!'

She unwound her legs from the stool and brought her feet to rest on a higher rail. She leaned her elbows on her knees and rested her chin on her cupped hands, her eyes staring into space. The storm within her had died down. She felt a sense of over-exposure and knew now why women shun speaking out about their private lives. It must be a terrible sensation for the odd one who does.

And what had she gained from all that talk? What had she proved? Just that she was as prone as any bride-to-be to pre-marriage nerves, to judge from her incredulous, patient but embarrassed listeners. She had succeeded in stirring up doubts and suspicions she thought she would never entertain or contemplate concerning the important and vital step that she would soon be taking. The saddest part of it all was that not one woman supported her in what she had said. Surely there was one woman or one man who could have agreed with her on some small point, if not seeing eye-to-eye with everything she spoke about. Was it because she had been too personal? But then they were all indulging in personal comments for the greater part of the evening. What had she said that was wrong? Why had no one come forward to agree with her? Even if one woman of all that were there had said: 'Look, everybody, what Sally has said is hard to swallow, but it's true.' Even Vienna had let her down. But then, she couldn't very well say anything, could she? It would be opening up old wounds and she would want to avoid that. Perhaps that was the answer to her question. Nobody could come forward because there was an area in their lives each one wanted to avoid uncovering. And you couldn't blame them for that.

Oh Pam, I've just made a fool of myself. Nobody cares and nobody wants to be reminded that they ought to care, not only about you, but about themselves. About the thousands of other women all over the world who are subjected to so much indifference and unkindness by the very people who are supposed to love them. Surely to be loved is not to live in bondage.

She was roused from her thoughts by Vienna nudging her gently. She held out a drink. Her face was pale and tired-looking but she smiled at Sally. 'You need it. I think we all could do with a drink.'

She accepted it gratefully but it would take more than a drink to restore what she had lost. She sipped her drink slowly. She wanted to get down from her stool and mix with the crowd, pretend nothing had happened, but her legs refused to move. The party was over.

'Good lord! Is that the phone ringing?' Vienna exclaimed. 'Who could it be at this hour? Michael, will you answer it?'

As Michael went out the door Vienna came over to Sally. 'I hate phone-calls late at night. I always expect to hear something terrible has happened and it usually has.' She remembered the sudden death of her father, the motor-accident of her youngest brother. She let down the last of her drink in one gulp.

Michael returned and came over to her. He whispered: 'It's for Pat. Martha is on the phone.'

Vienna's eyes widened in apprehension. Sally looked quickly from one to the other.

'What's wrong?' she asked.

'Martha wants to speak to Pat.'

Vienna's eyes dropped slowly. The worst had come. Then she roused herself.

'Tell him he's wanted on the phone. That's all you can do.'

As Michael made to move away Vienna raised her head. She had thought of something. She gripped him urgently by the arm.

'Don't say he's wanted on the phone. Tell him Martha wants to speak to him. That sounds better.'

Sally and Vienna watched the two men go out the door. They had seen the look of agonised uncertainty leap to Pat's eyes as Michael whispered his message. It seemed to them only right that Michael should accompany him. As the door closed behind the two men Sally and Vienna joined the silent, waiting guests.

Chapter Fourteen

Immediately Pat felt the hand on his shoulder and looked into Michael's troubled eyes he braced himself to hear the worst. He too had heard the phone ringing and immediately he was filled with a strange sense of foreboding. Michael telling him the call was for him confirmed his fears. Silently he accompanied him to the hall where the receiver lay awkwardly on its back entangled in its own flex. Automatically he disentangled it slowly and carefully, patiently unwinding once again the coil that sprang back as soon as he extended the abbreviated length. Michael looked on in wonder as he watched the long fingers efficiently working on what appeared to him as something stupidly trifling. How could he know that time spent in unnecessarily correcting even such a minor defect was for Pat time borrowed from the fleeting moments, moments that were now in possession of the dreaded news he held back from hearing, but which were still trouble-free and to which he clung because they told him nothing. At last he lifted the receiver. Beads of perspiration had gathered on his forehead and his voice came out low and croaking.

'Yes, Martha? This is Pat. What is it?'

Martha was evidently crying. 'Oh, sir, it's the missus. She's back. She has just come in.'

'She... she... shhe's... what?'

Pat had braced himself for a shock but he had not expected this. He felt an extraordinary weakness encircling him which began at the base of his spine and which pulled him down into the seat behind him. Michael, who had just decided to leave, stayed when he saw his reaction. He would hold on for a minute or two in case he was needed. Pat let his elbow fall on the table with a bang and cradled his forehead in the palm of his hand. He cleared his throat to speak but his voice faltered and he had an unaccountable desire to weep like a child.

'Tell me all. Please.'

He wanted to ask where Pam was now. How was she? Why didn't she come to speak to him? But the words refused to come. Martha was now recovering somewhat from the shock and her tearfulness was replaced by excitement.

'Oh, sir, she's only in five minutes. I awoke with the doorbell ringing and when I went to the door I called out who was there. The missus said, "It's me. Pam." Oh, sir...'

She was beginning to cry again.

Pat let her sob until she felt sufficiently recovered to speak. While waiting he covered the mouthpiece and looked up at Michael who still stood beside him and whispered: 'It's about Pam. She's come home. Thank God.'

Pat was too absorbed in his thoughts to notice Michael leaving. He heard Martha blow her nose.

She said: 'When I saw her standing at the door to tell you the truth, sir, I didn't know what to do. Whether to throw my arms around her or go down on my knees to thank God for her safe return.'

These were not the details that her listener wanted but he heard her out with patience. But where was Pam, he wondered. Why didn't she come to the phone?

'She looks very tired, sir. Very tired.'

'Where is she now?'

'She's in the kitchen getting a cup of tea. I wanted to get her one while she rang you but she said she would get it herself, for me to ring you.'

'Thanks, Martha. Tell Pam I'm leaving right away.'

Should he add: 'Tell her I love her? That I'm happy and grateful she has come home?' He would leave it.

'Martha, you go off to bed. You must be dead tired.'

'Oh, I wouldn't dream of going to bed. Not until you come home. Don't worry about me.'

He did not argue. He knew Martha would be hovering around Pam until he got home.

He left down the receiver. He must get his thanks and goodbyes over as quickly as possible.

Pam lay on her back, hands clasped behind her head. Daylight was seeping through the curtained windows. Her eyes were wide with wakefulness though her head ached with a dull pain and her whole body was soaked in total weariness.

She listened to her husband's quiet breathing, then moved her head to watch him. His body was turned towards her, one arm stretched over the bed in her direction, his head resting on the angle made by the other arm. In the faint light she could make out his face relaxed in sleep, as peaceful as a child's. In a detached kind of way she envied him the effortless ease with which he could turn on his side and fall asleep immediately in spite of the turmoil he had experienced, in spite of what further turmoil he might face on awakening.

How did she feel now? What damage had been done to Pat? To herself? She smiled bitterly. Her decision to return home had bereft her of every shred of human pride. She wondered had animals a sense of pride. If they hadn't she had cast her lot among them. She had nothing left now.

She traced each moment that had passed since she took the taxi to the airport to catch, as she had led Mrs Howard and the others to believe, the flight to Dublin. She had acted her part so well that she was beginning to believe that she was actually catching that plane, so much so, that when the time came and the announcement was made she started from her seat, then remembering, sat back feeling foolish and looking guiltily at her watch.

In a mood of bravado she decided to have some coffee. It was a token of confirmation to herself that she was not moving until her flight to Malaga was announced. She had just a little under four hours to fill in until then. She would read the morning papers and the magazines she had bought, and by the time she had lunch and freshened up there would be little time in which to feel uneasy or bored. One small detail niggled her: she had promised them at the hotel she would phone them as soon as she arrived home; even though she had the foresight to add jokingly that she hoped they would understand if by any chance they didn't hear from her when expected, it would only be because with all the excitement it was temporarily forgotten. And they had told her not to worry, they would hear from her in time. Still she knew they would expect the call.

She disliked herself for the deceit that was beginning to wind round and round her and be so much part of all her actions. To lie at all or to involve herself in underhandedness was foreign to her, and to deceive those people who had been so good to her, the only people in the world to whom she could have turned at the climactic moment was something she could not dwell on without a feeling of distaste.

She was here in a world of people, stationary in a moving crowd and there wasn't one to whom she could speak. She had been grateful for the smile from the attendant in the toilets when the catch of the zip in her skirt wouldn't budge and she had asked for help. Time was moving fast, faster than she really wanted. She was caught in a world of shadows. Nothing was tangible now. She, too, was only a shadow. She tried to inject some life into herself, to become the person on whom her future was based. This was her chance of a new life, a life that offered some hope, some faith in herself. This was no time to falter. She reached for her hand-luggage. It included all the clothes she had in her possession. But no matter. She would buy more later.

After her lunch she went in the direction of the departure lounge that was leading her to a new life that was unknown, uncertain. This is what it must feel like to be dying and to be conscious of it; the journey must be made on one's own.

She watched the airport clock ticking away the moments: in a few hours I'll be in Spain; in a few hours I'll have put my feet down in a world of my own choosing. She was a free woman. That in itself was a good thought. Excitement and tension were mounting within her. It was extraordinary what strength had returned to her body in the last few days, as if the enervating atmosphere of the hospital had discouraged the real intense urge to get stronger quicker. Would it have made any difference to her if she had gone home first? Could she have had the strength of mind to go ahead with her plans in the environment of her home? Courage to map out her future and set it in motion? She shook her head. Now her mind was alternating with the urgent desire to be on the plane and the wish that time would stand still or, that somebody would stop her from going ahead. If she took this plane she knew she had left the old life forever. She could not play around with the emotions of her children; they must not be used as pawns in the life and death struggle of a marriage.

She joined the crowd in her section of the departure lounge. There was laughter and talk all around. It seemed she was the only one who had nobody to talk to. Nobody to share smiles and jokes with. A woman with twin boys of about four years was sitting beside her. The little fellows kept darting from her whenever something new caught their eyes. The mother looked Spanish, so did the little boys, but all spoke English. She supposed the father was English and that the three were off to Spain to visit relations.

In front of her was an elderly couple chatting to each other. They seemed to be seasoned travellers, probably retired. There was none of that excitement, partly suppressed, partly exposed, even a little fearful, which is the hallmark of the inexperienced traveller.

There was a group of students, boys and girls, standing about. All Spanish. They were inclined to show off, as though they had need to make sure that those about them knew that they were there. It was their hour. At home they melted into the crowd and went unnoticed. Here they stood out because of their foreignness.

A little hand was thrust confidently into hers. One of the twins was standing in front of her a little to the right and leaning against her knees. He stood like that for an instant and then turned suddenly around: 'Mummy, see that boy,' then he realised his mistake. Two big brown eyes opened wide in astonishment as he stared at her. Without another word he slipped into the seat on the other side of his mother. She heard the urgent whispering of the little fellow, the answering laughter of the mother before she turned her head, eyes brimming with mirth and apologised light-heartedly for her son's mistake. She was delighted at the opportunity to talk to the mother and the twins were momentarily halted in the exploring of their surroundings. When she had asked them their names, their age and were they going to school the twin called Antonio said: 'Have you got children? Have you twins too?'

The mother reprimanded them rapidly in Spanish but Peppi, the little fellow who had mistakenly taken her for his mother and who seemed to think this unorthodox introduction gave him a special claim on her attention, was not at all abashed by the rebuke. He stared at her thoughtfully:

'I bet you're a nice mummy.'

She turned in the bed to face the window. It was now bright. Pat was still asleep. Even now, she could hardly remember what happened after that, and what she did remember was confused and disconnected. Did she dash immediately from the lounge without an apology or explanation or did she wait to tell the Spanish mother and her little boys why she had to leave them in a hurry? Had she done one thing and thought she had done the other or was it the other way about? She would never be sure. All she was certain of was that she had taken refuge in the ladies' room behind the locked door of the toilet. It was the only place that offered itself for her to sort out her pent-up emotions. Her two children had spoken through the voice of a strange little Spanish boy. How often had she heard Rosemary and Robert say: 'You're a nice mummy,' or 'We have the loveliest mummy in the world.' She would never be able to get away from her children even if she went to live on the moon. She had tried to tell herself they would be better off without her as things stood between Pat and herself.

She couldn't stay in the toilet much longer. She left and stood before a mirror. She put a comb through her hair. She looked at her watch. Then suddenly all the reasons she had built up so steadily for making this change in her life toppled. She found herself once more in a no-man's land. Not able to go forward and afraid to go back. If only she had no children how easy it would all have been. Children were like blackmailers. You were never free of them. There was no getting away from them no matter how you tried.

Their demands on the wealth of your love, time and attention were never-ending; it would never occur to Rosemary and Robert that someday the source of all that richness might dry up; she had known she could never forget them but she had thought she could get away from them.

What would she do now? Where would she go? Should she call Auntie Kit and say she had missed her plane to Dublin? No, she was sick of lies. She could return to the hotel and tell the truth. Wait a few days until she had sorted herself out and then make up her mind once and for all and stick to that decision. That wasn't good enough either. Let her get her facts straight: she was not able to take the plane to Spain. There was still time but she couldn't take that step. Next fact: she had to return to her children. But then her tortured mind turned over and over possibilities, solutions, a way out for herself so that in going back home her position there wouldn't be made more impossible than it had been.

But no matter how she examined and searched for an answer she came back to the one thing – there was no way out for her. She might as well get used to the realisation that once she went home, whatever position she had there, even though it had been almost negligible, was now gone. Pat would see to that. He might even go so far as to tell her that since she had already taken steps to desert her children, to get out of their lives and not come back. He didn't want her and the children could do without her. Could she face that? Was her love for her children that strong? She slapped her comb down with a bang. She looked at herself in the mirror and saw anger and determination blazing in her eyes. Yes! Her love for her children was that strong and that strength would overcome anything.

She put her things together and walked to the door. Dimly she remembered cancelling her flight to Malaga. How she explained this sudden decision to the official she couldn't recall even now, One thing stood out; her relief that there was a seat available on a later flight to Dublin. It occurred to her at some stage while she waited for her flight that her aunt might have phoned home. That collapse of her's would be on her aunt's mind. She pushed that problem to the back of her mind.

It was almost an anti-climax when Martha opened the door and stood there mouth open, eyes blinking, not yet fully awake. She had expected Pat to answer the door; their bedroom was nearer the hall door and so he was more likely to hear the bell ringing than Martha. After Martha recovered sufficiently to be coherent she told her that Pat was at a party that Michael and Vienna were giving for Sally. Her heart sank. So that was the way it was.

Her absence didn't cause him a bother. Out enjoying himself and having a terrific time because she wasn't hanging around. But what did she expect? To Martha's anxious enquiries she answered as best she could, but she was tired and she was thirsty. She would make herself a cup of tea, go to bed and Martha could ring Pat and tell him she was home. She couldn't bear the thought of speaking to him: the prodigal wife returning shame-faced and interrupting the merriment and fun: 'Pat, please forgive me. I am not worthy to be called your wife. Make me one of your hired servants.'

She was in bed smoking a cigarette when she heard the car pulling up outside the front door. She heard the key turn in the lock, Martha's hurried steps in the hall followed by a brief conversation and Pat running up the stairs. He flung the door open, took a step or two inside and stood there, his eyes fastened on her. She prepared herself for the storm.

I am waiting, her thoughts ran. *Let's get it over and done with. I'm not answering you. I'm not going to involve myself in lengthy arguments at this hour.*

But her husband Pat seemed to have no wish to speak. He stood motionless, face pale, eyes filled with pain. Her eyes followed the movement of his as they travelled all over her face. Then his shoulders sagged as a deep sigh escaped him. He came over to her, his lips curved in a wistful half-smile, knelt on the floor and lifted her into his arms. He pressed his cheek against hers and whispered: 'Thank God, you've come back.'

If he had beaten her she would have been less shocked. He did not ask any questions nor did she offer any explanations. Her cheek was wet with tears. His tears. She fingered them wonderingly and said: 'Get into bed. It's very late and you must be tired.' He got up slowly. His face looked older.

She did not know that he had longed to rush to her with overwhelming relief when he came into the bedroom, but that he was afraid. Afraid that if he took one wrong step it might be a fatal one. He went despondently to the bathroom, changed and got into bed beside her. He wondered what he should do. Oh God, if only she could help him out. There were a million things to tell her and she looked as if her mind were a thousand miles away. He could stand it no longer.

'Oh Pam, I love you.'

Her body jerked. He had given her a start. She looked at him and he put out his arms longingly and drew her to him. Old habits die hard and she found herself putting her arms around him. She never knew men could cry like this; that it was possible for a man to lose control. She should have been able to cry with him. They should have been of comfort to each other at this critical moment. But she remained unmoved, absorbed only with this phenomenon. He moved within her arms, hands fumbling, muttering something about the whereabouts of his handkerchief. Reaching awkwardly back, as she was still in his arms, she strained for the locker and brought out a packet of tissues knocking down some small items as she did so. She drew out a couple of tissues and placed them in his hand. He switched off the bedside lamp.

'I don't like you seeing me like this.'

'I have seen worse,' she said, with an unconscious touch of irony.

She let him talk after that. He talked and explained until he was weary, until his voice grew hoarse.

'I won't ask you where you have been or what you have done. If you want to tell me later, you can. But whatever you did, you had to do it. I know that now.'

He accused himself of many things, took all the blame for the breakdown of their marriage. She didn't agree with this though she did not say so, because not so long ago she had come to the conclusion she had contributed to the breakdown, however indirectly, by not remaining true to herself, the person that he first met and fell in love with. If she had remained that person all this might have been avoided. Giving in to Pat on all occasions in the early years of their marriage was not a true sign of love though she thought it had been. It had succeeded in avoiding arguments and rows then, but how much had been lost.

'I'll make it up to you,' Pat was saying. 'I promise I'll do everything I can to try and make you forget what has happened. That won't be easy. I mean, making you forget. But I'll spend the rest of my life trying. I know you don't feel any love for me now. How could you! But perhaps in time you will. I pray that you will. Because if you have stopped loving me then life isn't worth living, and I'm not just feeling sorry for myself saying that. I'm saying it because I realise now and I hope it's not too late, that the only thing that counts is our love for each other.' He was silent for some time. 'Everything else follows,' he added, almost to himself.

It mustn't have come easy to him, she thought, baring his soul to a woman he had seemed to despise all those years. She felt sorry for him as she would feel sorry for any person in the same situation. Everyone has a right to his or her own special image of themselves. It is this image that makes people feel good. If a crack appears in the image it is better that they see it first. If they fail to see it, all one can do, if one is in a position to do so, is to point out the fault. And how carefully one must go about doing that. This is what she had tried to do with Pat in later years but she had failed miserably. On the other hand Pat had no hesitation in smashing the image she had of herself, over and over, and every time she had tried to salvage the broken pieces to build the original image she found more and more of the pieces missing.

Her personal dignity had been trampled upon and she herself had by her own act, destroyed the last vestige of what had remained. Because now it was always possible that this last act of hers could be used by Pat in the future as the strongest piece of evidence against her as wife and mother. For had Pat really changed?

But had she actually destroyed everything? Was not the very act she had thought as the last in self-destruction really a cornerstone on which to build her future life? She would and must try to build a future for the children, for Pat and for herself. She would work hard at it.

She thought of the ordeal Pat had gone through a short while ago and for the first time pity for him swept over her. Pity for Pat, the man who was her husband. In a frightening, self-inflicted kind of brain-washing he had exposed so many faults and weaknesses. It was an unhealthy reaction. What would he think of himself in the cool light of day? Would she be able to help him regain his self-respect?

The sun was now brightening the room through the drawn curtains. What would this day bring for the two of them? What would the future have in store for them?

She stretched herself in the bed and yawned wearily. She was tired. Terribly, terribly tired. She pulled up the bedclothes, buried her head in them and fell asleep.